The Mazes of Magic

A Conjurer of Rhodes, Book 1

Jack Massa

Published by
Triskelion Books
www.triskelionbooks.com

The Mazes of Magic

ISBN 978-0-9976461-8-4

Print Edition published November 3, 2018

Cover design by Mirna Gilman, BooksGoSocial.

Dedication

In Memoriam,
Kathryn Fernquist Hinds
priestess, author, poet, scholar, friend
"worthy vessel of the Goddess"
#InHerName

...It was only in these temple societies that the indigenous Egyptian upper class still survived; they remained the principal centres of the national civilization and script and craftsmanship, enabling the ... traditions of Egypt to resist obliteration, and remain largely independent of the imported Greek culture. These survivals were encouraged by the Ptolemies ...

- Michael Grant
From Alexander to Cleopatra,
The Hellenistic World

The gods take many shapes,
And bring forth many fates.
What men expected did not come.
Instead the will of the god was done
In a way no man expected.
And that is the lesson of the play.

- Euripides, *The Bacchae*

Prologue

He had died once. He knew that much for certain.

He had wandered the shore of the River Styx, but for some reason not crossed over. Instead, he had returned to the mortal world—he knew not how or why.

Whole segments of his memory from that time were lost, or else scattered in fragments that made no sense, sharp fragments that cut at him like broken glass. His mind must have been damaged on that journey back from the Underworld.

The heat was stifling. How long had he been trapped in this cell with its dusty brick and searing black iron? He drank the water they gave him, but seldom touched the food. Better to starve, he had decided, than live a moment longer than he must in this place, this slave yard.

How had he become a slave?

Each effort to force himself to remember brought dizziness and headache, his mind swirling down into whirlpools of bewilderment and fear. Madness. He flailed like a drowning man, desperate to remember who he was.

Now he stood at the tiny window, staring through the black grate at the sun hovering on the horizon.

Helios, Lord of the Sun. Patron deity of Rhodes.

Yes, he was a Greek, from the island of Rhodes. Korax was his name, Korax son of Leontes. Those memories were clear enough. He had grown up in a prosperous merchant family, studied at the finest school in *Rhodos*, the island's capital city. Like all male citizens of Rhodes, he had spent his seventeenth summer at the oars of a galley, training to serve in the navy. He had been brave, reckless, full of life, passionate about theater and music. He sang and played the lyre.

Indeed, in one of his last memories he was practicing to play at a festival. But something about that night was different. As the dizziness welled in his brain, he fought to remember. He saw his fingers attacking the strings, evoking music that was wild, exquisite, but not his own.

Divine music.

Yes ... Outlandish, fearful, yet he knew it to be true.

That night, he was possessed by a god.

Chapter One

T**he disk of the sun blazed at the top of the sky. Merciless heat radiated down on white walls and dusty streets. It was late summer, the hottest time of year on the Delta.**

Nebrus the slave seller sat in the shade of an awning at the front of his warehouse. Cringing from the heat, he squinted along the thoroughfare—all but deserted this time of the day. Nebrus himself would have preferred to be taking his ease in the cool of his garden, sipping well water beside the lotus pool or dallying with one of his concubines.

But today an important customer was calling.

Why certain temple dignitaries insisted on conducting business in the heat of the afternoon was a mystery. Perhaps they wished to show their contempt for physical discomfort, to impress the populace with their mystical vigor. Nebrus snorted. Who was there to impress when the streets were empty because all sensible people had fled to the nearest shade?

Whole cadres of priests and temple functionaries were passing through town these days—returning to their cities upriver after the annual Synod in Alexandria. Mostly they were grim and sour men, disaffected with their lot and the state of the country.

Nebrus understood why. For many generations the priestly caste had controlled enormous wealth and power in Egypt. But all of that had changed with the coming of the Greeks. Alexander, called the Great, had won possession of the land from the Persian Empire. On Alexander's death, the Macedonian general Ptolemy had made himself King of Egypt—and had promptly confiscated most of the arable land in the Nile Valley. His son, the present Ptolemy II, had gone even further, establishing a royal monopoly on almost all manufacture and trade. To be sure, the temples still administered vast holdings, but now they did so at the pleasure of the king—and paid him heavy taxes in grain, oil, and coin for the privilege. In just over a generation, the Greeks had overhauled the whole economy of Egypt. Nebrus' own city, Zau, was just one example. The town had been a prosperous temple center when the Greeks still lived in huts. Now it was a backwater, like all the old cities of the Delta. All riches now flowed northwest to Ptolemy's splendid capital at Alexandria.

A movement of traffic around a nearby corner interrupted the slave seller's musings. A train of men in white garments and white sandals appeared, marching in slow procession to the beat of tambourines and drums. Muscular porters in white kilts carried a gilded litter in the shape of a sacred boat.

Nebrus climbed to his feet, leaning on a staff. He shouted to Nacht his clerk that the customer had arrived. He waited until the parade had stopped in front of his awning before venturing out into the sun.

The priests and their subalterns nodded to him in formal greeting. The younger men carried various parcels and satchels and wore plain black wigs to protect their shaven heads from the sun. The elders wore elaborate plaited wigs, along with amulets, sashes, and pectoral collars that indicated their office and rank.

A herald tapped his painted wand three times on the hard-packed ground. "I present his Excellency Harnouphis, second servant of Ptah in his Mansion at Mem-Nephir, Superintendent of Inventories and Records, Minister of the God's Accounts and Correspondences."

Nebrus bowed, eyes to the ground. Harnouphis' office placed him near the summit of power at one of the greatest temples in Egypt. More importantly, he administered most of the temple's wealth.

Attendants parted the gauzy curtains of the litter, and Harnouphis stepped from his cushioned seat. He was a short, broadly-built man of perhaps forty, dressed in exquisite gowns of white linen trimmed in gold. He moved with the alacrity of a much younger man and smiled with the practiced friendliness of a politician.

"Nebrus, my old friend. How have you been this past year?"

"Well, by the will of the gods, your Excellency. You do me great honor to greet me thus. May I offer you and your entourage the poor comfort of my garden?"

Harnouphis clasped the slave seller's hand vigorously. "Your hospitality does you credit in the eyes of Ptah. Regrettably, our time is short, so I must beg your forgiveness and ask that we proceed immediately to business."

Nebrus kept his countenance neutral but inwardly smiled with relief. "Of course, my honored guest. In what ways can my humble establishment assist the servants of Ptah?"

Harnouphis cast a sidewise glance at one of his subalterns, who took a step forward. "My chief scribe, Mehen."

Mehen, a long-faced and solemn man, drew a papyrus sheet from his beaded satchel. "The Mansion of the Spirit of Ptah has need of gardeners, two; porters and doorkeepers, five; kitchen slaves, one or two, especially if skilled in cooking or baking. In addition, we have pressing need for scribes or any man who can be trained in the reading and writing of Greek script."

"That last is a most urgent requirement," Harnouphis commented. "Pharaoh—May he live a thousand years—has decreed that henceforth all our letters and reports be scribed in the Greek."

"An onerous burden indeed!" Nebrus responded with wide-eyed sympathy. "I am certain my shop can supply the temple's needs in the first three categories. And now that I think of it, I also have one man that might be suitable as a scribe."

Nebrus led the high priest and his assistants through the gates of his warehouse. The clerk Nacht awaited them at the edge of a broad, dusty courtyard. Iron grates set along the brick walls enclosed scores of cells, most of them occupied by slaves awaiting purchase. A few stunted palms cast the only feeble shade.

For the next half-hour, Nebrus displayed his wares to Harnouphis and his entourage. Slaves were summoned from their cells, examined, prodded, questioned about their origins and abilities. Offers were made, prices quietly haggled over. Nebrus closed the sale of six men and a kitchen maid. He began to regard the time spent in the brutal heat as a worthwhile investment.

"You mentioned one who might serve as a scribe." Mehen reminded him.

"Oh, yes. This way if you please."

Nebrus conducted the party to an isolated cell in a far corner of the yard. Inside the cell, the slave lay on a bed of straw, his face to the back wall.

"This one is a Greek. My colleagues in Alexandria had high hopes for him—educated and a musician, they said. But, for whatever reason, he did not sell there. They sent him on to me after only a short time."

"What is he called?" Harnouphis asked.

"I don't know, some Greek name. I'm sure we have it in our records. Nacht, get him to stand up."

The clerk called out to the slave in *koine*, the common Greek dialect: "You there! Stand."

The slave shifted his shoulders but did not rise.

Nebrus sighed. "He's given up, you see. Certain types simply cannot abide the life of a slave. They refuse all food and simply wait to die. Sorrows are many under the Eye of Ra." He made a pious gesture. Then he poked his staff through the grate and prodded the slave roughly.

The slave jumped up, put his back to the wall and glared. Dressed in a grimy loincloth, he stood bony as a beggar, ribcage rising with his breath. His unwashed black hair hung long and tangled. The patchiness of his beard showed that he had not yet reached full manhood.

Mehen gazed at the slave with repugnance, but Harnouphis studied him with keen interest.

"You say he can read and write?"

"Oh, don't be fooled by his wretched appearance," Nebrus answered. "I was assured that he is well-bred and educated."

"Mehen," Harnouphis addressed the scribe. "Ask him if he can read."

Mehen cleared his throat and spoke to the slave in koine. "Young man, we are told you can read and write the Greek. Is this so?"

Korax stared through the iron grid at the Egyptians. He only wanted to be left alone, to return to the peaceful half-dream where he could almost ignore his misery.

The Egyptian with the satchel spoke again: "Young man, did you understand my question?"

But it was the other one, the elder in the splendid wig and gold-bordered gown who seized the Greek's attention. That one's eyes seemed to bore into him, to examine the very marrow of his bones.

Korax glared back defiantly.

After a few moments the elder shrugged, said something in Egyptian, and turned away. The others moved to follow.

Korax sucked in a breath, seized by panic. Some inner spirit prodded his wits: *an irreplaceable chance was about to be lost.*

"Yes," he rasped from a dry throat. "I can read and write. Quite well, in fact."

The Egyptians paused. The lavishly-dressed elder said something to his assistant, who took a papyrus sheet from his satchel and handed it through the grate.

"Tell me what is on this page."

Korax stepped forward and took the sheet from the man's hand. The shapes of inked letters brought sharper clarity to his mind. How long since he had seen a page of writing? No matter. He read it with ease and spoke with calm assurance. "The upper half is a script I do not know ... But I seem to think it is Egyptian? The lower half is Greek. It is an inventory: items received into the storehouses of the Temple of Hephaestus in Memphis on the Nile; in the month of Hekatombaion, in the ninth year of the Reign of Ptolemy II. Barley, 530 bushels. Wheat, 260 bushels. Flaxseed oil, 47 jars. Shall I continue?"

"No. That is sufficient. And you can write as well?"

He had to think a moment, but answered, "Of course."

The assistant took back the papyrus, rolled it deftly, and placed it in his satchel. He said something to his master, who again fixed the young Greek with a penetrating gaze. The Egyptians conversed among themselves. After a few moments they strolled away, still chatting.

Korax collapsed against the grate. The sun-heated iron burned his forehead. He let it rest there until the pain grew unbearable. Then he slumped back to the straw bed and lay down.

What did it mean? Would the wealthy Egyptian buy him, make him a scribe? At least that would remove him from this cursed cell that was like an oven. But to spend the rest of his days as a slave? Unthinkable!

Sometime later the slave seller's clerk came and unlocked the cell with an iron key. "Up with you, Greek. You're a fortunate man. You've just been sold to the priests of Memphis."

Korax followed the clerk through the courtyard and out into the street. Inside him, wariness and fear competed with a dull curiosity. What might the Fates have in store for him now?

Priests and attendants, all dressed in white, stood before a gold litter chair. Nebrus the slave seller was bowing and bidding them farewell. An overseer with a brass-fitted baton motioned Korax to a place behind the litter, where the other newly-purchased slaves stood. A drum started beating, and the litter chair was lifted up on the shoulders of porters. The priests departed in a measured walk. Herded by the overseer, Korax and his fellow slaves fell into step at the rear of the procession.

They marched through the streets and arrived at a high-walled temple by the river. The priests and their subalterns proceeded through the pylon gates. The overseer directed the slaves along the muddy riverbank to a small gatehouse at the rear of the enclosure. They entered an area of courtyards, storehouses, and outbuildings, shaded in places by palms and sycamores. The new slaves were taken to a pool, stripped, and herded into the water.

Korax had a few moments to enjoy the cool bath. Then an attendant came and roughly scrubbed him down. His nails were clipped and his mouth rinsed out with a solution of salty water. He was led to a bench beside the pool, where a barber shaved his head and anointed him with oil. Along with the other slaves he was given a loose, sleeveless tunic with shoulder straps and a pair of straw sandals.

Next, the slaves were ushered to a barrack beside the donkey stables. Straw mats lined the plaster walls. The slaves were directed to sit and rest. A while later, they were fed—platters of barley bread with lettuce and tumblers of beer.

Korax found himself a place in the corner, away from the other slaves. He watched them gobble their meals, but stared at his own plate with grim indecision. The urges of his belly warred with his lingering resolve, his determination to escape this life by starving.

But the events of this day had opened a new path. Perhaps it would lead him back to full possession of his mind and memory— perhaps even to freedom. It seemed foolish not try that path, to at least see where it led. Hesitantly, he nibbled a piece of crust, then washed it down with a swig of the thick, bitter beer.

His stomach churned, then settled. Soon he was eating and drinking eagerly. He finished everything then stretched out on his mat, enjoying the unfamiliar sensations of a full belly and clean, oiled skin.

He closed his eyes and drifted off to sleep.

Chapter Two

*H*e walked along a colonnade on a bright afternoon. He was leaving the library of the academy, the School of Bellerophon, in his last year as a student. As he walked, he gazed beyond the slope of the school property and down the long hill of the city—a sweeping view of green treetops, white walls, and red-tiled roofs—all the way down to the sea. There, sunlight glittered on the blue water and gleamed on the giant gold statue of the sun god, standing above the three harbors of the city.

Helios, Patron of Rhodes.

But today, Korax's mind was on a different god.

A warm breeze blew along the portico, a faint perfume of flowers mingled with the salt air. Spring had come at last. After months of dreary, landlocked days, the sailing season would soon begin. But first, the Festival of Dionysus: five days of processions, revels, poetry, and plays. The entire town would be decked in wreathes of spring flowers and filled with laughter, flute playing, and song. A young man of eighteen such as Korax could take full part in the revels, and he fully intended to enjoy himself.

Turning a corner, he saw throngs of students exiting through the front gates of the school. But instead of hurrying away as usual, most of them gathered in a crowd across the street. From his vantage point on the colonnade, Korax could see why.

In an open space before a grove of olive trees, lads and girls in bright-colored costumes danced to the music of flutes and drums. A line of young women clapped cymbals and sang in a chorus. Korax hurried down the steps to hear them better.

At first he thought they might be an acting troupe, newly-arrived in Rhodos for the festival and touring the streets to raise interest in their plays. But as he squeezed through the crowd he realized they were something even better—courtesans from the Guild of Aphrodite.

The girls and slender boys wore light chitons, scarlet or orange, cut high on the leg and fitted tight to show their figures. Dancers and musicians alike wore garlands of violets in their hair, their eyes lined and eyelids painted. Even from the edge of the crowd, he could smell a dizzying mixture of perfumes.

He searched the performers in the rear of the group and then grinned. The one he was looking for was there—a flute girl, sweet and slender, with creamy skin and gorgeous, wild red hair. Berenicea was her name, a girl of Celtic blood. He had glimpsed her twice before, once in a procession outside the guild hall that served as the temporary temple of Aphrodite, and on another occasion like this one, when her mentor, the courtesan Emerine, had paraded some of her young talent in the street to stimulate business.

He had heard his schoolmates speak of Berenicea as well. There was even talk of a wager among some young blades as to who would be the first to bed her. Though she had been raised in the house of Emerine, she had just this season come of age. Korax wondered with a yearning heart what a night in her arms might cost.

Now the music stopped. Two of the painted boys pranced forward and set down an ebony stool. They assisted an obese, florid-faced man in a great purple tunic to step up. He unrolled a proclamation, cleared his throat, and began to read.

"Young men of the School of Bellerophon: I address those who are of military age and fully vested in the rights of citizenship. From the Guild of Aphrodite and in the name of the most desirable hetaira Emerine, mistress of the guild, Cleonides, steward to Emerine, brings you greetings! Hear this

announcement and invitation: the Goddess of Love pays homage to her brother, the God of Wine, Plays, and Revels! On the first night of the Dionysia, all cadets in training with the Navy of Rhodes are invited to a night of revels in the Guild Hall of Aphrodite. There will be wine and music, delicacies from the finest kitchens in Rhodos to tempt the palette, and of course"—the steward waved his hand to indicate the troupe—"delicacies of the fleshy kind to tempt a young man's other appetites."

The crowd hooted and cheered as the courtesans waved and blew kisses. Korax, like all students his age, had already spent one summer training with the Navy of Rhodes, and was considered a cadet.

"And here is more," Cleonides continued. "Young poets, bring your lyres! A competition of song will be held. No less than two grand prizes will be awarded: one for the best hymn in praise of Dionysus, the other for the best to honor Aphrodite. And, listen well, young gentlemen, for you will not believe the generosity of Lady Emerine in donating these prizes. Both winners will receive—Are you listening, young captains of Rhodes? For I tell you, you must listen well if you are to believe me. Both winners will receive, as reward for their excellence in song, an entire night, absolutely free, in the arms of the girl or boy of his choice from the house of Emerine!"

A whooping shout went up, the young men applauding and clapping each other on the back with raucous laughter.

"All this, all this," the fat man shouted above the din, "Wine, song, food, and poetry, all yours for the paltry admission price of five obols per man. You heard me correctly, a mere five obols for a night of revelry and song such as no young sailor will want to miss. The companionship of our lovely ladies and boys will be available for the usual additional fees, of course. All profits of the evening will be donated to the Guild's fund toward building the new Temple of Aphrodite in Rhodos. Thank you, young gentlemen, for your attention. Please stay and listen to our music, and feel free to approach and meet anyone of our troupe who takes your fancy."

The steward rolled up his scroll and was assisted to step down from the stool. The music started up again, the young dancers capering before the crowd.

Korax smiled to himself as he watched Berenicea dip and sway.

Soon the older, more confident young men of the school walked over to mingle with the courtesans, exchanging pleasantries or grasping a hand to kiss. Korax was considering introducing himself to Berenicea. But then he saw a group of young cadets approach her and her fellow musicians.

"By all the gods," he muttered. It was Patrollos and his gang!

Patrollos was tall, broad-shouldered, and handsome, a son of one of the ruling families of the city. Everyone at the school considered him a natural leader, a future admiral. A troupe of sycophants followed him everywhere, all of them decked out in naval cloaks and jeweled armbands. Korax considered them all dull-witted bullies.

Lacking the brawn of most young men his age, Korax prided himself on his wit. Just two days ago, he had bested Patrollos in a classroom debate, mocked him in fact, so that students and teachers both erupted in laughter. Pride wounded, Patrollos had retaliated later in the day, cornering Korax on the exercise field and pummeling him, nearly breaking his jaw.

Korax hung back a moment, hesitant, as he touched the still-swollen spot below his ear. But he was possessed of a reckless and defiant courage. No matter how often he was bested by bullies, he never allowed himself to back down, never let them see him afraid.

Steeling himself, he marched over to within earshot. The young gallants were simpering at the pretty musicians, trying to engage them in conversation.

Patrollos laid a hand over Berenicea's hand, stopping her from playing. "And what is your name, my little beauty? It wouldn't be Berenicea by any chance?"

She smiled with surprise. "It is indeed, my lord. But how did you know?"

"Oh, I've heard much talk of Berenicea," Patrollos said. "Her flaming hair, her sea-blue eyes. It is said that Lady Emerine keeps her hidden indoors for fear that Aphrodite might espy her beauty and grow mad with jealousy."

Korax rolled his eyes in disgust.

Patrollos let his hand drop to touch the girl's bare thigh. "My pretty little red flower, I look forward to opening your petals with tender and appreciative fingers."

Berenicea smiled as she pushed his arm away.

Korax could stand no more. Impetuously, he stalked forward and interposed himself between Patrollos and the girl.

"Dear Berenicea, you are wise to disdain the clumsy advances of our would-be admiral here. For though he is tall and strong, his touch lacks all subtlety." Grinning, Korax fingered his bruise. "I can assure you of this, from personal experience."

Berenicea smiled mirthfully. "Indeed? And what is your name, young sir?"

"His name is 'Stumbles-in-the-Mud,'" Patrollos growled.

He grabbed the shoulder of Korax's garment, twisted him aside, and shoved hard. Korax staggered backward, slipped in a muddy patch, and fell on his backside. His spine struck a tree root, and he groaned in pain.

"Oh, do not worry about him," he heard someone say amid the hoots of laughter. "We knock him down all the time. He's rather like a target we practice on."

"Now, now, no violence, gentlemen, please." The fat steward in purple hurried over to quell the commotion. One of his boys helped Korax to stand. The steward and the slave boy together brushed him off.

"I hope you're not hurt, young sir. No harm was meant, I am sure," Cleonides said.

"I am not hurt." Korax answered, choking back his humiliation.

He glanced over at the line of musicians. Patrollos and his companions had turned their backs on him. For an instant he thought he caught Berenicea's eye, but he quickly looked away. Angrily, he waved off the solicitous attentions of the steward and turned to depart.

Stalking down the streets toward home, Korax nursed his rage. He would make them pay for this, Patrollos and all of his followers. Somehow, he would turn the tables and make them the objects of jeering and scorn. Korax swore he would do this before the moon waned and the ships in Rhodos harbor took sail.

He always believed he could do anything he put his mind to, and now he had put his mind to this.

Chapter Three

Korax woke in the night, panting with rage. He stared at the unfamiliar room, a barrack full of men sleeping on mats, lit by dim starlight slanting through narrow windows. The dream of Rhodes possessed him as if a daimon had seized his mind.

Not just a dream, a memory. The school, Berenicea the lovely girl, Patrollos the arrogant bully. All of it was true, he was certain.

Somehow, that incident had led to the loss of his life in Rhodes, his enslavement here in Egypt. Somehow he had died, returned from death, ended up here. He fought to slow his breathing, to stamp down the panic he feared would lead to another spell of madness.

He stared at the ceiling, pulled his thoughts into order. The Fates had brought him out of the slave yard, given him a new opportunity. Somehow, he would cure himself, regain his full memory. Somehow he would find his way back to freedom, back home to Rhodes.

He always believed he could do anything he put his mind to, and now he had put his mind to this.

He was still awake at daybreak when the slaves were roused. Overseers marched him and the others outside the temple enclosure to a landing on the river. Three barges were moored there, swaying gently in the current. As a son of Rhodes, Korax clearly recalled sailing on both Greek freighters and naval galleys. He scrutinized the Egyptian boats, noting the differences. These were broad-beamed craft, with benches for a hundred oarsmen and roomy cargo holds. Stout masts supported impressive yards, with sails nearly as wide as the barges were long.

Korax waited with the other slaves while porters loaded cargo and crewmen made ready to sail. After a time the servants of Ptah arrived, filing down the narrow street in their white gowns and white sandals. The parade consisted of many more priests, attendants, and functionaries than Korax had seen yesterday. It ended at the quay, the temple entourage gathering in groups. Chattering in a babble of voices, they boarded the barges using broad, railed gangplanks. Korax and the other slaves were herded toward the rearmost craft, but then a messenger came and issued crisp orders to the overseer. Korax was directed to follow the messenger. They stepped through the crowd to the first barge, where Korax recognized the scribe who yesterday had handed him the papyrus through the grate of his cell.

The man displayed a tight-lipped smile. "You are the Greek. I scarcely recognize you clean and shaven."

Guardedly, Korax nodded his head.

"I am Mehen, chief scribe in service to his Excellency Harnouphis. For now, you will take your orders from me. Come."

Korax followed him up the plank and onto the wide deck. The lead barge was larger and more ornate than the others, with capacious deck houses built along the center line. The highest-ranking priests were making themselves comfortable there, while porters collapsed and stowed their litters. Mehen led Korax toward the stern, past tents and awnings where a crowd of subordinates and scribes were storing their gear. He found a place for Korax against the rail, not far from the steps of the rear gallery.

Mehen called out orders to a slave, who brought two straw mats. The scribe sat cross-legged on one of the mats and gestured for Korax to do the same. From his satchel, Mehen took a wax tablet and stylus.

"We have your Greek name from the slave seller's records. However, a barbaric name is not suitable for a servant of Ptah. Therefore, his Excellency Harnouphis has decreed for you a new name, *Seshsetem*. It is written thus." He scratched the name in the wax, first in Greek letters, then in the Egyptian script. "This name means 'obedient scribe.' Live up to this name, and your days will be peaceful and fruitful in service to our god."

He handed the tablet to Korax. "Write the name in both scripts as I have done."

Korax took the stylus. He easily etched the name in Greek, then laboriously in the Egyptian characters. Mehen watched him critically. He pointed out several places where the characters were improperly shaped. Reaching into the beaded satchel, he produced a papyrus sheet.

"Continue writing your name in our script until you can do so perfectly. Then begin to practice from this sheet. It shows common words in both Greek and Egyptian. Later, a scribe will come and begin to teach you the sounds of our letters. You must become fluent in our language—reading, writing, and speaking—if you are to properly serve our god."

The chief scribe rose to his feet. "Apply yourself diligently, Seshsetem. In our tradition, a scribe who does not learn quickly enough is beaten with the rod."

Mehen marched off to attend to other business. Korax returned his attention to the tablet. Frowning with concentration, he copied the name 'Seshsetem' in Egyptian several times. Then he wrote it once in Greek and spoke it quietly.

"Sesh-se-tem."

His new name. His *slave* name. Perhaps his name for the rest of his life.

He scowled with a flash of anger. He glanced about to see that no one was watching then deliberately etched a different name on the tablet.

Korax.

The barges of the Temple of Ptah departed, crewmen straining with poles to push off from the landing. Other men took the oars and rowed against the current. Once the barges were away from shore, the huge sails were unfurled and filled by the steady north wind.

Korax sat in his place by the rail and practiced the Egyptian writing. From time to time he stood to stretch his legs and observe the passing shoreline. South of the town, the Delta spread away from the swollen Nile in an endless sweep of marshlands, interspersed with islands of fertile fields and palm groves. Occasionally the river widened as the branch they sailed on met another channel.

Korax took his dinner on deck: brown bread, peas, a few figs, a tumbler of dark beer. Servants and scribes eating nearby glanced at him with curiosity or indifference. They spoke among themselves and laughed at jokes he did not understand. As soon as he finished the meal, Korax returned to his mat and resumed the writing practice.

At sunset, the priests came on deck. They poured libations from gold vessels, gestured with long-handled incense burners, and chanted prayers. Korax stood with the rest of the ship's company in quiet attention. The ritual concluded as the huge orange sun sank below the horizon.

In the twilight, the helmsmen steered for the shallows. As the barges drifted close to shore, the crewmen reefed the sail and dropped anchors. Korax surmised that, even with the rising full moon, sailing the river at night was deemed too dangerous.

The north wind blew unrelenting, and the temperature dropped. Lying on the mat in only his thin tunic, Korax huddled against the chill. He would have welcomed a blanket but none was offered. He was too proud to ask, even if he had known the word in Egyptian.

When the moon rode at the pinnacle of the sky, he woke to a vision. A woman stepped across the deck toward him, passing through shadows. She was small, but strongly built, dressed in a black robe and silver headpiece. Her appearance nudged his memory, and as she drew close he recognized her: *his mother*. Kneeling beside him, she looked younger than he recalled, lovely in a vivid and unearthly way.

"You are pained, my son," she murmured.

He felt on the verge of weeping. "Mother, I am lost. I don't know how I came to be here."

"You were reckless," she answered. "Partly, it was my fault. I did not conceal my arts from you. I allowed you to learn too much, without teaching you proper piety."

Her arts. The memories came flooding back. Anticleia was his mother's name. She hailed from Thrace, a wild, mountainous land famous as an abode of witches. As a child, Korax had witnessed the magic rites she performed, often with two handmaids who had accompanied her from her homeland. Later, when he was older, he had snuck from his bed at night and spied on her rituals.

"I have paid for my mistake," Anticleia said. "And for you, my son, there may be a way back, a way to regain what you have lost— if you will make reparation."

Korax set his jaw. "What must I do?"

His mother stood. The image of her flowed and rearranged itself before his eyes. The figure became unbearably bright, incomparably beautiful. Her skin shone like gold, her hair glossy black beneath a curved crown. From her shoulders sprouted wings of yellow flame. Suddenly Korax recognized her, from a sailor's shrine he had seen once in Rhodos—the Lady Isis, queen of the Egyptian pantheon.

She spoke to him: "Are you willing to serve the gods?"

His heart drummed in his chest. To regain what was lost he must serve the gods. As he pondered this, the world around him shifted. He found himself floating in the sky, gazing down from a tremendous height. The Nile wound like a silvery ribbon far below, bordered by fertile bands on either shore, then desert to the horizons. Villages and cities, palaces and temples glinted in the moonlight. In his heart he sensed myriads of paths, endless possibilities.

Abruptly he sat up, wide-awake. The stout form of an Egyptian watched him from across the deck. The man wore a loose tunic with shoulder straps and a gold collar. Korax clearly perceived his eyes, glittering, penetrating. Then Korax knew him: the high priest, the one called Harnouphis.

They stared at each other for several moments, neither moving. Harnouphis seemed to be studying him, pondering some mystery. Then the priest turned and slipped away, quiet as a feather.

The temple ships journeyed on against the sluggish current of the Delta. More frequently now, mounds of dry land rose along the marshy shores, marked by villages and stands of palms and acacia trees. Trading vessels and cattle barges sailed past on the river, heading north.

Korax concentrated on his work, diligently copying Egyptian documents. Under Mehen's instructions, temple scribes took turns giving him lessons. They taught him the sounds of letters and made him say them aloud. They wrote words on the tablet, then pointed to teach him what things the words named: sky, river, boat, hand, eye, heart. Korax pronounced each name, straining to commit it to memory. The continual effort stimulated the disused channels of his mind. More and more, he felt alert and present, his fear tempered and under control.

But by afternoon his brain felt saturated. He took a rest from copying and wandered across the deck. Leaning on the rail behind the oarsmen's benches, he watched the river. The sun burned overhead in a cloudless sky, and the water sparkled. As he listened to the steady splash of the oars, his mind drifted off.

He began to hear voices, hissing, moaning. He could not understand the words, but he sensed the beings who uttered them—spirits of the land and the river. They were old, so old it taxed the mind to think about. In their whisperings, Korax sensed immense knowledge, for the spirits remembered all the ages that had passed. He also perceived a boundless, untiring strength. The spirits lived eternally, reborn each year with the flood.

A flock of water birds waded along a reedy stretch of shore, pecking in the mud with curved bills. Closer to the barge, a dark shape drifted in the current. At first Korax took it for a log, but then he spied pointy teeth and small, baleful eyes that watched him as the creature floated past, inciting in him a primordial terror.

"Seshsetem, what are you doing?" Mehen grabbed Korax's shoulder and spun him around. "Why are you wasting time?"

"I'm sorry." Korax didn't know how long he had been staring at the river. "I just needed a rest."

"Come with me," Mehen replied curtly.

Korax followed him across the deck. Mehen shouted to scribes who sat beneath the awnings. They stirred themselves and assembled before Mehen, smirking.

"I warned you about applying yourself to your work," Mehen told Korax.

Two of the scribes seized Korax's ankles and two others grasped his arms. They stretched him belly-down over a bench, holding him immobile. Twisting his head around, Korax saw that Mehen had been handed a stick, long and thick as a spear shaft.

"For shirking your studies," Mehen told him, "you will be punished with ten strokes of the rod. Learn from your error, Seshsetem, and do better."

He lifted the rod over his head with both hands and brought it down with force. It cut through the air with a whooshing sound and landed with a thud on Korax's back.

Korax's gasped, his body thrashing. But the four scribes held him firmly. The next blow struck his buttocks, the crowd of men laughing and grunting with satisfaction. Korax gritted his teeth to keep from crying out.

He would not bear this. As soon as they released him, he would run to the rail and throw himself in the river ... No! The pain and humiliation hardened into cold rage. He would endure it. And he would find a way to revenge himself on the cruel and vicious Mehen.

After the fifth stroke, a commanding voice interrupted the punishment. Korax turned and squinted through teary eyes. The high priest Harnouphis was speaking in a low mutter to Mehen. Red-faced, Mehen scowled with angry disappointment, but nodded obediently.

The men released Korax and backed away as Harnouphis himself came and raised him to his feet. The high priest smiled benevolently and touched Korax on the head as though conferring a blessing. Then Harnouphis turned, still smiling, and walked quietly away. The scribes muttered and dispersed.

Mehen faced Korax, brandishing the rod. "By the merciful intercession of our master Harnouphis, you have been spared the last five strokes. But I urge you to learn from your punishment, Seshsetem. Do not expect such leniency to rescue you in the future."

Chapter Four

Next day the barges sailed past the fringes of the Delta and into the broad main channel of the Nile. The marshlands receded behind them. Now the shores stretched in an unending panorama of flooded and irrigated fields. Behind the fertile swaths, settlements rose along the base of dusty hills and crumbling, sandy plateaus, the beginnings of the desert.

Bruised and sore, Korax kept to himself. His rage had cooled in the night. He would neither forget nor forgive his beating by Mehen, but he would use the pain to fuel his purpose. The vision of the Goddess Isis lingered, filling him with a sense of power and promise. He would regain his memory, discover whatever crimes he might have committed, and make fit retribution to the gods. He would find his way home.

He fixed his attention on his work, studying the rolls of Egyptian script and speaking the words aloud as the scribes instructed him. He copied lines of text again and again, seeking to mimic perfectly the curious curl of each letter. Mehen stopped by in the morning and mentioned Korax's diligence with stern approval. Korax did not look up from the tablet.

Toward noon, a murmur of excitement spread across the deck, and some men gathered at the starboard rail. Korax stood and gazed at the shore. His body stiffened with wonder at the view.

A desert plateau loomed above the river, stretching away to the south as far as one could see. Tombs beyond number reared up on the plateau, arranged among temples, monumental statues, and causeways of stone. Towering in the northern district of this vast necropolis stood three huge manmade mountains, perfectly angular and sparkling white against the blue sky. Korax recalled reading about the pyramids of Giza in the *Histories* of Herodotus.

But no written description could have prepared him for the giant majesty of the sight.

Memphis lay south of the great necropolis. The appearance of the tombs signaled the temple staff to pack their belongings and prepare to disembark. Crewmen ambled along the deck, stripping down awnings and unlashing bales. Korax was given a satchel to store his tablet and scrolls. He rolled up the straw mat and tied it with papyrus cord.

In another hour, Memphis came into view. Warehouses and boatyards stretched along the riverbank behind landings crowded with vessels. Massive white walls ran for miles, concealing the city except for the highest roofs and obelisks. Called Mem-Nephir by the Egyptians, Memphis was the ancient capital and still one of the most populous cities in the land. Korax remembered seeing Athens and Ephesus, two of the grandest cities of the Greek world. But Memphis was larger and far older. He gazed at the city with a blend of trepidation and awe.

The barges anchored at a broad quay of gray stone. A runner was dispatched to the temple to announce their arrival. Priests with their servants and subalterns disembarked. A crowd of spectators gathered to watch as the procession formed. First went musicians, beating tambourines and drums and chanting a sacred song. Behind them floated the gold litter chair of Harnouphis, his attendants and subordinates marching dutifully behind. Last went the servants, guardsmen, and slaves.

Walking along with the other scribes, Korax peered in all directions, drinking in the sights. The procession moved through gates forty-feet high and onto an avenue lined with sphinxes. Ahead in the distance stood massive pylon gates painted with hieroglyphs and flanked by statues of seated Egyptians in royal crowns. By the time they reached those gates, Korax could see that the statues must each be fifty feet high.

Inside, the parade crossed an enormous courtyard bordered on three sides by colonnades. Twin obelisks towered near the center of the courtyard. Ahead stood another set of pylon gates as large as the first and carved with figures in bas-relief. These gigantic figures depicted not men, but the strange Egyptian gods—human of form, but with heads of birds and animals. Korax craned his neck, still examining the images as he passed through the gates.

Inside the next courtyard, the procession halted in front a gallery supported by red pillars topped with white lotus forms. Priests lined the monumental stairway, arrayed in white pleated robes with hats, pectorals, and sashes of gold. An army of subordinates and attendants stood behind them, holding wands, scrolls, and ceremonial vessels. The arriving priests mounted the steps and formally greeted their brethren. Conversing together, they entered the sanctuary through massive doors of polished bronze.

The rest of the procession now dispersed in a dozen directions. Korax followed Mehen and his scribes to a side colonnade. They marched through a series of pillared halls and open courtyards arranged with gardens and pools. They entered a wide structure with plain, white-plastered walls. Within, they traversed a long passageway where lamplight flickered on ancient, peeling murals.

Finally, the party arrived in a broad hall where daylight flowed in through clerestory windows set below the ceiling. Shelves three times as tall as a man lined the walls of the chamber, stuffed with papyrus rolls. More than a hundred scribes sat on straw mats in neat rows, writing with ink pens on papyrus. Korax noted with surprise that a few of the scribes were women.

"This is our scriptorium," Mehen explained, "where you will spend most of your time."

A number of scribes approached Mehen and exchanged words in Egyptian. Korax gathered they were the chief scribe's subordinates, foremen in charge of various groups or sections. Mehen tilted his head in Korax's direction as he spoke with one of the foremen, a round-faced fellow with cheerful eyes and a comfortable layer of fat on him.

"This is Katep," Mehen said to Korax. "He will be your supervisor and will explain your duties."

"Welcome to the House of Records, Seshsetem." Katep spoke to Korax in Greek.

"Obey him as you would obey me," Mehen admonished Korax. "Remember the lesson of the rod."

Mehen issued a few crisp commands to Katep, then turned to other matters.

Katep smiled at Korax and gestured him to follow. "I am so happy to have another scribe who understands Greek," he said. "Chief Scribe Mehen informs me you are making good progress in learning our language."

"I am happy he says so," Korax replied. He was gratified by the compliment, and relieved to find Katep such an agreeable man. "There is a great deal I have to learn."

"We have much work before us," Katep affirmed. "Between the two of us, we must either translate all of our government reports and letters, or teach other scribes enough Greek to accomplish this."

"You speak my language very well," Korax commented.

Katep beamed. "Thank you! I studied for three years at a temple school in Alexandria—a majestic city to be sure. Have you been there?"

Korax tightened his mouth. His time in Alexandria had been spent in a slave pen and filthy cell. "Not long enough to appreciate the sights."

The foreman gave Korax a place beside his own to unroll his mat. Katep reviewed the lessons Korax had learned so far and spent an hour teaching him to read and pronounce new words in Egyptian. He introduced Korax to the other scribes in his section and scheduled each of them to spend time working with him in the days ahead.

Seated cross-legged, the wax tablet balanced on his thigh, Korax resumed the task of copying and memorizing the Egyptian letters. But after some time his concentration faltered, his mind and body exhausted from all he had experienced the past few days. A thrumming sounded in his ears, and his vision blurred. Squinting and dizzy, he gazed around the scriptorium, then back down at the papyrus. The black letters quivered and crawled on the page like swarming beetles.

With a cry of terror, Korax stumbled to his feet and fled.

"Seshsetem, are you feeling better now?"

Katep's round face stared at him with concern. They sat on a stone bench in a garden. Korax blinked, fingertips clutching his forehead.

"I am sorry. I seem to have lost my wits for a moment. I ... have been troubled lately by spells of madness."

Katep nodded solemnly. "I thought as much. Such sicknesses are known here. My honored wife, Hetepher, would say you are touched by the gods."

"Yes. Some in my country would say the same." Korax gazed around the sunny garden, the air fragrant with strange blossoms of purple and yellow. "When it happened to me on the barge, Mehen beat me with a stick."

Katep winced, then shook his head. "The chief scribe is a harsh man. But do not worry. If this happens again in the scriptorium, I or one of my scribes will stay with you till it passes."

His heart touched, Korax murmured, "You are very kind to a slave."

Katep waved a hand. "Some here are slaves, many more are free. It doesn't matter, so long as we do the work. And you are important to us. We need your help."

Korax stared off beyond the green garden at the tall porticos and sandstone walls, gleaming under the deep blue sky.

"You are progressing very well for someone new to our language," Katep said. "Do you have any questions for me?"

"Yes, I have one. I am learning your cursive script, but I do not understand how it relates to your other writing, the glyphs I see painted on walls and carved on monuments."

"Oh, that is the sacred writing," the scribe answered. "Most of us cannot read it. It is reserved for religious texts and magic spells. Don't worry," he added with a chuckle. "You will not need to learn that."

Korax contemplated a distant obelisk covered with the glyphs. The symbols fascinated him at some instinctive level. With their aura of power, they seemed to call to him.

"How does one learn the sacred writing?"

Katep laughed aloud. "It takes years. There are over 700 symbols, they say. It is taught only in the Houses of Life."

"The Houses of Life. What are they?"

"The sacred scriptoriums. Each great temple has one. But only initiates may enter. It is for the priests and their acolytes, not for ordinary scribes like you and me."

"I see." Korax rose from the bench. "How does one become an initiate?"

As he stood, Katep laughed again. "You are too curious, Seshsetem."

These words tugged at his memory. "No doubt you are right," Korax answered glumly. "I suspect it has caused me trouble in the past."

Chapter Five

Korax stood at the window of his bed chamber, staring down at the dark city.

A long line of torches pierced the blackness, winding up the streets in silence. Tonight was the eve of the Dionysia, the Bringing In of the god. By custom, the young men of Rhodos carried the god from his temple in the harbor district up the wide hill to the theater. There Dionysus would be installed in a shrine to watch the plays and performances and preside over the revels.

Korax watched in reverent quiet as the procession passed below his window. Young men in satyr masks carried torches to light the way. Priests clad in red and purple robes walked behind, swinging censers smoking with incense. Three other priests held the tethers of black goats, to be sacrificed at the end of the procession. Next, amid a blaze of torchlight, youths in masks of horse and mule pulled the sacred cart, overflowing with grapevines and blossoms. Within the cart rode the statue of Dionysus, the graceful, long-haired god, dressed in a panther-skin and holding his vine-wrapped wand.

In past years Korax, lover of plays and aspiring poet, had walked in the torchlight procession. But tonight he waited until the last marchers had passed, then quietly closed his shutters. Tonight he had a private appointment with the god.

Korax left a lamp burning on his bedside table. He lay down but did not sleep. All of his plans and preparations were complete. He only had to wait and gather his courage.

In an hour midway between dusk and dawn, when he was certain all others in the house were asleep, Korax crept from his bed. He picked up the lamp and noiselessly opened the door of his chamber.

He stepped down the passageway, past his father's room. There the hallway opened onto a gallery overlooking the courtyard. The waxing moon of Dionysus rode high in the west, silvery light glinting on roof and vine. But ahead the passage was walled again, and Korax crept with the utmost care past his mother's door. He turned the corner into the women's quarters, where the female servants slept and did their weaving and mending. At the end of this hall, he paused before a thick, black door. He pushed it open cautiously, wincing as it creaked on its hinges. He glanced anxiously behind him, then slipped inside.

The chamber was large, with high rafters opening to the eaves of a slanted roof. It was built to be a weaving room, but Korax's mother had long ago claimed it as her private domain.

When Korax was a young child, his mother had slept in this chamber, and he in a small bed in the corner. His earliest memories were of playing here as a babe, of watching his mother at her loom. Until age six, he had also witnessed the magic rites she performed here, often in the company of handmaids who had accompanied her from Thrace. Korax had gazed with fascination as his mother wielded a crooked wand or a bronze dagger glittering in the firelight. He had listened, entranced, as the women invoked the Great Goddess with sonorous Thracian chants that he only half-understood.

When Korax had reached school age, he had been moved to his present bedroom, at the opposite end of the house. It had felt like an exile, and he had trouble sleeping for many nights.

But within half a year, he had found his way back to the mysterious realm of the witches. The family sometimes slept on the roof in the heat of the summer. Korax discovered a loose slat where the flat roof that covered most of the house bordered on the sloping roof above his mother's chamber. Thereafter, on nights of new and full moons, he would often sneak from his bed and climb the ladder to the roof. Removing the loose slat, he would watch unobserved from his high vantage point as Anticleia and her maids performed the rites of Hecate.

Korax remembered enough from those spying missions to know how to conjure a spirit or god—or so he believed. But first he needed to borrow a few of his mother's instruments.

A small altar covered in black cloth stood against the far wall. There he found the serpent-handled knife, laid before the gold statue of Hecate and the smaller, wooden figures that represented Anticleia's ancestors and household deities. Searching through casks and baskets nearby, Korax took scented candles and a cake of incense.

He left the black door ajar and hurried, quietly as he could, back down the passageway. The blood was thumping in his ears by the time he reached his own door.

His writing table, set before the open window, would serve as the altar. He had already laid it out with ivy, the vine sacred to Dionysus. Now he lit two candles from the flame of his oil lamp and set them on the table's edge.

From a storeroom downstairs he had taken a brass brazier, the size of a large wine bowl. This he lined with a layer of charcoal, then lit it from one of the candles. Now three fires were burning.

On a chest nearby, a thrush fluttered in its tiny wicker cage, wakened by the shuddering light. Korax had purchased the bird from a stall outside the Temple of Dionysus and smuggled it into the house under his cloak.

Korax paused to calm his mind. What he was about to attempt was dangerous, some might even say blasphemous. He wondered, after all, if he should stop. But then he felt the sore place in his jaw, and remembered the cause of that injury. He thought of all the times he had been hurt and humiliated by Patrollos and others like him.

With a trembling hand, Korax reached for an incense cake. When he dropped it into the brazier, the flames shot up a brilliant orange and spat a gout of perfumed smoke.

"If fiery destruction be the fate of Korax, son of Leontes," he whispered to himself, "then at least he will singe a few enemies before he burns."

Not a bad conceit, he thought, as he picked up the dagger.

Outside the window, Rhodos lay quiet in the glimmering moonlight—the city asleep, all unaware of Korax and his magic. He traced in the air symbols of invocation he had watched his mother use. Then he spoke the words he had prepared, pitching his voice at a low murmur so as not to waken the household.

"I call upon you, Dionysus, lord of many voices, patron of players and poets, god of the wild places and the wild heart. I, Korax, son of Anticleia of the Thracian tribes, child of the witches of Hecate, summon you now in all your power and might to come before me. By flame and smoke, I conjure you to appear."

His hand shook as he put down the dagger. The fire in the brazier sputtered and writhed, seeming to glow brighter, to blaze with the very presence of the god. Korax stared entranced, and for several moments forgot what he intended to do.

Then he remembered the singing contest at the Guild of Aphrodite. Patrollos and his friends would be there to try to win the prize.

And Korax would be waiting for them.

He steadied himself and reached for the birdcage. Opening the top, he grasped the thrush tightly and pulled it out. Gritting his teeth, he held the fluttering, struggling body close to the fire as he picked up the knife.

"I entreat you, Dionysus, to bend your power to my will. Inspire me with your brilliant music and fill my heart with poetry. But discomfit my enemies. Reduce their songs to foolish babble. Stitch their tongues inside their mouths and bind their wits like the hooves of fatted lambs. Rain laughter and derision on their efforts and bring them only shame. Thus I conjure you, Dionysus, god of poets and players, lord of many voices: Do thou as I will!"

Gripped by a fearful ecstasy, Korax lay the bird on the table and cut off its head with a stroke. Blood spurted, and he squeezed the quivering body in his fingers and poured the blood into the fire.

☥

Korax moaned and flung out his arms with a cry of distress.

Where was he? What had he done?

He clasped his shaven skull with both hands. He lay on a pallet bed, in the small room he'd been given in the temple barracks.

The dream, the calling of the god ... The memories came flooding back, squeezing his vitals with an icy, superstitious dread.

What a fool he had been! To tempt the gods for his own petty revenge ...

No wonder there was terrible retribution to pay.

Chapter Six

The awful dread stayed with him the next day. Grim and subdued, he strained to concentrate on his work in the scriptorium. The intense labor of writing and reading mostly kept his thoughts away from the memory of what he had done in Rhodes. Still, he was grateful when the long day ended.

As he had the previous night, Korax took supper on a terrace outside the main kitchens, seated with a host of servants, porters, gardeners, and clerks. Along with the standard brown bread and beer, the meal included figs, melons, and chopped pieces of roasted goose and duck—leftovers from the priests' tables. It was the best fare Korax could remember since his life in Rhodes, but tonight he had small appetite.

He returned to his tiny room, in a barracks of brown brick and crumbling plaster. The platform bed, a lamp, and a small palm-wood chest were the only furnishings. The bed had one of the curious wooden headrests that the Egyptians favored instead of pillows. Korax had found it impossible to lie on comfortably and thrown it on the floor.

He had stretched out on the bed and was trying to find a comfortable position when his door swung open. Mehen came in, attended by a servant with a lantern.

"Seshsetem, our master Harnouphis summons you."

Korax strapped on his sandals and followed the two men, his unease mingling with curiosity. Why should the high priest want to see him? The sullen Mehen offered no explanation, and Korax judged it prudent not to ask.

They crossed a succession of gardens and courts, the grounds growing more splendid as they went. They approached a gate lit by torches and guarded by watchmen with spears. The guards seemed to recognize Mehen and let the party pass without challenge.

After crossing another garden, Mehen led the way up a long flight of steps with a stone balustrade. They strode along a high gallery, past tall doors with chiseled carvings. Finally, Mehen stopped and pulled open one such door by its bronze ring.

Inside, the servant bowed to Mehen and departed. The chief scribe conducted Korax down a corridor with polished floors and walls paneled with costly cedarwood. They crossed a perfumed antechamber furnished with sumptuous rugs and wall hangings. A slender young woman in a gauzy gown sat on a cushion, idly plucking a lute. She wore a doleful, languid expression and lowered her gaze when Korax's eyes met hers.

"This way," Mehen said.

They entered the next room, a study crowded with scrolls and elegant furniture, illuminated by numerous lamps. Clad in a sleeveless black tunic, Harnouphis waited at the edge of a tiled terrace. Behind him, Korax glimpsed a view of roofs and courts, stepping down to the dark waters of the Nile.

The high priest smiled amiably and gestured Korax to a chair set before an ebony table. Harnouphis took a shallow white bowl, carved of alabaster, and filled it with water nearly to the brim. He poured in droplets of dark oil from a green faience flask. He stirred the bowl with a delicate stick of chased silver, then placed it on the table in front of Korax.

"Stare into the bowl," Mehen said in koine. "Tell us if you see anything."

Korax eyed them both for a moment, then obeyed. At first, he perceived nothing except the swirl of oil spinning off in faint, iridescent colors. But as he watched, the swimming colors began to form an image. Heat pulsed in Korax's skull, and he heard a faint keening, like the call of a bird or animal somewhere in the night.

Then he saw a face, a huge feline face with bristling muzzle and tawny fur. Staring, he realized that the lion had the body of a woman, bedecked in robes of red and gold and holding a staff.

"I see a woman with a lion's head," he muttered. "It is one of your goddesses, is it not?"

"The Goddess Sekhet," Mehen affirmed.

He interpreted Korax's words for Harnouphis. The high priest faced the terrace, his back to Korax. He spoke and Mehen directed Korax to look at the bowl again.

The colors whirled, as though stirred by an unseen hand. Korax scrutinized the bowl for a few moments.

"I see another figure, a man's body, but the head of a bird. Another of your gods, I think."

Mehen spoke a single word to Harnouphis, who nodded triumphantly. Korax sensed that the high priest had somehow cast the images into the bowl, but he kept that insight to himself. Harnouphis took the bowl away and brought out a decanter and goblets of painted pottery.

Mehen relayed his words. "His Excellency begs your indulgence for not acting as a better host. He asks you to join him in a cup of wine."

"Thank you." Korax shifted in his chair, unsure what tone to strike now, what role he was expected to play.

Harnouphis poured red wine into three cups. He handed one each to Korax and Mehen. Again the chief scribe translated: "He asks your opinion of this vintage. It comes from your Greek island of Sicilia."

Korax sipped from the delicate cup; the first wine he had tasted since before he was enslaved.

"It is excellent. I am most honored. But may I inquire why his Excellency confers such honors on a lowly slave?"

Harnouphis gave no answer, changing tacks instead. Mehen continued to translate in the exchange that followed.

"We know that in foreign lands people follow certain Mystery cults, which derive, we believe, from our own ancient rituals. Are you an initiate of any such rites?"

Korax answered guardedly. "I know of the Mysteries. But so far as I know, I am not an initiate."

"So far as you know? How can you not be sure?"

"My mind is ... confused. Some of my memories have been lost."

Harnouphis plainly found this interesting. "Well then, do you recall any experience with the divine arts—what you might call 'magic?'"

Korax swallowed, his mind racing. Plainly the high priest was impressed with his talent as a seer. There might be many ways Korax could turn this to his advantage. He spoke from the memories that had recently surfaced.

"My mother practiced certain arts. I think I may have learned from her, a little."

Harnouphis scrutinized Korax with his piercing eyes before speaking again.

"There is more. What happened to the back of your head?"

Korax instinctively put his hand there. The touch brought a flash of memory: *Lying on the street, a snarling face above him, hands gripping his hair, smashing his head against the cobblestones.*

"I must have been attacked, badly injured ... I believe I may have died—if that is possible."

"What do you remember of that experience?" Harnouphis wanted to know.

"Not much. Darkness, wandering. I think I have been mad ever since. My mind loses track of where I am sometimes."

Hearing the translation of these words, Harnouphis stroked his chin and pondered. Abruptly, he smiled and spoke briskly to Mehen.

"You may go now," Mehen told Korax. "I shall summon the servant to guide you back to your quarters."

Korax lifted himself from the chair then paused. "Can you help me? Can his Excellency help me?"

Mehen translated his words and then the reply.

"What help do you seek?"

"To regain my memory, to make my mind whole again."

Harnouphis stood at the edge of the terrace. Behind him, the moon had risen over the eastern desert. On hearing Korax's words as interpreted by Mehen, the high priest smiled benignly, stepped around the table and laid a hand on Korax's shoulder.

"My dear young friend," Mehen repeated the priest's speech in koine. "I believe we can help each other. What you call madness is both a curse and a gift of the gods. I shall help you master it, and you in turn will use it to help me serve our god. Will you agree?"

Korax trembled inwardly. The words of Isis returned to him: *Are you willing to serve the gods?* Exaltation surged in his heart. He bowed to Harnouphis with the deepest respect.

"I am your servant, my lord."

The attendant came with his lantern and conducted the Greek from the study. When they had gone, Harnouphis dropped into his chair and leaned back, grinning. He pulled off his wig, tossed it on the table and massaged his shaven scalp with stubby fingers.

Mehen had lingered. He stood grimly awaiting further orders.

"What is it, Mehen?" the high priest asked, his eyes closed. "Why so sour?"

"Forgive me, your Excellency. You read my inner thoughts, which I would not presume to express."

"Except that I encourage you to express them now. Please, be at ease, my friend." Harnouphis waved at the chair across from him.

The chief scribe gripped the back of the chair, but remained standing. "I despise this Greek. I know you have discovered abilities in him. But I cannot believe that any good will come of employing an unpurified foreigner."

Harnouphis cocked his head with sardonic amusement. "You are parochial, Mehen. Do you really think the gods care about a man's nationality?"

The chief scribe's face went rigid. "Forgive me, Excellency. I should not have spoken."

"No, not at all. It is I who misspoke." Harnouphis flowed from his chair. "I did not mean to insult you, my friend. And I understand your concerns."

He lifted the cup that he had poured earlier for Mehen, but which the abstemious scribe had never tasted. He handed the cup to Mehen, who took it reluctantly.

"This Greek," the high priest continued. "It does not matter where he comes from. His *gift* is what matters. Perhaps it is because he came so close to death, but whatever the reason, his vision easily pierces the net of appearances. Other men, schooled in our arts, must trace mazes to reach that place of clarity. For him, it is like walking an open corridor. What comes to us in a trickle is to him a stream that flows unbidden into his mind."

Harnouphis resumed his chair and sat back languidly. "I will teach him to control that stream, and he will be a wondrous tool for our purposes. I am certain of it." The high priest raised his goblet. "Be cheered, my loyal Mehen. Let us drink to the future!"

Chapter Seven

The sacred lake lay behind white walls near the great sanctuaries of the temple. Four ramps of bleached stone sloped down into clear, clean water. Priests taking part in the daily rites of the god were required to bathe in the lake twice each day and twice each evening.

Harnouphis arrived at the lake an hour before sunrise, a slave lighting his way. The shore of the lake shone brightly with lanterns. Dozens of priests could be seen bathing in the water. Others sat on stools along the bank while barbers shaved their heads or attendants rubbed their bodies with ointment.

Only a handful of priests were actually required to perform the daily rituals. These assignments rotated on a monthly basis. Except for priests with current duties, attendance at the rites was optional. But Harnouphis always walked in the processions when able. Naturally, it was important for a man of ambition to be seen as pious and dedicated, especially by the first servants of Ptah, the priests of the Inner Circle. But Harnouphis also found attending the rites helpful in keeping track of his fellow second- and third-degree priests—prospective allies and rivals in the ever-shifting politics of the temple hierarchy.

He removed his linen dressing gown and waded naked into the lake, wincing at the cold. The temperature of the sacred water never felt comfortable. He had just started to scrub himself with a cake of natron when a man nearby noticed him, a tall priest with the trim musculature of an athlete.

"Harnouphis, is that you? My esteemed brother! Welcome back to the Mansion of Ptah."

"Greetings, Paramses." Harnouphis grinned companionably. Paramses was a second servant and a man of rising status. He frequented the libraries of the House of Life and was rumored to be a skillful magician. Certainly, he was clever and ambitious, like Harnouphis himself. Unlike Harnouphis, Paramses came from the nobility. For recreation, he drove a chariot and hunted in the desert. In his current post, he was commander of the temple watch.

"How went the Synod?" Paramses asked in hushed tones. "How heavily will Pharaoh's foot press on our necks this year?"

So the game was pretended confidences, Harnouphis thought. He would play readily, without telling Paramses anything he could not easily learn elsewhere.

"May Pharaoh live a thousand years," he pronounced with subtle sarcasm. "I do believe the priests of Egypt held our own this year. Quotas were not raised, except the one on wines produced in the Delta. And the mining tax was actually reduced by a tenth of a tenth."

"That is holding our own." Paramses seemed impressed. "Pharaoh's coffers must be full."

"They are continuously replenished, I am sure," Harnouphis said dryly. "But tell me, dear brother, what transpired in the three months of my absence from Mem-Nephir?"

"Oh, you know. Nothing much changes here." Paramses brushed droplets from his arms. "Wise Amasis still reads as Hierogrammat in the House of Life. And of course, the most esteemed Neksapthis still serves the god as Master of Artisans—despite his wondrously advanced age."

"May he live forever!" Harnouphis intoned. Neksapthis was the Sem-priest, the supreme cleric of the temple. When he at last "passed into the West," one of the nine first servants would advance to take his place. This in turn would open a seat in the Inner Circle. Thus it was an event that many priests had anticipated for many years.

"May you also serve the god long and well." Paramses smiled heartily and took his leave.

Harnouphis completed his bath quickly, then found a seat on the bank. While a barber scraped a bronze razor over his scalp and neck, Harnouphis contemplated. Paramses was definitely a man to be mindful of.

By tradition, 29 men held the rank of second servant of Ptah, and there were 59 third servants. Fully two-thirds of these men were nonentities—unimaginative creatures who had inherited their places in the temple and cared only to preserve their comfort and security. To Harnouphis, such men were sheep and of little concern. It was the remaining one-third who interested him, and they were of several types. A few were authentically holy, mystics who truly loved Maat, the Divine Law, and lived to serve it—men like Amasis, the master of the House of Life. These men were falcons, aloof from worldly affairs and, because of their aloofness, generally not a concern. Other men had ambitions, desiring wealth, prestige, power. With varying degrees of ruthlessness, they would use any means to attain their ends—bribery, flattery, pandering, blackmail, betrayal, and of course magic. The ones drawn to magic were the most interesting of all. Some were like lions, powerful, but not clever enough. Others were jackals, cunning but not strong. Then there were the serpents—stealthy, wise, formidable.

Harnouphis styled himself a serpent. From a poor scribe, the son of a laborer, he had risen to second servant through excellent work, subtle political maneuvering, and even subtler magic. Paramses acted the part of the lion, but he just might be a serpent in disguise.

Shaved and anointed, Harnouphis donned his ritual vestments. He slipped into a long tunic with shoulder straps. Servants tied white sandals on his feet and a scarlet sash around his waist. They affixed a heavy gold pectoral collar over his breast. A plaited wig went over his head, covered with a ceremonial headdress. The servants handed him a ritual scroll and staff.

Arrayed for the rites, Harnouphis marched with his fellow priests along a path of white paving stones. His mind moved quietly, sinuously, like a serpent through deep rushes. Understanding the minds and motives of men, their strengths and weaknesses; tapping mystic energies to strengthen your own mind and will; coaxing gods and spirits to reveal their secret knowledge; combining all of it—understanding, will, knowledge—into a design of your desire, then impressing that design onto the malleable flow of events. That was the game, the ancient game of pharaohs and wizards that Harnouphis relished playing.

And where did this young Greek fit into the game? A most intriguing question. A player could make all the best moves and still never advance past a certain point—unless he was given the right chance, by fate or the gods. Harnouphis had waited years for such a gift to appear. A small, eerie thrill at the base of his spine told him that this was the role written for Seshsetem, his obedient scribe.

The sky reddened in the east. Harnouphis arrived at the front steps of the main sanctuary. Colossal red pillars loomed overhead. The servants of Ptah assembled at their various posts. Some prepared incense burners, some filled vessels with holy water, some tightened the strings of sacred harps.

Harnouphis moved easily through the crowd, greeting fellow priests he had not seen these past three months. He conversed affably with all, regardless of their rank or status. Harnouphis cultivated his reputation as a good friend to all.

He noticed Shepseskaf standing on the portico, conversing with another high priest. Shepseskaf was the temple chief treasurer and Harnouphis' immediate superior. Harnouphis had spent all of yesterday afternoon giving the man a complete report on the Synod in Alexandria. Still, Harnouphis made it a point to approach and greet him this morning. As he drew near, he saw that the other priest was Peherenptah, another member of the Inner Circle.

"Greetings, your Excellencies." He bowed.

"Ah, Harnouphis." Shepseskaf exhibited a brief smile. He was an aristocrat of ancient priestly lineage but no particular intellect or ability. He regarded Harnouphis as a social inferior, though a talented and useful functionary. Harnouphis in turn regarded him as a sheep who pretended to be a lion.

"Good morning, Harnouphis." Peherenptah's eyes shone. "I've heard excellent news about the success of your mission to Alexandria."

Harnouphis shrugged diffidently. "The credit belongs to the priests of all the temples. Of course, I did my humble best to represent our interests before Pharaoh and his ministers."

Peherenptah laid a hand on his shoulder. "You are too modest, my brother. Your skill and hard work are inestimable assets to the mansion of our god."

Harnouphis bowed, pleased at the approbation. Peherenptah was the temple's chief steward and a formidable member of the Inner Circle. Some counted him the frontrunner to replace the current Sem-priest. Harnouphis had his doubts. Peherenptah was a potent magician, but also a notorious libertine. Neither lion nor serpent, he seemed more like the powerful hippopotamus who wallows too much in the mud. Of course, that beast's true nature often remained hidden below the surface. And when roused to anger, the river horse could be terribly dangerous.

Meditating thus, Harnouphis courteously withdrew to allow the two first servants to continue their conversation.

Presently a procession appeared at the gates, coming from the outer courtyard. Temple bakers, cooks, and brewers carried offerings of bread and cakes, roasted flesh, beer, and wine. Gardeners brought bowls of fruit and flowers. Arriving at the base of the steps, the marchers presented their offerings to the priests who would carry them into the sanctuary. The gold vessels, bowls, and platters they bore were immeasurably old and exquisitely crafted. Ptah was the great artisan god who had fashioned the world. The artifacts of his temple were renowned as the finest in all Egypt.

From a gallery high overhead, a horologer priest called out a chant to announce that the sun was rising. The priests arranged themselves before the tall doors to begin the morning rite. Harnouphis took his position among the second servants. He watched Neksapthis, the frail and withered Sem-priest, step to his place at the forefront. Leaning on a ceremonial staff, Neksapthis chanted the opening prayers in a quavering voice. Harps and cymbals sounded. The assembly of priests chanted replies in chorus.

Thou art risen, Great Ptah
Risen in peace!
Arise! Arise in peace!

The great doors swung inward with a groan of bronze hinges. The Sem-priest led the procession into the first chamber, a vast hypostyle hall containing a forest of rose-colored pillars. Flickering torches lit the way through the darkness. At the west of the hall, the procession halted before doors of gleaming bronze. Attendant priests fumigated the air with incense and sprinkled holy water over the offerings. Neksapthis sang more prayers, and the chorus answered.

They passed into the next chamber, a gallery not quite so vast, where only consecrated priests could enter. Painted statues lined the walls and stood before supporting pillars. The priests set offerings before some of these personages—different ones being honored each day of the month. By the time the procession reached the far wall of the sanctuary, the sun had risen high and daylight slanted through the clerestory windows under the distant ceiling.

Now it was time for the climax of the rite. A first servant would break the clay seal and enter the sacristy. Alone in this sacred place, he would bathe the statue of Ptah, clothe him in new raiment, and serve his morning meal.

But as Neksapthis ambled toward the golden doors, and the priests chanted the holiest invocations, disaster nearly struck. The aged Sem-priest stumbled and started to fall.

The assembled priests sucked in their breath. This would be a terrible omen indeed. In the crucial moment, Harnouphis saw that Shepseskaf and Peherenptah both stood within reach of the staggering Sem-priest. But both remained rooted in their places. Instead, it was the nimble Paramses who darted forward from the ranks of the second servants and saved Neksapthis from falling.

Steadied, the supreme cleric smiled benignly at his rescuer and clasped him by the arm. Paramses bowed respectfully before backing away.

Yes, Harnouphis reflected, Paramses was decidedly a man to be watched.

"Our master Harnouphis commands me to educate you in certain practices," Mehen said to Korax. "These are basic exercises that will improve your mental stability and balance your life-force, which we call *ka*. Listen to me carefully, Seshsetem."

Korax nodded eagerly. They stood inside his tiny room, dusk thickening outside the window. Korax had returned from his third day of work in the scriptorium to find the chief scribe waiting.

"Stand with your feet together, thus," Mehen instructed. "Straighten your back. Now stare at the lamp. Concentrate solely on the flame. Breathe slowly and deeply."

Korax continued this activity for several minutes. Then he was told to shut his eyes and visualize the flame, placing it above his head. Gradually, he willed the flame to gleam brighter, until it shone like the dazzling sun. Next, he envisioned a ray of this sun descending to create a second light at the center of his head. After a time the light lanced down again, igniting a pulsing sphere at his throat, then his heart, then the base of his spine, and finally the space between his feet.

Korax experienced this inward sunlight with a numbing intensity. The radiance seemed almost to lift his body and make it float in the air.

Finally, Mehen told him to open his eyes.

"Repeat this exercise each morning and evening," he said. "Consider it part of your duties. Do not fail."

When the chief scribe had departed, Korax stretched out on his bed. His mind was dazed, yet calm and relaxed. A strange power thrilled inside his body.

He had felt such power before.

Chapter Eight

*I*n the twilight, a gentle breeze floated through the streets of
the harbor district. Sounds of song and feasting flowed
from the open doorways of taverns and inns. Korax
marched along in his navy trappings, a leather headband
confining his black hair, a sword in bronze sheath hanging from
a baldric, his lyre in a drawstring bag tucked lovingly under his
arm.

All day he had strolled through the city, enjoying the revels of
Dionysus. He had marched in processions, danced in jubilant
crowds, played and sung on street corners. Always, he felt the
presence of the god he had conjured, throbbing in his veins, filling
his mind with poetry, his heart with wild joy.

He crossed the Square of the Colossus, where torches burned
brightly amid groups of revelers, their boisterous laughter
drifting through the dusk. Below the statue's huge pedestal, a
circle of women dressed as maenads danced barefoot in the
shallow pool, kicking up water while the crowd around them
whooped and cheered.

The guild hall of Aphrodite stood on a narrow street at the
edge of the temple district, not far from the main harbor gates. As
Korax approached the brightly-lit portico, he could hear music
within and smell the clematis vines draping the entryway.

Inside, he found a tiled antechamber illumined by cressets.
Young women and boys of the prostitute's guild stood in a line,
wearing short, diaphanous costumes. Coronets of polished
bronze sparkled on the heads of some, while others had flowers
woven in their flowing hair. The sensuous music of flutes drifted
from the inner hall.

Behind a wide table facing the entrance sat Lady Emerine's enormous steward Cleonides, a wreathe of ivy on his head. He was flanked by two muscular giants with folded arms. They were made up with brown body-paint and horns to look like satyrs, but the stout clubs at their sides were not just for ornament. They were guards, assigned to keep order.

"Welcome, young sailor!" Cleonides cried. "We are honored by your presence." He waved to indicate the smiling boys and girls behind him, who regarded Korax with knowing eyes. "All sensual pleasures await you within, for the small donation of five obols to the goddess."

Korax took the purse from his belt. He counted out five obols, dropping them into the fat man's palm, then added a sixth. "For your trouble, good steward."

Cleonides smiled with delight. "Oh, a noble youth indeed! May the Lady of Love favor you always."

He put the coins away and clapped his hands sharply. A boy and young girl skipped forward to take Korax by the arms.

"Treat this one with special attention, my lovelies," Cleonides told them. "He is a gentleman of the finest breeding."

The young courtesans led Korax to a fountain at the rear of the chamber. They removed his sandals, washed his feet with a sponge and basin, dried them with a soft towel. They tugged felt slippers onto his feet. Korax stood, enjoying the softness against his toes. The boy took his cloak and the girl removed the sword belt from his shoulder.

"I will keep the lyre," Korax said.

The courtesans conducted him to the doorway of the main hall, a large rectangular chamber with pillared alcoves along the sides. Graceful friezes of mythical love scenes adorned the upper walls under gold-painted cornices. At the front of the hall, a lifelike statue of Aphrodite smiled down from behind a flower-draped altar. In the absence of a true temple in Rhodos, this hall served for worship as well as celebrations.

Couches and tables were spread along the walls in front of the alcoves. Places were set for perhaps a hundred dinner guests, many already occupied. The young cadets of the Rhodian navy lounged on pillows or stood in small groups chatting, each with a wine cup in hand. Korax scanned their faces, saw some he knew from the School of Bellerophon, others he recognized from his naval service last summer. Patrollos and his followers were nowhere in sight.

Courtesans of both sexes glided about the hall, carrying pitchers of wine or trays overflowing with grapes, pears, and pomegranates. A trio of flute girls stood in the center of the floor, playing a sweet, languid air. Berenicea was not among them.

Korax found himself an empty couch before an alcove, an inconspicuous location. He accepted a wine cup from a serving boy, but took only a sip. With the god's presence throbbing in his blood, he needed no more intoxication.

Presently, Patrollos and three of his band arrived, marching across the open floor and taking couches near the front. Their faces were nervous, as though striding into battle, though the plush slippers on their feet made that impression incongruous. Among the party was Cimon, a tall and brawny kinsman of Patrollos; Lyceas, the son of a wealthy banker; and Amynias, a cousin to Korax, though never his friend. Korax bore grudges against them all, but especially against Amynias. His cousin was the worst kind of fraud and parasite. Amynias seemed to believe he could join with Patrollos and his band in humiliating Korax in public, yet still pretend friendliness to him whenever family occasions brought them together.

Korax caressed the strings of his lyre. These four enemies had no idea what lay in store for them this night.

Shortly, a trumpet flourish sounded at the front of the hall.

"Young gentlemen of the Navy of Rhodes," a herald announced, "your hostess, the Lady Emerine."

The famed hetaira appeared from a doorway, leading a train of guests arrayed in rich and colorful costumes—leaders and friends of the courtesans' guild. These dignitaries were accompanied by the prettiest boys and girls of the house of Emerine. Korax sucked in his breath when he saw Berenicea. She wore a short lilac tunic and high-strapped sandals. Her red hair was piled on her head, tied with a purple scarf and a wreath of wild daisies.

The guests took their couches, the young courtesans attending behind them. Lady Emerine sat in a cushioned chair at the center, a commanding woman of legendary beauty. Her costume deliberately imitated Aphrodite: a sheer gown of white silk cinched by a golden girdle, earrings and coronet of gold set with coral and rubies.

"Young men of the Navy of Rhodes, I bid you welcome," she announced. "The Guild of Aphrodite is honored by the presence of so many handsome and gallant young sailors."

A rowdy cheer started up from several quarters, and soon guests and courtesans alike had joined in. Smiling, Emerine waited for the applause to subside.

"As promised, we offer you the finest wine and feasting and the prettiest companions to be found in Rhodos. And I also know there are many skilled poets among you who are ready to entertain us with their hymns composed for this occasion. To judge the lyric contests, we are honored to have as our guests three preeminent performers and poets: Anasicrates and Moerocles of Rhodes, and Apollonius of Alexandria."

These three gentlemen stood, waved their hands with elaborate flourishes and bowed, first to Emerine, then to the hall.

Emerine stood as a boy brought her a goblet on a silver tray. She poured a libation to Dionysus, then a second one to Aphrodite.

"And now, let the feasting begin!"

Parades of servers appeared from several doorways, carrying baskets of bread and heavy, covered dishes. A clatter of pottery echoed through the chamber as the dinner guests served themselves. As promised, the feast offered delicacies of every kind: roasted beef and mutton, sea bass and perch, crayfish and eel. The courses were served with sauces of every description, both sweet and briny—cooked from olive oil, garlic, spices, cheeses, fruits, and honey.

As the feasting commenced, the actor Anasicrates called all poets who would sing in honor of Dionysus to come forward. Korax noted that the line included Amynias, Cimon, Lyceas, and about ten others. The young men drew lots from a clay jar to decide the order of performance.

Next, the poet Moerocles invited all who wished to sing for Aphrodite to approach. Korax lay still and watched as Patrollos and six others walked to the front of the hall. Patrollos was the only contestant from the School of Bellerophon. He had actually discouraged other students from entering the competition. As was well known, he hated losing any contest, and no one at school wanted to earn his enmity. It was even whispered that he had paid the school music master to secretly write a lyric for him. Patrollos had boasted that when he won the crown of Aphrodite, he would claim Berenicea as his prize.

Korax stayed in his place. At the prompting of the god, he waited until the last of the competitors was drawing. Then he jumped to his feet and strode briskly to the front table.

"Forgive my tardiness, esteemed Moerocles," he announced. "But here is one more to compete. I am inspired by Dionysus that I should sing for Aphrodite."

"Well-spoken," said the poet. "And what is your name?"

"I am Korax, son of Leontes." He bowed deeply to Lady Emerine, who answered the gesture with an amused nod.

"Well, Korax son of Leontes," Moerocles said, "since only seven came forward, I placed only seven lots in the jar. Certainly, it would be unfair to ask the others to draw again. So what am I to do?"

"I will sing in whatever place you deem fair." Korax's shrug expressed his complete indifference to the issue.

Moerocles conferred in whispers with his fellow judges. After a moment, they nodded.

"Then you shall sing last," the actor declared. "And though some may deem the last place advantageous, it will not be so in this case. The judges agree that you will need to outshine all others in great measure to win from that position."

"I am content," Korax answered. "Since I expect to outshine all others immeasurably."

A few jeers and catcalls erupted at this display of audacity. Korax bowed to the judges and allowed himself a quick glance at Berenicea. She met his eyes, and a faint smile passed over her lips.

Korax returned to his coach, heart pounding with excitement.

He leaned his back against a cushion and placed the lyre on his thigh. He grew very still, feeling the presence of Dionysus within him. He watched impassively as the first contestant sang. At one point, he glanced over at Patrollos and the others. They muttered to one another, eyeing Korax with hooded, distrustful expressions.

The feasting continued as one performer followed another. Korax touched neither food nor drink. The aura of stillness about him only deepened.

The fifth man to perform was Cimon. As he walked to the front of the hall Korax's fingers suddenly moved, gliding noiselessly over his lyre strings. His lips whispered something, but if asked, he could not have told what words he spoke, or even what language.

As Cimon made ready to play he abruptly jerked his head in Korax's direction, and their eyes locked. Korax felt a surge of power tighten every muscle of his body.

Cimon blinked, collected himself, and began his song. But his fingers twitched, missing some notes, striking others harshly. The effect was a dreary cacophony that contrasted starkly with the words of the hymn, which celebrated the sweet pleasures of wine. The effort received awkward, shallow applause. Cimon slunk back to his place with his head hung.

Korax relaxed and watched the next two performers. Then it was Lyceas' turn.

Lyceas marched to his place with a belligerent air and deliberately avoided looking at Korax. He strummed forcefully, but as soon as he started singing it was plain his throat was tight. His voice screeched at the high notes, and he had to stop and cough halfway through the song.

Korax returned to his normal frame of mind as several more poets sang. But then Amynias' name was called and Korax stiffened, his hands clutching the lyre like claws. He stared balefully at Amynias, who strolled to the singer's place with his usual frosty self-possession.

Amynias plucked two sweet notes. But as he opened his mouth to sing, he struck a third note and the string snapped, the end *whipping up and striking him below the eye. He let out a gasp, his hand flying up to cover his cheek.*

A few snickers of cruel laugher sounded in the otherwise quiet chamber. Grimacing, Amynias examined a smear of blood on his fingers. He looked helplessly at the judges.

"Pardon me. I ... I cannot continue."

Korax emerged from his trance. He reached for his cup and found that his hand trembled. He steadied it with an effort of will and took a small, calm sip.

Two more contestants sang hymns to Dionysus. Then an intermission was held while the judges conferred. More dishes were served. Dancers performed to the music of cymbals and flutes. Berenicea stood playing with the other flute girls. Korax was lost in watching her when a dark shape loomed at the corner of his eye.

Patrollos stood over him. Korax sat upright, but Patrollos' close position prevented him from standing.

"I don't know what you are doing," Patrollos said, "or how you are doing it. But I vow to you: it will not stop me from performing and performing well."

His voice was quiet and meant to sound menacing, but he was clearly strained by frustration and fear. Korax almost pitied him. For a moment, he thought about putting an end to his plan. But as soon as the thought occurred, he knew it was too late. He had set a god in motion, and that motion must run its course.

So he merely stared at Patrollos and said not a word.

Presently, the contest for the hymn to Aphrodite was announced. Korax resumed his pose of deep stillness. As the first four poets took their turns, Korax breathed slowly and deeply, trying to keep himself relaxed. The god's energy curled within him, a panther ready to strike.

The fifth man to sing was Patrollos. When his name was announced, Korax abruptly stood and backed into the alcove behind his couch. The motion caught Patrollos' eye, and he paused. When he proceeded, his steps were slower, less certain than before.

Korax crouched in the shadows, knees bent, hands squeezing the curved frame of his lyre. No one in the hall could see him. His lips moved, silently uttering angry, baleful syllables—a curse in an ancient language he did not know. His hand made jerky tearing movements close to, but not touching the lyre strings.

At the front of the hall, Patrollos plucked three notes and began to sing. His hymn was an elegant poem in the classic style, restrained and balanced. His voice was strong, if a bit deep. He sang the first two lines perfectly. Then on the third line he missed a note, and on the fourth his tongue stuttered over the words.

Patrollos glanced anxiously at the black alcove where Korax worked his magic. The fact that he could not see Korax seemed to drain his poise. His playing grew strident and faltering. On the second verse he missed several words, and on the third he forgot an entire line. Unnerved, he finished in disastrous fashion, striking notes in the wrong places and slurring the poetry. He slumped back to his place amid feeble applause, an image of utter defeat.

Korax staggered from the alcove, drenched in sweat. He collapsed on the cushions, arms flung wide.

A serving girl approached. "Are you all right, young sir?"

He answered with an exhausted laugh. "I have never felt better."

The next contestant began to sing. Korax slowly recovered his strength. When the hymn ended and the applause faded, Moerocles the judge called his name:

"Korax, son of Leontes. Our last contestant of the evening."

Korax rose and brushed back his hair. "Time for the climax of the play," he muttered.

Coolly, he walked to the spot before the judges' table. "Esteemed judges," he announced in his best oratorical tones, "elders of the guild, fellow guests: it has been a memorable and inspiring evening. I am inspired, in fact, to offer the following review of some of the performances we have heard."

He plucked a strong note and began, singing words whispered to him by the god:

> *The panther-clad god wishes to thank*
> *All who offered him their poems*
> *But he views with scorn a few of their rank*
> *And wishes to bid them now go home*

As he played, Korax strolled over to where Patrollos and his group were seated. He wanted to leave no doubt as to whom he was singing about.

> *One called Cimon, with his clumsy thumbs*
> *He sang of wine and languors sweet*
> *But his playing sounded woefully sour*
> *He might play better with his feet*

Cackles of laughter rippled through the hall. The revelers were by now quite drunk and not averse to hearing some mean invective.

> *Now Lyceas is a handsome youth*
> *Whose downy beard the god finds pleasing*
> *But his lyric was crass and tedious*
> *And his voice like an old sow wheezing*

The laughter swelled. In front of Korax, his victims looked about in shame and consternation. In the street or on the athletic field, they would have jumped him by now and used force to still his mockery. But here in polite company, they had no choice but to take it.

"Sing on, good satirist," someone shouted. "Tell us more!"

Korax turned to his beloved cousin.

Now Amynias is a glib young man
The love of rich friends he craves to win
He's willing to follow them like a slave
And more than willing to betray his kin

But the god disdains men who are false
And does not care to hear them sing
So when Amynias started to play
His finger slipped and he broke a string

Now the feasters were roaring and stamping their feet to urge him on. Korax sidled up close to Patrollos, who stared back at him with helpless rage.

But the most embarrassing hymn tonight
Came from Patrollos, the noble and strong
He thought to buy his way to the prize
By paying a teacher to write his song

Patrollos sang for the Goddess of Love
His purchased lines shone like glass
But his tongue stumbled like a three-legged goat
And his lyre would have pained the ears of an ass

A crescendo of raucous laughter followed these verses. Patrollos balled his hands into fists and stood. With a curt bow to Lady Emerine, he turned and marched stoically toward the door. Amynias and the others rose and hastened after him.

Exhilarated, Korax watched his enemies retreat from the hall amid clamorous jeering. Because of his family, Patrollos was known to everyone present. Tomorrow, the story of his disgrace would spread all over the city.

"I fear you have driven away some of my guests," Lady
Emerine remarked as the laughter and applause died away. "I
must admit it was done with cunning rhymes. But this is not the
night of the Comedies, master Korax. You were supposed to
present a hymn of love."

"And so I shall, gracious hostess," Korax answered gallantly
as he strode back toward her throne. "Forgive me, but I was
compelled by the god to rid the hall of some ignoble ruffians."

Emerine returned his glib smile with a placid look that
managed to communicate both amusement and disapproval. "It
is usually folly, young man, to credit the gods for our own base
deeds. However, we will hear your hymn now."

Korax inwardly called to the god. Instantly, his mood
swooped down from the heights of triumph to a sober place of
contemplation. As he sang, his entire soul seemed to flow into
each plaintive word.

They are wrong who claim the Goddess of Joy
Looks down on mortals from above
For I know she lives within me
And in the one I love

Korax paused between verses, letting his lyre sing. He stared
at Berenicea, making sure he caught her eye.

When I gaze on her I love
Small fires burn beneath my skin
Pleasant yearning wrings my bones
Aphrodite breathes within

Fair Goddess born of ocean foam
Lift my song with your sweet grace
Let it win for me my love
I see your light in her bright face

Korax ended his song gazing at the red-haired girl. Berenicea
stared back, her chest rising with each breath, her eyes wide and
shining.

A long moment passed before Korax realized that the chamber was filled with deafening applause.

Chapter Nine

Korax wandered the temple grounds under the stars. The latest memories, bubbling up in his dreams, had left him too restless to sleep or even lie still. Enflamed with guilt, dread, wonder, he had risen from his bed and ventured into the night.

How shamefully he had behaved! How cruelly he had wounded Patrollos, Amynias, and the others. And yet, how wonderful the magic, the power of the god pulsing in his blood, inspiring such glorious music and cunning rhyme.

Struggling to find a place of balance amid these conflicting passions, he walked along the deserted paths and galleries. He avoided the places patrolled by watchmen—mainly the gates that led to the sanctuaries and priests' quarters. This still left a sprawling labyrinth of buildings, gardens, and courts, all empty and quiet.

Fortified walls enclosed the temple compound, but the parapets mostly stood unguarded. Korax climbed steps at the northern edge of the complex, mounting to a high terrace. Sitting at the base of a pillar, he looked out over the suburbs of Memphis to the desert and the vast necropolis. A waning moon hung parched and yellow in the west. Monuments and mortuary temples stretched away to the northern horizon, where the great pyramids shone small and ghostly in the distance. Korax imagined what lay beyond them—the vast Delta, the sea, Rhodes.

Magic. How marvelous it had felt. He recalled his mother's rituals, the power she wielded. His parents never spoke of it openly, but it was said among the servants that her witchcraft protected the fortunes of the house, safeguarded the family's ships at sea, guided all of their business decisions.

That same talent lived in Korax—he knew it now—an inheritance from his mother, a gift of the gods.

But he had used the gift wrongly, impiously.

And yet, if he could learn to use magic for noble purposes, as his mother did, surely that would pay for his foolishness. Under the starry sky the words of Isis came to him again: *Are you willing to serve the gods?*

Korax bowed his head.

But he was merely a slave, trapped in this desert place so far from his home. How could he hone his talent, learn all he would need to know of the divine arts?

How?

The next time Korax was summoned to his master's chambers, Harnouphis was clad in a black gown and a folded headdress. He wore a gold pectoral collar, a scarab amulet carved of garnet, and seven gemmed rings on his fingers. Chief Scribe Mehen stood nearby, eyeing Korax with his usual pinched expression.

Harnouphis smiled amiably and handed Korax a tumbler of wine. He spoke and Mehen translated.

"Our master Harnouphis bids you good evening. Tonight he has a new and important exercise he wants you to try. Be seated."

He gestured to a chair before the wide writing table. But Korax set down the wine cup and remained standing.

"Before we begin, I have a request to make of his Excellency."

Mehen frowned. "And what might that be?"

"His Excellency has shown that he values my talent as a seer. I would wish to develop that talent, in service to the gods. I wish to study the divine arts, to be initiated in the House of Life."

"Impossible!" Mehen flared angrily.

But Harnouphis questioned him, and Mehen replied in Egyptian. Hearing Korax's request, the high priest evinced surprise and a shade of anger. But he quickly masked his feelings and answered in a tone of mild caution. He and Mehen exchanged several remarks in low voices. Then both of them turned to Korax, and Mehen spoke with exasperation.

"Our noble master forgives your effrontery, Seshsetem. He instructs me to say that your ambition is laudable, but that you must remember that you are both a foreigner and a slave, making it extremely difficult to grant your wish."

Harnouphis spoke again, and the chief scribe continued with obvious reluctance. "Still, due to his boundless generosity, his Excellency does not refuse your request. He says that, if you work diligently, and continue to perform these special tasks he occasionally asks of you, he may, in time, consider your worthiness for what you ask."

A flimsy promise at best, Korax thought resentfully. But he could see no advantage in pressing further at this point. Harnouphis gestured at the chair, and Korax sat.

On the table before him stood two rows of white candles. Each burned before a rectangular mirror of polished copper. Set upright on the table, the mirrors formed a miniature corridor, closed at one end but open at the front facing Korax. Harnouphis muttered something and pointed at the cup.

"Drink the wine," Mehen said.

Korax picked up the tumbler and swallowed the draught. He noticed a tickle in his throat and a smear of powder lingering in the cup.

"The wine has a mild drug," Mehen explained. "Do not be alarmed if you feel a slight drowsiness or hear a buzzing in your ears. Just relax and gaze at the candles."

Korax suppressed his feeling of alarm and did as instructed. Harnouphis sat down across the table and began a chant, intoning words in a voice that rose and fell hypnotically. The candles sputtered and blazed brighter.

Korax slipped into a reverie. He imagined the corridor of mirrors to be a passageway where he walked. On each side he could see his reflection. Candles the size of torches blazed off into infinity. Then another figure appeared in the mirrors. Tall and angular, it had the body of a trim, broad-shouldered man and the black head of a dog or jackal. Korax knew him from paintings and carved reliefs—the God Anubis, the guide of the dead.

The god turned and trod silently down the passageway. Afraid, but unable to resist, Korax followed. Anubis turned a corner, his animal tail sweeping behind him. Korax paused, sensing another presence. He turned and saw Harnouphis. The high priest gestured urgently for Korax to go on.

Korax proceeded around the corner and saw the god ahead of him. Steadying his nerve, he followed. This corridor had no mirrors. Instead, the walls were covered with painted scenes and hieroglyphs in vivid, glossy colors. Anubis reached a crossing in the passage and turned. Korax increased his pace, Harnouphis on his heels.

They followed the god through a maze of passageways, all of them lit by torches and covered in shiny murals. Korax sensed that he must keep the jackal-headed god in sight or that he and Harnouphis would become hopelessly lost.

Finally, the god stopped at the end of a long corridor. Standing before a pair of gold doors, Anubis turned and, as he did so, changed. The jackal-features transformed, flowing into a mass of white feathers. The face of a bird peered down through tiny yellow eyes. Korax knew him as Thoth, the god of scribes and magicians.

Korax halted, daunted by the god's glistening stare. But Harnouphis strode forward. He gesticulated with open hands, gave a half-bow of obeisance, and uttered a chant. For a moment, Thoth regarded the high priest with an unfathomable expression. Then the god pointed at the gold doors, which immediately swung inward.

Harnouphis raised a hand to Korax, commanding him to stay. Then the high priest straightened his habiliment and marched resolutely through the portal.

Korax put a hand to his lips, gazing up at the god. A wild impulse prodded him to disobey Harnouphis and follow him into the chamber. Korax brushed the thought aside, but it welled up, stronger than before. After all, his talent had led the high priest to this secret place. Why should Korax be denied the opportunity to pierce the mystery within? If Harnouphis would not teach him the ways of magic, he must take the risks to learn for himself.

Propelled by this reckless urge, Korax strode forward. He bowed his head hastily to Thoth and thrust himself across the threshold. Inside he found a vast chamber of gleaming white stone. At the far wall stood a huge statue cast from the brightest gold. The face was human and serene, surmounted by a skullcap and adorned by the narrow, ceremonial beard of a Pharaoh.

The statue was Ptah, the Great God. The Greeks equated him with Hephaestus, but Korax had learned that to the people of Memphis he was much more than the patron of craftsmen. Ptah was the Sun. Ptah was the Primal Artisan who had fashioned the world. Ptah was the demiurge who brought the universe into being by uttering the Great Word at the moment of the creation.

Harnouphis stood in the center of the floor, palms raised in supplication as he vocalized an invocation. The air hummed with mystic forces.

As Korax watched awestruck from the rear of the chamber, Ptah came to life. The god raised his scepter high overhead. The ankh at the tip glittered, flashing with the brilliance of the Egyptian sun. Ptah's mouth dropped open. In a mighty voice he uttered four syllables.

"Aaaa-tuuum faaaahh graaaal."

The stone chamber shook with the sound. The ankh burst into a blinding light. The world shattered and Korax fell into blackness.

Chapter Ten

*B*erenicea held Korax's hand in her soft fingers and led him along the narrow passageway. Her perfumed oil lamp cast a halo over them both.

Korax followed her as though in a dream. He had released his will to hers, as earlier he had released it to the god. Perfectly appropriate, he told himself, for Berenicea was his goddess of love. On that point, his inspired hymn had revealed a deep and mysterious truth. He smiled, reflecting on the flow of muscle in her sleek calves, the sway of fabric about her thighs. Berenicea glanced at him over her shoulder and giggled.

The judges had conferred for only a few moments. Korax— despite his insulting attacks on his fellow contestants—was the overwhelming choice among the singers to Aphrodite. Staphylus, a young man Korax knew from school, won for his hymn to Dionysus. Lady Emerine crowned both young men with laurel wreaths and formally invited them to choose their companions for the night. Korax of course chose Berenicea, while Staphylus chose a handsome boy. In the role of priestess of Aphrodite, Emerine pronounced a ritual blessing on the four young lovers. Then, in her role as businesswoman, she reminded her other guests of the many desirable companions available to them for a modest fee—all proceeds to benefit the goddess.

Berenicea unlatched a door and pushed it open. "I believe this chamber will please you, my lord."

Her lamp revealed a small, luxurious bedroom arranged in the Eastern fashion. A multicolored Persian rug made soft padding underfoot. In lieu of a bed, a pile of cushions lay spread against the wall, draped by gauzy hangings. Fresh air and moonlight drifted through an open casement.

"Why, yes," Korax told her nonchalantly. "I am pleased."

Berenicea set down her lamp and shut the door. Next moment, she pressed against him, twined her arms around his neck and kissed him fervently.

On the couch in public, she had kissed him shyly on the lips, allowed him to squeeze her waist and thigh, but had otherwise been reserved. Now, alone with her at last, Korax was overwhelmed by her passion. He hugged her tightly with one arm, his other still holding the lyre.

When she twirled away, his phallus stood up under his chiton like a pike. She gave him an amused glance, then gently took the lyre from his arm.

"Your hymn was very beautiful," she murmured as she set the instrument aside. "I'm sorry. I know I told you that already."

Korax clasped her two wrists. "I will never tire of hearing you say it. I will never tire of hearing you say anything."

She caught her breath, eyes appraising him. "I must confess, as a courtesan I am taught it is necessary to keep a certain distance. And I am not very experienced. But you are not at all like my other clients."

Korax grinned at her. "How am I different."

She lowered her gaze, her smile shy. "I don't know. Perhaps it was your hymn. It awakened something in me. Almost ... well, I imagined it was the goddess herself."

"Perhaps it was. I truly see her in you."

She regarded him skeptically, appraising again. "You are certainly an unusual young man. So gifted. But those verses you sang about the other poets—so cruel. You must hate them very much."

"They deserved it," Korax answered.

Berenicea nodded pensively. "I remember the other day outside the school, when Patrollos pushed you into the mud, and *the others laughed. And yet you came here tonight and confronted them all fearlessly."*

"To punish them," Korax said. "And to win you."

Did the black fury that seethed in him frighten her, he wondered, or arouse her? Perhaps a little of both?

Berenicea smiled her enigmatic smile and walked him gently to the cushions. Korax sat down awkwardly, and recollected that he was quite drunk.

The girl snuggled against his shins and started to pull off his slippers. "My, your knees are bony," she laughed.

Korax stiffened, injured by the remark. "I know I lack the brawn of some young men," he intoned with drunken dignity. "But I won the contest, and my ardor for you is unmatched."

"Oh! I meant no offence." Berenicea tilted back, horrified that she had hurt his feelings. "Forgive me, I am a stupid girl."

Before Korax could reply, she scurried to her feet. "Wait."

She fetched his lyre, pressed it into his hands and knelt before him. "Master Korax, you are a glorious singer, a brilliant poet, and I think a man of other talents of which I could scarcely guess. I am only a poor courtesan of the house of Emerine. My service is to my mistress and to the Goddess of Love. But if you will sing your lyric for me once more, I will love you not only with my body, which is my duty, but with my whole heart, which is my choice and my gift."

Korax swallowed before he could answer. "Adorable girl, you are as beautiful in spirit as you are in outward form. My heart has swelled into my throat, which can make singing difficult. But I assure you, I will try."

Korax left the guild hall at daybreak. Rain had fallen in the night, leaving the streets slick and scattered with puddles.

Threatening clouds still loomed overhead, shading the city in an eerie half-light.

But Korax's mood was bright as silver.

The spirit of the god had stayed with him, expanding his ecstasy, deepening his blissful union with the lovely Berenicea. Only when Korax kissed her farewell did he sense Dionysus withdrawing at last, leaving him drained and satiated.

Now, the laurel wreath set on his head, the bagged lyre tucked under his arm, he wandered happily into the Square of the Colossus. The plaza lay still in the gray morning, empty but for a few exhausted revelers who slept beside empty wineskins on the broad steps of the stoas. Korax stopped in the middle of the square and gazed up at the Colossus. His cloak flapping in the wind, he offered a prayer of thanks.

"Helios, god of Rhodes and patron of my fathers; Dionysus, god of players and poets; Aphrodite, mistress of all lovers: I, Korax, son of Leontes, thank you for this morning, and for the night that came before."

Behind the Temple of Helios, Korax crossed a wide boulevard and entered a tradesman's warren—a maze of narrow streets, close-packed houses, and apartment blocks. This way would take him straight across the lower city and up the hill, his most direct route home.

In the damp morning, shops and storerooms stood shuttered along the deserted streets. An old man dozed under a ragged cloak at the mouth of an alley. A gray cat lay curled on a doorstep and watched him pass with wary, golden eyes. Once Korax thought he heard footsteps moving faintly behind him. But when he turned there was nothing.

The cramped street slanted upward. Ahead, a long public stairway climbed a steep stretch of hill. As Korax approached the base of the steps, two cloaked figures emerged from behind a building.

Patrollos and Cimon.

Korax whirled his head to look behind him. The others had appeared from a side street: Amynias and Lyceas.

Korax groaned with weary resignation. In those brief moments when he had allowed himself to think beyond his night of triumph, he had known there must come a reckoning—and, little doubt, another drubbing. He just hadn't expected it so soon.

Too tired to even try talking his way out of it, Korax just stood his ground as they paced toward him. Their hair hung wet and tangled, their cloaks wrinkled and stained. Lyceas and Cimon carried collapsed wineskins over their shoulders. Apparently they had stayed out all night drinking, licking their wounds, plotting to corner him on his way home.

"We know you used witchcraft." Patrollos' voice was a hoarse whisper. "Amynias confirmed that your Thracian mother is a witch."

He grabbed Korax by the front of his garment, lifted and slammed his back against a wall. Dropping the lyre, Korax tried to wedge his fists up between Patrollos' arms, to break his hold. Instead, Cimon and Amynias each seized one of his arms and twisted them back. At the same time, Patrollos yanked and then shoved him backward, his head cracking against the brick.

Korax grunted, straining helplessly.

"We want you to admit it," Patrollos growled. "Did your mother cast the charm for you? Or did you learn it yourself, like a puppy learning tricks from his mother bitch?"

Korax spat into his face.

Patrollos gasped and his bloodshot eyes glazed over. He pulled Korax away from the wall with such strength that Cimon and Amynias were also thrown back. He lifted Korax's body in the air and flung him down hard. Korax landed on his back and Patrollos leaped on top of him, knees pinning his arms. Patrollos grabbed a handful of hair and smashed Korax's head on the cobblestones.

Korax yowled in pain, and tried to kick his way free. But he could gain no leverage. Roaring, Patrollos slammed his head down again, and again.

He could not tell if he was dreaming or awake. He seemed to be walking along a beach at night, through soft sand that slipped under his sandals. The faint murmur of running water sounded somewhere to his right. But then the same sound could be heard on his left and again, it seemed, behind him. Ahead in the distance he spied faint lights—lamps or torches burning atop a far citadel. He kept walking toward the lights, but never seemed to draw nearer.

He could not recall how he had come here. The last he could remember were voluptuous scenes of lovemaking with Berenicea, his red-haired Celtic girl. Thinking past that only made his head hurt.

He turned around and was confused to see the distant lighted hilltop behind him now. Wearily, he sat down, then stretched out on his back. Overhead the stars wheeled in a black, shimmering sky.

From far away a voice called his name. "Korax."

The stars turned faster, until they were spinning blurs of light around a central core of blackness. A roaring wind filled his ears, and it seemed the sky was falling around him—or he falling into the sky.

"Korax!"

The roar grew deafening, the light blinding. He gasped, and the rush of wind became the sound of air sucked into his throat. His body heaved and shuddered. His eyes flew open wide.

Trembling, he stared up at a bleak gray sky and an ashen face hovering over him: a woman. He wondered dimly who she was.

"My son," the woman uttered.

Yes, he knew her now. His mother.

A thought swam through his wounded brain: His mother's witchcraft had called him back from the dead.

Chapter Eleven

Korax awoke in his bed. A broad, solemn face stared down at him, a middle-aged woman. Puzzled, he remembered his mother's grave face against the sky of Rhodes. But this woman was Egyptian.

Seeing him awake, she touched his forehead with her palm. With a grunt, she reached over to a basin, wrung water from a cloth, and wiped his brow. When he tried to rise she pressed his shoulder down and spoke a single word he recognized from his scant Egyptian vocabulary.

"Stay."

Flat on his back, Korax watched her rise and leave his room. Memories from the dreams returned, floating uneasily through his mind, inciting awe, then horror. Patrollos had beaten him to death—or near to death. But somehow Anticleia's enchantments had called him back to life.

He sat up, then bowed his head and shut his eyes to let the waves of dizziness pass. Now he was Seshsetem, a scribe in the Temple of Ptah, a slave. He still had no idea how he had come to Egypt. Whatever happened after he woke on that street in Rhodos was still a void, a long and empty oblivion.

The door opened and the Egyptian woman reappeared, carrying a pitcher and a wood platter of bread and dates. She set them down beside the bed, brought a drinking cup from the shelf, filled it with water.

"Eat now." She turned and left again.

Korax picked up the cup and drank. He had a powerful thirst, and hunger as well. How long had he been unconscious? As he nibbled the bread, he remembered his last visit to the apartment of Harnouphis, the vision of the maze, the hall of Ptah. He had impetuously entered the god's chamber, ignoring his master's command. No doubt Harnouphis and Mehen both would be displeased with him.

After finishing his breakfast, he stood and stretched. He felt whole and hearty enough. He seemed to have suffered no ill effects. He placed his feet together and stood erect. Closing his eyes, he began the exercise he was ordered to perform each morning and night, visualizing the sun above his head.

The cell door opened again, snapping him to alertness. Mehen appeared, carrying a walking stick, his face taut and angry.

"So, you are awake at last. Do you realize you slept an entire day and night?"

"No," Korax answered, taken aback. "I was not aware."

"Foolish, despicable scribe." Mehen brandished the stick. "Were it not that Harnouphis forbids it, I would beat you till you bled."

Korax clenched his jaw, suppressing a wild urge to wrestle the stick away and beat Mehen instead. But that would bring him no help, only worse trouble.

"Our master Harnouphis is severely displeased with you. He said you had the effrontery to disobey him in the mystic maze, to enter the holy sanctuary of the god. And you, a foreign slave. Should he wish it, he could have you beheaded for such blasphemy."

Korax lowered his eyes. "I am sorry."

"You wish to initiate in the House of Life," Mehen sneered. "After this disobedience, it will be a long time indeed before Harnouphis even considers such a thing. And I promise you: I intend to use whatever influence I have with our master to ensure that it never happens!" He waved the stick in the air. "Now dress yourself and return to your duties. You have lost one whole day. I shall see that your work is doubled to make up the time."

The chief scribe whirled and stalked out, slamming the door behind him. Korax stood with fists clenched at his sides, gripped by impotent fury.

Seeking to calm himself, he took several long breaths. He did not dress immediately as ordered. Instead, he returned to the mental exercise. Mehen had commanded him to perform this practice each morning and night, and so he would comply.

As the envisioned spheres of sunlight descended his spine, his anger faded. A sense of divine power grew inside him, and with it came knowledge: This exercise was itself a step toward the magic he craved to discover. That thought consoled his heart. To attain the freedom he longed for, he must follow this path with humbleness and patience. It would not be easy for him. He was rash and reckless by nature. But that wildness had led to all his troubles and must be tempered.

Such was the duty set before him by the gods.

Korax clung to the idea of this duty with grim resolve. In the following days, he worked diligently in the House of Records and repeated the mental exercises morning and night without fail. Gradually, this regimen balanced his nerves, stilled his raging passions. The spells of distraction and madness grew milder and less frequent. At the same time, his concentration improved, his mind growing steadily more focused and clear.

Under the tutelage of the jovial Katep, his learning of the Egyptian language accelerated. Before long, he conversed readily in the native tongue and understood nearly all of what he heard. He soon mastered the writing of the cursive script and was readily translating Egyptian documents into koine. Side-by-side with Katep, he devised a course of instruction and began training his fellow scribes in the Greek letters.

Some evenings, Mehen or one of Harnouphis' servants would appear at Korax's cell and conduct him to the high priest's apartments. At first, Harnouphis treated him with severity, admonishing Seshsetem that he must be obedient and never repeat his foolish and blasphemous error. Korax hung his head and accepted the rebukes in silence, then did his best to follow his master's commands.

He would gaze into the scrying bowl and enter a state of trance. In visions, he met all manner of strange beings: creatures with bodies of mist or flame, animals that spoke with human voices, occasionally a god or goddess of Egypt. Prompted by Harnouphis, Korax would converse with these personages, repeating the high priest's questions and the answers given.

As Korax mastered the everyday Egyptian speech, he soon realized that the words he relayed were often of a different language, one completely unknown to him. He suspected it to be an ancient, magical tongue. He asked Harnouphis about it more than once, but the priest ignored his questions, pressing him instead to repeat every syllable precisely.

Sometimes, instead of the scrying bowl the high priest would direct Korax to stare at a candle flame. Harnouphis would utter a chant, and the flame would flicker and dance in response. Then Mehen would set down papyrus and pen and tell Korax to write whatever words came into his mind.

After a time, Harnouphis changed Korax's daily exercises, making the regimen more complex and demanding. Now Korax caused the inner sunlight to circulate, flowing to different centers within and around his body. With each envisioned sphere of light, he intoned a word or phrase over and over in a deep, reverberating voice. Korax recognized none of these words of power, but again suspected they must belong to the magical tongue. When he questioned Mehen about it, the chief scribe told him curtly not to ask, only obey. Clearly, Mehen resented teaching Korax these practices and only did so at their master's command.

The expanded exercises left Korax inflamed, his nerves vibrating. Some nights he found it impossible to sleep. Then he would rise and wander the temple grounds.

One night he returned to the high terrace that overlooked the northern wall. Leaning with his back to a pillar, he gazed out over the city and the desert beyond. Cruel longing pricked his heart as he thought of Rhodes.

More than four months had passed since his arrival at the Temple of Ptah. His life here was comfortable enough, the tedious labor in the Hall of Records leavened by the fascinating glimpses of magic in his scrying for Harnouphis. But it was still the life of a slave. No matter how resolutely Korax tried to follow the path of duty and patience, he yearned for his home, his family. He wondered if his parents were well. How much did they know of what had become of him? Were they even still alive?

That question raised ominous doubts in his mind. Did the home and family he remembered even exist? Or might they all be delusions born of his madness?

He must find out, must learn the truth of his past. He must get away from this cursed captivity.

As he had done many times, he tried to concoct a workable plan of escape. He now had considerable freedom to come and go within the temple enclosure, and he could speak Egyptian well enough to get by. But even if he slipped outside the temple walls, he would need money to buy passage downriver. He could think of no way to acquire any coin. Besides, the temple had its own police force, known for their efficiency in tracking fugitive slaves. They would quickly follow the trail of a runaway scribe—especially one with unusual talents that a certain high priest valued so highly.

Korax hung his head in frustration. Tears welled up from deep in his soul. For the first time he could remember, he wept without restraint, pouring out his loneliness and grief until all the tears were shed.

A few nights later, weary from roaming, Korax sat down under a sycamore tree. Nearby a desert spring fed a clear, round pool with a soothing trickle of water. Beyond the pool lay a long, low-roofed building faintly visible in the moonlight. Someone had told Korax that this was the House of Life. Of plain brick and white plaster, it looked more like a stable than the hall of sacred wisdom ...

Korax opened his eyes with a start. He didn't know how long he had been dozing. Across the garden, a door had opened in the wall. A figure emerged, an old man with a scrawny body and bare head. As Korax watched, the man closed the door behind him, and it seemed to disappear. The wall was cunningly designed indeed, Korax thought. He had never spotted the hidden door, even though he had passed this way in daylight.

The old man ambled toward the edge of the pool. He pulled his garment over his head and dropped it on the bank. Sighing contentedly, he lowered himself into the water.

Silently, Korax shifted into a crouch. He wondered if he could slip away without being seen. But then the old man called out to him.

"Don't worry about me, young sir. I'll not tell anyone I've seen you. To be frank, I'm not supposed to be here myself this time of night."

Chagrinned, Korax rose and stepped from his hiding place. Approaching the water's edge, he smelled a whiff of salty natron, which the old fellow was using to wash himself.

"I like to bathe here when no one is around." The man splashed happily. "Did you know this pool is fed by the same spring as the sacred lake where the high priests bathe? Except this pool gets the water first."

"No," Korax admitted. "I did not know that."

The old man squinted at him in the moonlight. "I don't believe I've seen you before. May I ask your name?"

"It is Ses—It is Korax," he answered—and wondered why he felt compelled to give his true name.

"*Korax*. How unusual. Sounds foreign."

"It is Greek."

"A Greek in service to an Egyptian temple? Now that *is* unusual." The old man pushed off with his feet and glided on his back.

"I don't believe I caught your name, grandfather."

"I don't believe I tossed it. Ha ha! I love that old joke. But you can call me grandfather. I like that. I don't have any grandsons of my own, you see?"

Korax squatted beside the pool. "Are you a scribe in the House of Life?"

"Not exactly. You might say I'm a doorkeeper there."

Korax considered this remark, which intuition told him not to take at face value. "That sounds interesting. You must observe much of what happens then."

"Oh, yes. Many scribes laboriously copying old manuscripts, placing them in their proper niches. Not very interesting, really."

"But the writings are magical, are they not? And sometimes new spells are written."

"Ah, magic! What is your interest in magic, grandson?"

Korax smiled ruefully. "I sometimes imagine it is my calling."

"Really? That must be intriguing for you. Perhaps a little frightening too?"

"Not frightening, but frustrating," Korax replied. "I know one must be an initiate to gain admission to the House of Life. But I've read of Greek travelers who claimed to have learned the Mysteries in the temples of Egypt. So foreigners must be admitted sometimes—unless those writers lied, which is certainly possible. Tell me, grandfather, how can I become an initiate?"

"You are in earnest then?"

"I am."

"Well, it's not difficult. First you must ask. Then you must be deemed worthy. Are you a free man?"

"No, a slave," Korax said. "Harnouphis is my master. He is a powerful magician, so I believe."

"Harnouphis, the second servant? Oh, yes, a noteworthy man, admired for his profundity and his generous spirit. I suggest you ask him to sponsor you."

"I have tried that," Korax said, shoulders sagging.

"And...?"

"He promised to consider it, but that was months ago. I think ... Well, Harnouphis uses me to scry for him. I fear he would prevent my learning magic, so he can keep my talents all for himself."

Surprised, the old man ceased his splashing. Growing very still, he stared hard, as if reading Korax's soul.

"That is an interesting idea," he said at last. "But I doubt it could be true. Such actions by a servant of Ptah would violate rightful principles."

Korax heaved a sigh, but said no more.

The old man floated on his back. "If you are in earnest, I suggest you speak to your master again. If Harnouphis sees true talent in you, he would be honor-bound to sponsor your initiation."

"I told you, I have tried."

"Ha-ha! Then try harder. As a doorkeeper, I can tell you this: the portals of the sacred knowledge don't always open the first time one knocks.

Chapter Twelve

Be seated, Seshsetem." Harnouphis regarded Korax with a fatherly smile. A mild breeze flowed into the study from the night-cloaked terrace at his back.

"Thank you, your Excellency." Korax sat in his usual chair at the ebony table. Taking hold of his nerve, he said, "Before we begin tonight, I would like to speak with you—to discuss the terms of my continued service."

Harnouphis' cordial expression declined into a frown. "Your *what?*"

"Seshsetem!" Mehen hissed. "You forget yourself!"

"No, no. Let him speak." Harnouphis waved a calming hand. "Continue, my young friend."

Korax cleared his throat. *Knock harder, the old man at the pool suggested. Tonight, he meant to force the door open if he could.* "As your Excellency knows, I have been in your service for over four months. I believe I have met all my obligations as a scribe in the House of Records, and I know that the services I've rendered to you in this chamber have also been of value."

"Go on," Harnouphis said.

"I feel I have the talent to offer greater service, if given the opportunity. I have asked once before and now I ask again: I wish to be initiated into the House of Life."

"Insufferable effrontery!" Mehen exclaimed.

Harnouphis ignored the chief scribe's outburst and spoke with quiet authority: "You have asked before, and I have answered. Such a privilege will not even be considered until you have proven your worthiness through long and patient duty. Your bringing the matter up again so soon does you no credit."

Korax kept his voice level. "I do not consider four months to be very soon."

"Slave, you forget yourself!" Mehen cried.

Harnouphis glared at Korax. His tone was deathly calm. "That is not for you to decide."

Korax set his shoulders into a posture of defiance and stared without flinching.

Harnouphis stared back, frowning. Abruptly, he gave a subtle smile. "I laud your determination and courage. But you must realize, our secret traditions are an ancient treasure of Egypt. They are almost never disclosed to foreigners."

"I understand that." Korax was ready for this objection. "But I am a servant in the Mansion of Ptah. And if your Excellency were to sponsor the request, I believe one of the rare exceptions could be made."

Harnouphis appraised him, frowning once more. "Do you realize, Seshsetem, that before you can truly practice the sacred arts, you must master the old language? This typically takes many years of study. Your mind is quick, but I doubt you have the necessary patience."

"Perhaps not, your Excellency. But as you say, I do have determination. If it takes me many years, then the sooner I can begin, the better."

Harnouphis pondered for a moment more, then rose from his chair. He stirred a mixture of water and oil in the scrying bowl. "I understand your request is important to you, and I will think it over. To be frank, I may decide that it is not in the temple's best interest or your own." He set the bowl down in front of Korax. "I hope you will understand if that is my decision."

Korax stared pointedly at the high priest. "As your servant, I will accept your decision, of course. Only, I worry that my disappointment might make it difficult for me to see accurate visions for you in the future."

Korax heard a grunt of rage from Mehen, but his eyes stayed fixed on Harnouphis. The second servant glared at him for an instant, pure malice in his eyes. Quickly, Harnouphis concealed the emotion.

"You have made your point, young man." His sudden smile was unnerving, reminding Korax of a serpent. "As I said, I shall consider your request again. Now, let us begin the scrying."

Mehen returned to his quarters that night in a mood of black rancor. The audacity of this Greek jackal knew no bounds. For months, Mehen had watched the Greek's star rise in the estimation of his master Harnouphis, had seen Harnouphis grow more and more dependent on the Greek's ability as a seer. Mehen had despised Seshsetem from the start. This latest episode only proved his instincts correct.

Unlike most officials of his age and rank, Mehen still resided within the temple enclosure. As he had never married, he had seen no need to acquire a house in the city. Instead, he occupied several rooms in a residential precinct near the western wall. The simple apartment suited him well enough, and the proximity to the House of Records was an advantage. Mehen worked many hours in his capacity as chief scribe, not to mention long evenings of study in the House of Life. His diligence and dedication were impeccable, and esteemed by many.

Entering his foyer, Mehen removed his wig, sash, and collar and handed them to his manservant. He told the servant to extinguish the lamps in the outer chambers and then dismissed him for the night. Mehen took a candle and proceeded to the small room that served as his study.

The room was furnished with only a rack of scrolls, a straw mat, and a low table. On the table stood statuettes of Ptah and his consort, the Goddess Sekhet. Between them stood a wax figure, crudely carved—a man with the head of some indeterminate animal.

Mehen sat cross-legged on the mat. He lit a cake of charcoal from his candle and placed it in a clay censer. He added a lump of gummed incense, which fizzled and spawned a column of gray smoke. Mehen shut his eyes, took deep breaths, stilled his thoughts.

Presently, he started chanting in a quiet voice. "Aukert-khetet-ast. Aukert-khetet-ast. I call you now before me, creature of the desert pool. I, Mehen, know your true name. I command you to appear."

Mehen had prepared and studied many years to attain the ability to call a magical ally. Even so, there were nights when the creature did not answer the summons, or when it seemed that the responses he gave were illusory, merely the voice of Mehen's own thoughts.

Tonight, however, Aukert-khetet-ast spoke to him clearly, his utterance like the croaking of a frog.

"You are troubled tonight, O servant of Ptah."

"Anger burns in me. My master Harnouphis is ready to allow the Greek slave to be initiated into our Mysteries."

"That is peculiar. But it would seem to be Harnouphis' decision. Why does it enrage you?"

"Because the slave is a contemptible foreigner. And because ... he has usurped my place of prominence in my master's eyes. Harnouphis says he may turn down the request, but I know how much he depends on the unpurified one. He will lower himself, degrade our Mysteries even, because he sees advantage in using the Greek."

"Then your anger is justified."

"Yes. But Harnouphis is my master and mentor. And there seems to be no swaying him. That is why I called you. I want to know how you see the future of this matter. How high will this foreigner rise?"

Aukert-khetet-ast held silence for a time, then: "I see you are correct. The foreigner seeks to conceal his motives. He has no loyalty to Harnouphis or your god. He longs to return to his homeland, and will use any means to escape."

"I knew as much. It is plain to see."

"Still, I counsel you to patience, Mehen. A day will come when the foreigner overreaches."

Chapter Thirteen

Stomach fluttering with anticipation, Korax approached the House of Life.

A portico of gray columns shaded the main doors, while hieroglyphs ran along an entablature beneath the tile roof. He had never seen the east façade of the building. It stood in a precinct he never visited by day, and the area lay behind guarded gates, so his wanderings at night had also never brought him here.

Harnouphis walked beside him. Having agreed to request Korax's initiation, the second servant now acted the part of benevolent sponsor.

"Remember to be open and honest in all your answers, Seshsetem. His Excellency Amasis will immediately perceive any attempted deception. I have spoken to him on your behalf, but of course the final decision must be his."

They climbed five steps, crossed the portico and passed through the tall portal. Inside, they proceeded along a narrow, vaulted hallway. Doorways on either side led to broad chambers filled with daylight and lined with shelves. Korax glimpsed a few men reading scrolls or writing with reed pens on papyrus. Otherwise the libraries stood empty. Korax knew that most of the priests and acolytes who studied in the House of Life performed other duties during the day. In the evening these chambers would be more crowded.

At the end of the corridor they turned into a dark, cramped passageway. Harnouphis knocked on a door, and a voice called out permission to enter. Harnouphis ushered Korax into a pleasant office lit from an adjacent terrace. Beyond the terrace lay a lovely garden of ferns and oleander.

An old man, seated on a mat, rose as they entered the chamber. Korax's stomach, already tense, twisted into a knot. He recognized the scrawny old man from the bathing pool. Harnouphis tapped his staff on the floor and gave a formal introduction.

"I present his Excellency Amasis, Hierogrammat, Supreme Scribe of the House of Life in the Mansion of Ptah. Your Excellency, this is Seshsetem, the young man I mentioned."

"Ah, yes." Amasis nodded pleasantly. "You seem somehow familiar, young man. Have we met before?"

Korax opened his mouth, hopelessly uncertain how to reply.

"Ha-ha!" Amasis laughed. "Forgive my playing with you. You are my lost grandson from the bathing pool." He clapped Korax's shoulder with startling force.

Harnouphis' face expressed bewilderment.

"Oh, I met Seshsetem once before," Amasis explained. "He wanders the grounds late at night, and sometimes so do I. But I'm not sure why a healthy young man should be so restless." He turned a meaningful look on Harnouphis. "Almost as if his nerves were charged with unusual stimulation."

Harnouphis' smile seemed plastered on. "He never fails to surprise me."

Korax found his voice. "It's true I sometimes have trouble sleeping. It seems to harm no one if I walk about a little."

"No harm," Amasis assured him. "I see no harm whatsoever in this young scribe. Come, let us stroll in the garden."

Amasis put on a disheveled wig and picked up a walking stick. He led his guests down the terrace steps and along a winding path of white pebbles. Ferns and palm fronds filtered the bright sun, casting speckled shade. Insects whirred in the flowering shrubs.

In answer to Amasis' questions, Korax repeated his reasons for seeking initiation: that he felt an inner calling from the Goddess Isis, that he had mastered his current duties and sought to offer higher service. He made no mention of his scrying for Harnouphis, though of course Korax had already disclosed this activity to the old "doorkeeper" at the bathing pool.

Harnouphis in turn affirmed that Seshsetem had proven himself a dutiful scribe, and that his talents might indeed benefit the temple should he receive training in the sacred scriptorium.

The three men rested at the side of a cement pool, where silvery fish swam lazily beneath floating lily pads.

"The recommendation of your esteemed master bears much influence in the House of Life," Amasis told Korax. "But before we decide on your request, I want to be sure you understand what it would mean. As a candidate, you will first undergo an initiation ritual, which we call the *Welcoming at the Threshold*. Most men find this experience unnerving; many are utterly terrified. The rite has been known to drive some weak-minded individuals to such a state of distraction that it took them months or even years to recover. Obviously, those men were not meant to study here."

The knot in Korax's belly tightened. "I understand."

"After you have passed initiation, you will be given scrolls to copy, to introduce you to the sacred writing. You will also be assigned daily meditation rituals, which will begin to attune your body and mind to a higher kind of functioning. In all this, you will be guided by a mentor, who will answer your questions and oversee your progress."

"I have volunteered myself as your mentor," Harnouphis said.

"Yes, an extremely kind offer for a servant with so many other duties," Amasis remarked.

Korax detected a note of reserve in the statement, as if Amasis would have preferred to assign a different mentor but could not refuse Harnouphis' offer.

"When you are judged perfect in your knowledge of the sacred writing, you will be eligible for advancement into higher grades of initiation. The first phase normally requires several years to complete—the exact time being dependent on the candidate's talent and how hard he works."

Amasis set a hand on Korax's shoulder. "In all your efforts Seshsetem, you must strive to adhere to *Maat*. As ours is not your native language, I must make certain that you understand this concept. Maat is the name of a goddess we worship. She personifies truth; that is, the divine truth behind the net of appearance that makes up the visible world. Maat is order; the divine order that regulates the daily journey of the sun and the yearly rise and fall of the river. Maat is law; the divine law that shapes the destinies of all. As you progress in our sacred knowledge, Maat will be revealed by your studies, by your mentor, and by your own inner guidance. Sometimes it is hard to adhere to Maat and tempting to stray. But departure from Maat introduces impurity; and impurity leads inevitably to failure and chaos.

"Having heard all this, Seshsetem, are you still determined to enter the House of Life?"

His certainty had only strengthened during Amasis' last speech. "I am, your Excellency."

"Splendid! I will make the arrangements. Your initiation will commence at dawn three days hence."

"That is amazing news indeed!" Katep exclaimed. "Congratulations, Seshsetem."

Korax nodded, smiling as they sat together in the scriptorium. "It will not alter my duties here. We will continue to work together."

"I am glad of that," Katep said. "When the harvest comes, we'll need you more than ever. But we must celebrate your accomplishment. Why not come to dinner tomorrow at my house?"

So it was arranged, and the following afternoon Katep and Korax left the scriptorium together. They exited the temple complex through a service gate in the south wall. Except for a few formal processions, it was the first time since his arrival that Korax had been able to venture outside the Mansion of Ptah. He wore a fresh linen tunic, gray sash, and white sandals on his feet. On his head was a plain black wig, which he had been given but seldom wore. He had stopped short of applying rouge or darkening his eyelids with kohl, as a young man might typically do for a social occasion.

Still, he knew he looked very much the Egyptian scribe that he had become. The thought both pleased and needled him, pride at his adaptability mixed with a gnawing dismay at the dwindling of his Greek self.

The two friends walked past broad plazas and ceremonial avenues with their pillared halls and towering obelisks. They entered a residential district of close-built houses and winding streets. A fat orange sun was settling over the roofs when they reached the house of Katep.

Shouts of excitement greeted them as they entered the foyer. Katep's two little daughters ran up and hugged their father's legs.

"Here are my darlings, Ipwet and Kiya!" Katep cried with gleaming eyes. "And here is my son, Baufre."

The boy, older than his sisters, greeted the two men with a dignified bow. Baufre had the traditional shaven head and sidelock of a preadolescent Egyptian boy.

"And this is my dear wife, Hetepher." Katep touched her lovingly on the hip and kissed her cheek.

Hetepher was a slender woman with dark, serious eyes. She extended her hand, palm down. "Welcome to our home, good sir."

Korax touched her fingers lightly and bowed in courteous greeting. "I am honored by your invitation."

Hetepher smiled. "My husband has told us much of Seshsetem. Your knowledge and hard work have spared him much trouble and worry."

The lady ushered them through a comfortably-furnished living room and out to a tiny garden. Stools had been arranged beside a small lotus pool, and low tables set with bread, dates, and tumblers of beer and water. The aroma of roasting meat drifted out from the kitchen.

The party relaxed beside the pool, Hetepher sitting on a footstool and leaning against her husband's knee. The little girls played in the garden, running over occasionally to receive a caress from their parents. Baufre sat nearby, listening attentively to the adults' conversation.

At first Katep and Korax discussed their work. With the harvest approaching, their labors would intensify. Many of the scribes would be dispatched to the temples' far-flung estates to assist auditors in counting and recording. At the same time, more correspondences would need to be written and long inventories tallied and reported.

But after the steaming plates of roast lamb had been served and everyone had eaten their fill, Hetepher requested that the conversation change. "Dear husband, you can talk about your work with Seshsetem any time. Tonight is a celebration."

"You are right, of course," Katep said. "What should we talk about then?"

Hetepher offered a coaxing smile. "Well, we know Seshsetem is a well-traveled man. We would love to hear him tell us about the places he's visited."

"Yes, please!" Baufre exclaimed, as though he had been dying to hear that suggestion.

"Now wait." Katep held up his hands. "He is our guest. We must not impose."

"Not at all," Korax replied. "It would be my pleasure."

He still could not remember what happened to him after he was attacked by Patrollos, still had no idea how he had come to Egypt as a slave. But memories from his earlier life were steady and firm. For the next hour, he drew on those memories, recounting his travels in the Aegean and Greece. From his early teens, Korax had sailed on the family's trading ships in the summers. He entertained Katep's family with descriptions of the fabulous tomb of Mausolos in Halicarnassos, and the towering beauty of the Parthenon in Athens. He talked about differences and similarities in how people dressed and spoke, what they ate and drank, how they worshipped the gods.

But when the subject turned to his homeland of Rhodes, Korax's heart grew leaden, his tone wistful. "Rhodos is not the largest or most splendid city that I can recall. But to me, it is most beautiful."

Quiet settled over the garden, now lit by flickering oil lamps. The little girls dozed against their father's knees. Young Baufre stared at Korax with rapt attention.

"Perhaps you will have the chance to return someday," Hetepher remarked softly.

"Perhaps," Korax said. "It is a strange fate that has brought me to this ancient city on the Nile. But at least I have learned one thing: good people and good friends can be found in every land."

"I drink to that!" Katep lifted his beer. "But you have learned many other things also, my friend. And now you will be initiated into the House of Life, and I am sure will learn much more."

"Yes." Korax's face brightened. "An opportunity I have longed for."

Hetepher shifted in her seat. "I am happy for you, Seshsetem. But I feel you would be wise to regard the opportunity also with caution."

"Now, wife. We don't need to worry him with that story," Katep admonished.

"I speak from my heart, husband. Would you have it otherwise?"

Katep frowned but held his tongue.

"Please speak, "Korax encouraged her.

Hetepher sighed, her voice taking on an edge of sorrow. "It concerns my older brother. He was a scribe at the temple, like Katep. He aspired to enter the House of Life, and when the chance came, he was initiated. For a few years, everything seemed well. He would not speak much about his studies, but he appeared bright and enlivened. Then things changed. When I saw him, he acted moody and short-tempered. It almost seemed he had become a different person. One night, when he had drunk many cups of beer, he boasted that his mentor raised powerful spirits, that these beings would bring all within his circle wealth and greatness. That was the last time I saw him alive. The following month brought the Festival of Ra, when Ptah is taken downriver to visit his fellow god at Iunu. During the return voyage my brother drowned in the Nile. They said it was an accident, but I feel in my heart that he might have jumped—or even been pushed."

"Or perhaps he simply got drunk and fell overboard," Katep said. "Most scribes who enter the House of Life do not end up drowning in the river."

"I did not say the case was typical," Hetepher answered. "And I don't mean to discourage Seshsetem. I simply urge caution. Not all the men who study in the House of Life are above evil magic. Not all of them are true servants of Maat."

Chapter Fourteen

Korax entered the House of Life in the still hour before dawn. Barefoot and bareheaded, he wore a tunic of black linen tied with a black sash. Harnouphis marched beside him, dressed in vestments of white and gold, a ceremonial headpiece augmenting his height. Tiny lamps flickered in niches along the corridor. Only their muted footfalls and the rustle of their garments disturbed the quiet. At the end of the hallway they stopped at what seemed like a blank wall. Harnouphis rapped on the floor with his staff. A moment later, Korax was startled as the wall panel slid aside, revealing a lightless passage. Harnouphis took out a strip of black cloth and tied it securely over Korax's eyes.

"Speak not a word," the high priest warned. He placed the end of a rope into Korax's hand. "Follow my lead, and tread carefully. We will descend many steps."

Korax heard his master move forward. When he felt a tug of the rope he followed. Heart pounding, he edged ahead until his toes touched the top of a step. Cautiously, he moved down the stairs, which seemed to turn in a spiral. The air grew cool and moist, possessing the sweet tang of incense. Finally, the steps ended. Korax followed the rope across an open space paved with smooth tiles, cold under his bare feet.

Abruptly a hand shot out and stopped him. A deep and hollow voice sounded. "This one is unpurified. He cannot enter our sacred hall."

Harnouphis spoke a ritual reply: "He is a man of courage and a devotee of Maat. I ask that he be purified."

Fabric whispered as another priest stepped close. Dense, perfumed smoke floated into Korax's face.

"I purify thee with fire and air, the gifts of Ra."

The smoke dispersed. Drops of cold water splashed over his head and hands. Another voice sounded.

"I purify thee with water and salt, the gifts of Geb."

The first of the voices spoke again: "Proceed, O seeker. Thou art justified."

The rope tugged forward, and Korax advanced. Through the blindfold, his eyes faintly perceived a brightening, as though they had entered a well-lit hall. He sensed many people standing and watching. From some distance ahead he heard the voice of Amasis.

"Who is the Enterer on the Threshold?"

Once more, Harnouphis answered: "Here is one lost in darkness who searches for the light."

The voice of Amasis drew closer. "To find the true light he must quit the scintillating darkness. To enter the House of Life he must die to the illusions of the world."

Harnouphis said: "His will is firm, and his heart is strong. He is willing to risk the terrible journey."

Abruptly, a hand lifted the blindfold. Korax saw Amasis inches in front of him, dressed in robes of scarlet and emerald green. About them stood a candle-lit hall, a crowd of men in white tunics. A large painted coffin lay on a platform a few yards ahead.

Amasis lifted an alabaster bowl. "Drink of the waters of the blue lotus, that your eyes may be opened."

Korax parted his lips as the drink tilted toward him. He swallowed as fast as he could, but some of the potion spilled over his chin. Amasis waited till the vessel was drained completely before taking it away. Harnouphis tugged the blindfold down.

"Let our brother be slain," Amasis cried, "that he may rise again."

Korax's feet were yanked from beneath him. Strong hands gripped his arms and shoulders. A drum started beating across the hall, and voices chanted. His body was laid on a stone and rolls of linen bandages wrapped around his limbs and torso. His arms were folded over his chest and more bandages used to secure them in place. Finally, the priests wound the bandages around his head, leaving only a small opening at his nostrils.

The chants mounted, loud and bellowing. Hands lifted him up and carried him, then lowered him into the coffin. Amulets were placed over his throat, chest, stomach and groin. Korax heard the coffin lid closing.

All was now blackness and silence.

He strove to hold on to his nerve. He reminded himself this was only a ritual. Yet terror loomed inside him. Suppose they left him here too long by accident? He would die of suffocation. His shade would wander forever on the banks of the Nile. He tried to slow his breathing, to regain his composure. The air was parched, his throat full of dust. The blue lotus had dried all the moisture from his body. Perhaps it was turning him into a mummy. Perhaps he had failed to understand the literal meaning of the rite. He actually was meant to die, to be transformed into an animated corpse, no longer human, no longer alive. Dread crawled along his spine and sank talons into his heart.

Korax never knew how long he lay, tormented by fear and the suffocating darkness. But suddenly it ended. The coffin lid creaked open. Daylight shone and he could see.

Amasis smiled down at him. "Get up, grandson! You've lain there long enough."

The blindfold and mummy wrappings had vanished. Korax wore only the black tunic and sash. The old priest gripped his forearm and helped him climb from the coffin.

"It's time to begin the ritual," he said. "Follow me."

Amasis started off, still clad in the dazzling robes of red and green. A gold *ankh* sparkled at the tip of his walking stick.

They proceeded across the now-empty hall and entered a winding corridor. The towering walls were ribbed with granite. The polished floor sloped gently upward.

After a time, they came to an iron gate. In front of the gate stood a monster with the sinewy body of a warrior and the head of a black hound.

"Who are you?" His growl made Korax shudder.

Amasis held up his staff, the ankh flashing. "I am one who wanders in darkness, seeking the light of Maat."

"No one can pass here except he speak my name."

"Creature of the Gate of Night is your name. Dark One of the Abyss is your name. I know you and fear you not."

The guardian shrank back. "Thou knowest me. Pass on."

When they had stepped through the gate, Amasis turned to Korax. "Release all fear from your soul, grandson. Respect and honor all beings, but fear not men nor beasts nor spirits nor even gods. To fear is to fail before you have begun."

They walked on.

A while later, they approached a gate of gleaming copper. A lithe, voluptuous woman in a purple gown and silver collar barred the entrance.

"You may not pass unless you know my name."

Amasis answered: "Bright One of the River of Life is your name; Child of Joy is your name. Though my heart yearns for you, I will pass on."

"Thou knowest me." The lady backed away into the shadows.

When they had passed the gate, Amasis said: "Embrace the fleeting pleasures of the world but lightly. For if you try to hold them, they will instead hold you, and your heart will shrivel with sorrow. Come."

After a time, they reached a third gate. It sparkled with silver encrusted with garnets and lapis. Its guardian had the head of a handsome young man and the body of a parrot.

"None may pass this gate who cannot tell my name."

"Son of the Wise Ones is your name," Amasis replied. "Proud Sphinx of the Desert is your name. I honor you, but we will pass on."

The guardian cawed, spread his wings and flew away.

Amasis led Korax through the gate. "That can be the trickiest test of all, grandson. Mystery, knowledge, power, wisdom—all can tempt you from the path. Only by placing your devotion to Maat foremost can you be sure that your steps are righteous. Now follow, the rest of the passage is easy."

A short walk brought them to a luminous hall. Hieroglyphs engraved in gold covered the pillars, walls, and ceiling. At the center of the hall stood a goddess with flaming wings, so beautiful that the sight of her squeezed Korax's heart.

Isis.

"Go on," Amasis said. "I need guide you no farther."

Korax walked a few steps, his legs trembling.

"Come forward without fear, Korax of Rhodes." The Lady's voice was sweet as music. "For you have been justified."

Meekly, Korax approached her, awe and thankfulness shivering through his spirit.

"You stand in the Hall of Coming to Wisdom," she said. "It is the first hall of many. In time, you may advance to other halls beyond this one, which are presided over by other gods. But first you must learn the lessons of this hall, which are written on the walls and pillars all around you."

Korax surveyed the glittering hieroglyphs that covered all the surfaces of the hall. How long must it take to learn so much wisdom?

The goddess held out her hand to him, beaming. "I welcome you to the Mazes of Magic, my brilliant child."

Korax stepped forward and touched her hand. At once, he fell to his knees in adoration, then prostrated himself and set his forehead on the floor close to her feet. Perfect harmony and bliss suffused his whole being.

The world changed. Noise groaned over his head. Cool air rushed in. Hands moved around him, lifted him up. Dazed, he realized they were unwrapping the bandages.

Many voices chanted, their words now in the common tongue:

Awake! Awake!
Your trials have ended.
You rise like Ra in the morning.
Night flees before your flashing eye.

They lifted him out of the coffin and set his feet on the floor. Hands steadied him as the last of the wrappings were unwound.

Isis covers you with her wings.
Osiris walks beside you.
Horus now is your brother.
The Word of Ptah is on your lips.

The blindfold was pulled from his head. Amasis and Harnouphis flanked him, wearing broad smiles. They faced a bright hall full of initiates, now decked in white robes with white sashes.

"Scribes of the House of Life," Amasis called. "Let us welcome our new brother, Seshsetem, to the Mazes of Magic, the paths of the sacred knowledge!"

The hall erupted in shouts and cheers. Looking down, Korax saw that his black tunic and sash had somehow changed to white.

Chapter Fifteen

Three days after his initiation, Korax was conducted back to the House of Life by Harnouphis. Over his white tunic, Korax wore a green sash he had been given at the end of his initiation rite—his badge of admission to the sacred scriptorium.

The high priest led him through the library rooms with their towering shelves of papyrus scrolls. Tall porticos admitted ample daylight. The warm, fresh air held the fragrance of garden blooms and traces of incense.

One library was set aside for medical texts, another for treatises on the construction and consecration of amulets. Several chambers stored invocations to the gods and various liturgies. Two rooms near the rear of the hallway held historical records—reaching back thousands of years according to Harnouphis.

"There are more libraries underground," he said. "But this is as much as may be shown to a neophyte."

He led Korax back to the first chamber and indicated some shelves close to the floor.

"These are your introductory lessons." Harnouphis removed a sheet and showed it to Korax. "The papyrus presents the same text in three different forms. One is the common language that you already know. Above it is the older cursive form that we call the sacred script. Above that, the message is transcribed in hieroglyphic."

Harnouphis rolled up the sheet and handed it to Korax. "You begin by copying each of these documents. Copy all three scripts in wax, at least seven times or until your hand is perfect. Only then should you venture to copy in ink. By repeated copying, you merge the activities of eye, hand, and mind. This is our time-honored method of learning the sacred language."

Korax examined the three scripts on the page. "I can see how this practice will teach me the meaning of the words and symbols. But how will I learn to speak the words?"

Harnouphis grunted with amusement. "You will not need to speak the sacred tongue until you actually practice ritual. That comes later, much later."

Concealing his disappointment, Korax quickly rolled up the papyrus.

Harnouphis was grinning. "Remember my admonishment to patience, Seshsetem. One does not learn the wisdom of the ages in a year, or even a decade. Now, so long as you satisfy your other obligations, you are free to come here and study whenever you wish, day or night. The House of Life is never locked, and the sentries will recognize your green sash. As for the spiritual exercises that Amasis mentioned, these are the same that I instructed Mehen to teach you and which you are already practicing. There is no need to alter the regimen at present. You look a bit crestfallen. I hope you are not disappointed by the reality of what you now face?"

Korax set his shoulders. "Not at all, Excellency. I am eager to begin my studies."

Despite his professed enthusiasm, Korax admitted to himself that the task before him seemed overwhelming. How long would the gods require him to stay here and study? Years? Decades?

Worse, he soon found he had little time to devote to the House of Life. As the harvest season approached, his work in the House of Records took nearly all of his time. The daily trickle of inventories, reports, and letters swelled to a flood that Korax and his fellow scribes waded through from dawn to dusk. Many nights, the lamps burned late in the scriptorium as they struggled to keep afloat in the rivers of papyrus. Korax often returned to his room hours after sundown, too exhausted to even practice his mental exercises.

Those evenings when he did dredge up the stamina to visit the House of Life, he found the studies arduous. After reading and writing all day, his back ached and his hand was cramped from holding the pen. Copying the arcane texts was challenging enough, understanding them even more formidable. Without word-sounds to associate with the writing, his mind found it nearly impossible to memorize the symbols.

Korax had always prided himself on his intellect, but this study seemed a vast, intricate puzzle beyond his ability to solve. Still he pursued it doggedly, sitting on his straw mat in the library late into the night, until sleepiness forced him to retire. Often he would dream of the hieroglyphs—stick figures of birds, snakes, hands, eyes—perpetually wandering about, seeking to find their place in some abstruse pattern, but never quite succeeding.

An imposing council chamber of pink sandstone stood in an upper story of the temple complex. Beyond its outer terrace, blooming gardens cascaded down toward the distant, muddy waters of the Nile. Occasionally, the chirping of birds fluttered in from the gardens, punctuating the relentless drone of speeches.

The purpose of today's assembly was to prepare for the annual Synod in Alexandria, when high priests from all the temples of Egypt paid homage to Pharaoh and reported on the conditions of their estates and cities. The Synod took place every year in the months following the harvest.

Harnouphis sat on a padded bench, in one of several rows of benches occupied by his fellow priests, administrators, and clerks. Awaiting the time to give his report, he half-listened to what was said, half-observed the men around him.

The nine first servants of Ptah occupied thrones on a curved dais facing the benches. Judging from their faces, some of the first servants appeared to have trouble maintaining interest in the proceedings. This seemed particularly true of Neksapthis, the ancient supreme cleric. Occasionally he nodded off, only to waken with a start when his head slipped heavily out of his cupped hand. Of all the first servants, only Amasis seemed both alert and content. The master of the House of Life observed each speaker with his customary bright-eyed serenity.

Currently addressing the assembly was Paramses, the commander of the temple watch. Harnouphis viewed Paramses as a potential rival, so he attended keenly to what he said and how the council reacted. Paramses reported on the number of peasants who had fled from the fields during the growing season and sought sanctuary in the Mansion of Ptah. By ancient tradition, commoners who found their workloads too heavy or conditions too desperate sometimes went on strike and "ran away" to the temples. The Ptolemies had never been so brash as to revoke the Law of Sanctuary, but everyone worried that if conditions worsened past a certain point, the labor unrest could easily spread out of control.

When Paramses finished his report, Imouthes rose from his throne among the first servants. He was short, broad-shouldered and belligerent, Paramses' immediate superior and in charge of all temple police, sentries, and doorkeepers. His title was First Warrior of the God.

"Brothers, Paramses' report underscores my continuing concerns about the level of taxation. I have seen letters indicating the number of sanctuary seekers in other temples is even higher. I believe the time has come when we must take a firm stand. At this year's Synod, we must not only insist that Pharaoh not increase quotas, but that he reduce our taxes."

A grumbling of voices spread through the hall. Harnouphis scanned the first and second servants to note their reactions. He knew which high priests sympathized with Imouthes' views, so he only checked for any changes in the usual factions.

Imouthes was a firebrand who favored militant tactics against the Greek rulers. Similar cadres of priests existed in the great temples of other cities, but their numbers usually stayed in the minority. At times they even advocated armed rebellion, though Imouthes' bluster had never gone so far. Harnouphis considered Imouthes like the lion of the male sex—more prone to roaring than to actual violence.

Shepseskaf, chief treasurer and Harnouphis' superior, raised two hands to quiet the assembly. "Brothers, brothers. All of us would wish our taxes reduced. But the number of sanctuary seekers is not really high when compared to historical standards. And preliminary reports on this year's harvest are most encouraging. There should be plenty of grain for Pharaoh, the Mansion of Ptah, and the peasants themselves."

A slight frown tugged at Harnouphis' mouth. Typical of Shepseskaf to upstage his delivery of the favorable inventory reports.

"The Synod will set the quotas for *next year's* harvest," Imouthes reminded everyone. "We cannot always count on years of bounty!"

Another round of muttering ensued.

Surprisingly, the Sem-priest Neksapthis spoke up in his cackling voice. "Brother Imouthes raises a valid concern. Every year's inundation is not the same. And we have also heard rumors that the sacred Bull Apis is refusing his feed. This might portend an unfavorable harvest."

Harnouphis' eyebrows perked up. This was the first he had heard of the sacred bull's lackluster appetite.

All heads turned to first servant Peherenptah, whose role as chief steward placed him in charge of the Apis Bull. The gregarious Peherenptah stood with a reassuring gesture.

"The god in his incarnation of Apis is well and content, I promise you. It is true he acted listless for a few days, but after his feed was changed to different stocks of emmer and barley, his ka returned to its usual robust vigor."

His easy chuckle found echoes across the council. But Harnouphis scrutinized the chief steward, trying to decide if the man concealed a deeper concern. Sickness of the Apis Bull would cause anxiety among the populace, and might signal trouble for Peherenptah and his circle. As Harnouphis was called to give his report, he made a mental note to go himself and visit the sacred bull.

The work at the House of Records had finally leveled off. Still, much remained to accomplish before Harnouphis and the other priests departed for Alexandria. So Korax was surprised when, in the middle of the afternoon, Mehen informed him that they must accompany his Excellency on an errand outside the temple walls. The surprise increased when Korax learned that the errand was simply to visit and observe the Apis Bull.

The sacred bull occupied his own small temple opposite the main gates of the Mansion of Ptah. The temple enclosed a shrine for offerings, luxurious stables for the bull and his consorts, and a fenced yard where Apis took his daily exercise.

A chattering throng of spectators filled the tiered benches overlooking the yard. Most of them were Egyptians, but Korax also noticed groups of men, women, and children in Greek dress—tourists from the new Greek cities of Egypt. He had seen almost no Greeks for many months, and he gazed at the tourists with an uncomfortable surge of feelings. Their apparel and postures seemed alien, yet painfully familiar. He pondered how much he had changed in less than a year. How much of Korax was still Greek, how much now Egyptian?

"Observe the sacred bull," Harnouphis commanded. "His movements are supposed to forecast the future. Tell me what impressions you receive."

Korax stared as the great black beast entered the yard. Sluggishly, the bull ambled a few steps then stopped, looked up at the crowd and lowed mournfully.

"He does not like so many watching him," Korax muttered. "He feels his privacy invaded, especially by the Greeks."

"That's not likely to change," Harnouphis remarked dryly. "The temple charges each citizen a silver drachma to pay homage to the god. Apis brings in valuable revenue."

"What about the future?" Mehen asked. "Does he express an opinion regarding the inundation?"

The bull padded over to the trough and drank lazily.

"The floods will come," Korax said, staring into the distance. "But not so high as last year."

"Will they be sufficient to nourish the land?" Mehen demanded.

Korax shook his head. "Doubtful. The god senses a presence rising, new in this time, but ancient. It spells danger for the land."

His link with the bull faded. Korax blinked, turned to glance at the two priests.

Mehen's face was pale with worry but, to Korax's surprise, Harnouphis wore a placid, thoughtful expression.

"Times of danger may bring opportunity," he said.

Chapter Sixteen

When the last reports of the harvest had been tallied and reviewed, the documents stored away, and copies packed in satchels for the trip to Alexandria, Harnouphis announced a celebration. All the scribes of the House of Records and their families were invited.

The banquet was served in a courtyard built around tiled pools. Colored lanterns illuminated the cool twilight and cast shimmering reflections in the water. Low tables brimmed with roasted meats, salads, fruits, breads, and cakes. Dark beer flowed freely. In a corner of the yard, a trio of musicians played quiet tunes on harp, pipes, and rectangular tambourine.

Korax dined with Katep and his family. They conversed with the easy conviviality of old friends, and reflected on how glad they all were that the season of intense labor had ended. Katep would be spending more time at home now, and his wife and children were obviously pleased. Beneath his fringed wig, Katep looked very tired.

The family left soon after dinner, claiming it was the children who needed to go to bed. Korax glanced around to see that all of the families with children and many of the married couples were also departing.

But the banquet did not end. Instead the musicians relocated to the center of the courtyard. A group of singers joined them, pretty young women in diaphanous gowns and glittering, beaded girdles. They pounded tambourines, swayed their hips, and sang a lively song about drinking and pleasure. In the midst of the song, dancers ran out from the gallery, lithe girls with flowing black hair. They posed and twirled, nude beneath short tunics of gilded netting. The scribes who remained at the banquet laughed and cheered. Korax reclined on a cushion and picked up his tumbler of beer.

While he watched the dancers, Harnouphis and Mehen approached him. The high priest and chief scribe were making the rounds in their role as hosts of the banquet.

"We are glad to see you enjoying yourself, Seshsetem." Harnouphis sat down rather heavily.

Korax nodded respectfully to Harnouphis and to Mehen, who knelt nearby. He noted with surprise that the high priest appeared a little drunk.

"You know, you have done excellent work for us this season," Harnouphis said. "It has not gone unnoticed. And now here you are, an initiate of the House of Life. We are all very proud."

"Thank you, your Excellency."

"I've been thinking about you, Seshsetem. I realized the other day that you are still living in some tiny room in the slaves' quarters. That is not appropriate for a scribe of the House of Life. Mehen, we must find more appropriate lodgings for him."

Mehen showed a rare, cordial smile. "There are empty rooms in the apartment block I occupy. I will speak to the steward in charge."

"Good. Good," Harnouphis said. "It is important that we keep Seshsetem happy. Is there anything else you are lacking, my young friend?"

Korax shrugged, disarmed by the unexpected solicitude. A pretty dancer skipped past, and his head swung to follow her.

"Ah ha!" Harnouphis laughed. "I just thought of something else … Let us discuss some subtleties of our theology, Seshsetem. The priests of Amun, in the great city of Waset, believe that their god created the Universe by an act of divine masturbation. As you know, we clerics of Mem-Nephir maintain on the contrary that our god Ptah created the Universe by speaking the Great Word. Now I ask you, which story is more dignified?"

Korax held his tongue, baffled as to where this was leading.

"In any case, unlike our colleagues to the south, we of the Mansion of Ptah do not place any particular value on masturbation. Nor do we consider celibacy a prerequisite to holiness, except of course on days when we actually do ritual in the temple. On the contrary, we regard a moderate amount of contact with women to be healthy and useful in balancing ourselves. Now, in light of all this, are there any of these young entertainers that you find especially appealing?"

Korax took a gulp of beer. "I find all of them especially appealing, Excellency."

Harnouphis snickered. "How about that little dancer over there? The one with the turquoise veil."

"Very limber," Korax declared, studying the curve of her spine as she moved.

"Ha-ha." Harnouphis clapped him on the back and rose unsteadily. "I'm glad to see you have a healthy interest! Enjoy your evening now."

Harnouphis and Mehen walked off to continue their rounds. Korax leaned back on the cushion, smiling and shaking his head. He sipped his beer and watched the dancers sway and cavort amid the colored lights.

After a while, despite the pleasant stimulation, his head grew heavy with fatigue. Regretfully, Korax decided he had best go home to bed. He left the courtyard of the pools and made his way across the gardens toward his quarters. A swelling moon hung bright and fair in the clear desert sky. Reaching the barracks, he shuffled down the dark hallway to his room.

He had just taken off his sandals and stretched out on the bed when a knock sounded. He opened the door to find the pretty dancing girl. Her turquoise veil was draped over her thick hair and fell down past her waist. It half-concealed, half-accentuated her delightful figure.

She tilted her head and smiled beguilingly. "You are the scribe Seshsetem?"

"Yes," Korax replied, rather stupidly he thought.

"My name is Itaji. May I come in?"

Korax opened the door wider. She stepped lightly into the room, a rustling of beads and fabric, a whirl of perfume. She lifted a green faience bottle in her delicate hand.

"His Excellency Harnouphis instructed me to deliver this flask of wine. He said you are a Greek and wine is the favored drink among your people."

"Thank you," Korax said. "His Excellency is extremely generous. Perhaps you will stay and share a drink with me?"

Her smile widened. "All right."

Korax found his only cup, filled it for her and took the bottle for himself.

Itaji sipped the wine, staring avidly into his eyes. She stood only as tall as his chest, her eyelids painted turquoise, her cheeks brushed with rouge. She had removed her veil and Korax gazed at her breasts under the gold mesh, the dark nipples rising with her breathing.

"Delicious," she said. "I seldom have the opportunity to taste wine. I don't really care for beer, you know. Besides, as a dancer, I must watch my figure."

She pivoted and stepped across the room, walking on the balls of her feet like a cat. Standing beside the bed, she set down the cup and twirled to face him.

"His Excellency also instructed me to provide you with private entertainment ... of whatever sort you desire. That is, if you find the idea appealing."

Korax moved close, stared down into her lovely face. "I do not know enough Egyptian to express just how appealing I find that idea."

Itaji giggled and pressed herself into his arms. Their mouths met in an ardent kiss. Boldly, she untied his sash and pulled the tunic over his head.

"Ah!" she cried. "So it is true! I've been told that Greeks have an extra skin, but I never believed it."

Korax grinned at her amazement. To his Greek mind the Egyptian custom of circumcision seemed as bizarre and barbaric as his unclipped manhood must seem to her.

Itaji touched his rigid member hesitantly, a look of fascination on her face.

"The extra skin is harmless," Korax laughed. "I promise you, I function exactly the same as an Egyptian man."

A mischievous grin flashed across her mouth. "I will judge that! I will let you know my decision later."

Korax sat on a broad balustrade outside one of the libraries of the House of Life. By the light of a rising moon and a lamp flickering near his feet, he read the text of his lesson.

> The vizier Ptahhotpe says to Pharaoh, sovereign, my lord, decrepitude has come; old age has descended; feebleness has arrived; dotage has appeared. I lie in a second childhood; my eyes are feeble; my ears are deaf; my heart is tired; my tongue cannot speak; my lips drool ...

Korax lowered the papyrus with a sigh. Sometimes the only thing more tedious than copying these texts was the texts themselves.

More than a month had passed since Harnouphis departed for the Synod. At first, Korax had wondered if, being a native Greek speaker, he might be assigned to accompany the delegation to Alexandria. But if Harnouphis had even considered this idea, he had obviously rejected it. Perhaps he feared that the sometimes willful Seshsetem might seize the opportunity to escape captivity by slipping away into the crowded Greek capital. Korax had to admit, the notion had occurred to him.

Mehen had not made the trip this year. Instead, Harnouphis had left the chief scribe in charge of the House of Records. Among his duties, Mehen was supposed to continue mentoring Korax. But the ungenerous Mehen had proven even less helpful than Harnouphis. All he did was check Korax's copies occasionally, then order him to keep working.

Dolefully, Korax gazed across the moonlit garden. On the other hand, Mehen had kept the promise about finding Korax better housing. The Greek now occupied two well-appointed rooms. The apartment even had a small terrace with potted palms and a woven chair. A manservant came every few days to sweep the floors, change sheets, and oil the lamps. Of more importance to Korax, the delightful Itaji continued to visit him every few nights. Well-rested, well-fed, well-caressed by the beguiling dancer, Korax fretted that he might succumb to the ease of his life here, lose his ambition to escape.

"Grandson, I thought that must be you. No Egyptian would sit with his legs draped so casually over the rail."

Korax jumped from his perch and bowed to Amasis, the master of the House of Life. "Good evening, your Excellency."

"And how are your studies progressing?"

Korax glanced unhappily at the papyrus in his hand. "Truthfully, not so well as I would wish. I consider myself highly intelligent, but I'm beginning to fear these studies might be beyond my capacity."

"Ha! Perhaps your Greek intelligence does not mesh well with our Egyptian knowledge?"

"Perhaps."

His downcast aspect brought a look of sympathy from Amasis. "Let me see what you are reading."

Korax handed him the sheet.

"Ah, yes. The sorry laments of Vizier Ptahhotpe. I promise you, grandson, the more advanced lessons are not so uninteresting."

"I only hope I may someday read them."

"Hmm. Is it the cursive or the hieroglyphic that cause you such perplexity?"

"It is both," Korax answered hopelessly. "I learned your common Egyptian quickly enough. But each day the scribes worked with me and taught me the sounds of the speech. Without sounds to match with the writing, memorizing the words is very difficult."

"The phonetic tablets are not helpful?"

Korax looked at him blankly. "What are those?"

Amasis brow flicked upward, and he stared for moment. "You mean Harnouphis only gave you the lessons and not the phonetic tablets? I see. Follow me, Korax. Bring your lamp."

Amasis strode down the portico, Korax hastening behind. They passed the portals of other libraries, then stepped into the hierogrammat's office. The room was cluttered with documents of every size and description. While Korax held the lamp, the old man shuffled through pages on one of the many floor-to-ceiling shelf cases.

"I'm sure I have them somewhere," Amasis muttered. "Yes, here."

He handed Korax a set of papyruses. Each page had three columns: hieroglyphs, the corresponding letters in the sacred cursive, and a syllable or two written in the common script.

"You see how it works," Amasis commented. "These sounds are the same for the sacred script and the corresponding glyph. You study these tables repeatedly and refer to them when you read the lessons. Pretty soon, you will be able to speak the words of the old language. Then I suspect the learning will come easier."

Korax scanned the pages with amazement. This was exactly the key he had been lacking.

"I don't know why Harnouphis failed to give you these tablets," Amasis remarked. "Each teacher has his own methods, and perhaps I am wrong to interfere. But your master has so many obligations, I am sure the matter simply slipped his mind. Still, it would be wrong to embarrass him by pointing out his omission. I think it best that we never mention to him that I gave you these. Instead, you can happily surprise your mentor with the accelerated pace of your learning."

He ended with a pointed, cheerful expression.

Korax regarded him levelly. "I understand you perfectly. Your Excellency honors me with your generous interest."

"Not at all," Amasis said. "A man must look after his grandchildren. Ha-ha!"

Chapter Seventeen

With the aid of the phonetic tablets, Korax soon learned the sounds associated with both the sacred cursive writing and the hieroglyphs. At last, the magical language had acquired a voice, a voice capable of teaching him.

Within a month, Korax had finished copying all of the introductory lessons. But when Mehen came to check on his studies, Korax warily showed him only a portion of his finished work. Since his masters were obviously contriving to thwart his progress, Korax considered it prudent not to exceed their expectations.

Instead, he worked through the assigned lessons rapidly, then used his extra time to range through the libraries, searching out additional texts. From subtle questioning of other neophytes, he pieced together a map of the established course of study. Generally, he followed this age-old curriculum. But he also leaped ahead at times, tracking a hint or reference in a basic text to a concept's culmination in a more advanced book.

Gradually, the flower of the secret knowledge unfolded to his mind. He learned of the Great Word of Ptah that had rushed forth at the moment of creation to establish the framework of the Universe; how the Great Word had divided into the distinct syllables of the sacred language—sounds that abided through eternity and formed the vibrational underpinnings of existence. At the same time, the Great Word was comprehended as light, the pure, dazzling radiance of the sun. Fractured by the will of the Supreme Artisan, the light formed all the myriad phenomena visible to man. It was this same divine light that Korax visualized each morning and evening in his mental exercises. Now he realized the true purpose of those practices. Gradually, they drew the light down into the initiate's body, attuned the light to his mind. Eventually, an adept became capable of wielding the light, shaping it to his will. Thus a magician could shape events, could share in the work of the Supreme Artisan, the ongoing creation of the visible world.

Immersed in these profound concepts, Korax hardly noticed the passage of time. He was surprised one day in the Hall of Records when Mehen announced that news had arrived from downriver. The Synod had ended, and their master Harnouphis would soon return. The disclosure sparked a realization in Korax and a mood of bleak despair.

He had been a slave in the temple of Ptah an entire year.

"What troubles you, Seshsetem?" Itaji asked him that evening, as she lay curled in his arms after lovemaking.

"My excruciating lack of progress," he grumbled. "I've studied for over eight months in the House of Life, yet my goals appear farther away than ever."

"Oh? What are these goals that frustrate you so?"

His mouth twitched. He could hardly disclose to her that he hoped to master enough magic to escape his enslavement. Besides, the notion had come to seem almost preposterous. "You would not understand."

Her finger caressed his cheek. "I would be very glad to try."

His head shook, mouth tight. *Why was he even trying to learn?*

Because the Mysteries intrigued him. And because of that promise from the goddess, and the thrill of magical energy it had sparked in his soul. But all of that now seemed distant, baffling. He could see why they called these studies the Mazes of Magic. He was wandering, blind and confused.

With a sigh Itaji rose, stretched her nude body. "Don't I still please you?"

"Yes, of course."

She was an exquisite mistress, to be sure. With her strong, supple body, she had introduced him to erotic practices he would never have imagined. Of course, as a professional, she bedded him for payment. A free scribe, drawing a salary, would probably have married by now, or at least found a concubine of his own. As a slave, Korax had to rely on the generosity of his master to finance his enjoyment of the dancer's attentions. Fortunately, Harnouphis still prized Korax's talents and wished to keep him satisfied. Sometimes Korax felt like a sacred beast—pampered with luxuries and used for other men's rituals.

The dancer dropped her arms to her side. Her voice was petulant. "Do you know what I think? If you keep on this way you will turn into a dried-up old mummy, like so many of the priests in this temple." She picked up her gown from the foot of the bed. "You should enjoy the pleasures of life and leave the great problems to the gods. That is the teaching of the goddess I serve— Hathor, the beautiful Lady of Love."

Korax looked up with sudden interest. "Do you also worship Isis?"

Halfway into her gown, Itaji shrugged. "Of course. Everyone worships Isis. She is the queen of heaven."

"I know," Korax muttered. "I once believed that she had spoken to me, pointed me to the path of the Mysteries. But it's been a long time since I've heard her voice or felt her presence. She has a chapel in the House of Life, and I visit her there sometimes. But she never speaks to me."

Smoothing her dress, Itaji glanced around. "You need to pray and make offerings to her daily. Set up a shrine here in your apartment."

Korax considered the thought. "I would need a statue or wax figure."

"Oh, I will bring you one from the marketplace." She reached for her girdle. "I will bring you a figure of Lady Hathor too. You would benefit from her presence in this dreary room."

Korax smiled as he watched her dress. She was a sweet mistress, to be sure. When she had strapped on her sandals, she pranced over and pecked him on the lips.

"Now try to be cheerful, Seshsetem. I will see you again in three nights."

When she had gone, Korax put his hands behind the headrest of his bed and glanced down at himself pensively. The sight made him wince. Long gone was the sleek-muscled body he had acquired on the exercise fields of Rhodos and at the oarsman's bench that summer in the navy. Instead, his limbs were spindly, his belly round and fat from drinking beer.

Korax the Greek was vanishing before his eyes.

Morosely, he stood and found his clothes. He put on a tunic and sandals and tied on the green sash, intending to go to the House of Life.

But after crossing the courtyard outside the apartment, his feet took him another way. The sun had set, the cloudless sky dimming from blue to gray, the first stars twinkling. He wandered past rows of granaries and store houses.

Korax the Greek was fading away. Although he clung stubbornly to his memories of life in Rhodes, he still couldn't recall how he had come to Egypt. Mostly, the time after his grievous injury was a blank. A few visions had come in his dreams, but they were fragmented and baffling. In one, he leaned on the rail of a sailing vessel, staring at the sea, hearing in his delirious mind the calls of dolphins or birds—or were they sirens? In another, he sat in a dim feast hall, surrounded by rough, bearded men and dark-eyed women .They wore the black garb of Cretans. It made sense that if Korax had been on a ship, it might have been taken by Cretan pirates, and he kept prisoner while they waited for ransom. But if that were the case, why had the ransom not been paid? Why had he been sold into slavery? In that dream, he had been playing an old tortoise shell lyre and reciting verses from the *Odyssey*. Homer's great hero was forced to wander ten years before reaching his home. Would Korax's exile last so long? Would he ever return to Rhodes?

Lost in these gloomy thoughts, he approached an auxiliary gate in the western wall. Though still a slave, Korax had learned that the initiate's green sash allowed him to pass most guard posts without challenge. Outside the gate, he wandered along the base of the white walls that enclosed the temple complex. He arrived at the grand avenue of sphinxes and turned toward the river.

An entire year since he first walked this way. Eight months since entering the House of Life. His mind roamed back to the sacred knowledge, dizzying in its immensity.

One book described Four Phases of Creation, each a distinct manifestation of the Great Word. Each constituted a world in its own right and was symbolized by one of four principles: Earth, Air, Water, Fire. Each of these worlds possessed its own vast array of rulers, spirits, forces, daemons. More: within the sphere of each world dwelled seven powers, akin to the seven planets of the night sky. Each of the powers had an associated metal, stone, plant, animal, color, fragrance, musical note, number, and hour of the day. In his art, the magician used those attributes to invoke a particular power. Powers could be raised by mental visioning, by chants and incantations, by intricate sigils written on papyrus or traced in the air.

Always there was more to study, whole rooms of scrolls, whole subjects scarcely touched: the five components of the human soul; astrology and the casting of horoscopes; the magic of herbs and the mixing of medicines, drugs, and potions; geometry and the sacred architecture; the construction of talismans and amulets and the spells to bind them with power. The priests of Egypt maintained that it took years to learn the beginnings of their sacred wisdom, many lifetimes to master it all.

Despondent, Korax had to admit that estimate seemed more and more accurate. He viewed himself as a man climbing an endless spiral stair, its summit forever hidden in cloud.

Or simply a fool lost in a labyrinth.

His steps had brought him to the river. The Nile was in flood stage, the people of Memphis watching anxiously to see how high it would rise—if the inundation would be sufficient to ensure an adequate harvest next year. Korax recalled that concern being raised in his examination of the Apis Bull.

Now, as he watched the dark, rushing waters, another memory came to him—the story told by Hetepher, Katep's wife. Her brother, an initiate in the House of Life, had drowned in the Nile. Perhaps, Korax thought, the man's death was not due to an accident or to evil magic. Perhaps the poor scribe had simply been driven mad by confusion and frustration, wandering the Mazes of Magic.

Contemplating that gloomy idea, Korax the slave, Seshsetem the scribe, stood beside the river as the last daylight disappeared.

Chapter Eighteen

From the center of the council chamber, Harnouphis gravely scanned the faces of the first servants on their thrones. The council knew already that the Synod had not gone well. Chief Treasurer Shepseskaf, with his usual oily shrewdness, had left Harnouphis the unhappy task of delivering the details.

"The negotiations proved unfortunate for all the servants of our gods this year," Harnouphis began tentatively. "Pharaoh's government plans major new expenditures ..."

"We don't need to hear about his library and pleasure fleet," First Warrior Imouthes interrupted from the dais. "Just tell us how much more we'll have to pay."

Mutterings spread through the ranks of the second and third servants. As ever, the militant Imouthes sought to exploit the taxation issue to stir up resentment against the Greeks. On this occasion, his task would not be difficult.

"Very well." Harnouphis read from the summary in his hand. "The quota of barley is increased by one twentieth, the quota of wheat is increased by one tenth. The temple's obligation to plant oil-bearing crops increases as follows: linseed, two thousand hectares; sesame, fifteen hundred hectares ..."

The grumbling swelled as Harnouphis continued down the list. It burst into an uproar when he announced the new taxes imposed on woven linen and papyrus sheet.

"Insufferable!" Imouthes shouted above the din. "We barely met our quotas last time, and all the signs forecast a lower flood this year. This Greek king will drive our god to destitution!"

Neksapthis, the old Sem-priest, raised a trembling hand to quiet the chamber. "This is ill news indeed, Brother Harnouphis. Is there nothing we can do to alleviate these terrible burdens?"

Harnouphis closed his lips over clenched teeth. As in previous years, his superior Shepseskaf had avoided the Synod, leaving the burden of negotiations to Harnouphis. The meetings had gone sour, through no fault of his own. Now the blame clung to him like a stench.

"As I started to say, Pharaoh's ministers were adamant that they must have more production. The king's military campaigns are costly. There is talk of building huge new war galleys. Believe me, the other temples suffer as much as we, or worse."

"Small comfort!" Imouthes yelled, leaping to his feet. "I say this weak-kneed pandering to Pharaoh must end."

Harnouphis repressed a shiver of rage, stung by the remark but lacking any useful response.

"And what do you suggest?" Shepseskaf demanded.

Imouthes paced along the dais. "I suggest we take a more forceful stand. I am reminded of a story from the 13th Dynasty. In a year of particularly onerous taxes, it is said that fire destroyed a third of the granaries of Mem-Nephir. But it was straw, not grain that burned. The clever priests of that day had hidden the grain in the temple cellars. That year, the servants of Ptah feasted well while Pharaoh's minions had to make do with less."

Slouching on his throne, Shepseskaf replied with acid irony: "So your solution is to hide Pharaoh's grain and burn our barns? And when word of this petty deception reaches Ptolemy's ear, I am sure you will negotiate forcefully with his Macedonian phalanxes."

"The tale is meant as an illustration," Imouthes shouted over the spurts of bitter laughter. "But I do contend that we must look for bold and creative solutions to our dilemma."

"My brothers, if I may be permitted to speak."

Harnouphis pivoted to see Paramses rise from a seat among the second servants.

"My family has a long history of dealing with greedy Pharaohs. I believe there are subtleties and tactics that we have forgotten in our present day." The agile Paramses strolled gracefully across the floor till he stood in front of Harnouphis. "We've spoken in the past about the issue of asylum seekers. But I believe this is a problem we can turn to our advantage. Instead of discouraging peasants who seek sanctuary, we should welcome them, and quietly encourage others in the fields to join them. Soon, few farmers will be left to harvest Pharaoh's crops. Then we will have some leverage for negotiating. We can offer to send the peasants back to the fields as soon as Pharaoh lowers the quotas."

A babble of voices followed this speech, with many of the first servants reacting and trying to be heard. Finally, Neksapthis, waving both his hands, succeeded in quieting the assembly.

The Sem-priest turned to Amasis, who till now had said nothing. "My brother hierogrammat, what is your view of this idea from Paramses?"

Amasis answered mildly: "I am certainly in favor of creative solutions—provided they are realistically thought through. I suggest we encourage Brother Paramses to develop his plan, and ask all other council members who are so inclined to do likewise. Let proposals be written in detail, with foreseeable contingencies and ramifications. Then let the Inner Circle discuss these proposals and decide on a course of action."

As soon as the council ended, Harnouphis left the temple enclosure. Resentment smoldering in his heart, he marched through the city gates and along the quays that lined the river.

In the cooling of late afternoon, dockworkers unloaded cargo; women carried bundles from the market stalls; children played on the pavement. All noticed the angry, storming walk of the high priest of Ptah and hurried out of his way.

Jackals and worms, Harnouphis thought. To have served the temple so long and well as he had done, and now to be so carelessly humiliated. Were it in his power at that moment, he would have every member of the council put to the torture.

He wandered beyond the warehouses and stone piers, into an impoverished warren built along the riverbank. Mud-brick hovels clustered at the base of the city walls, the homes of poor laborers and fisherman. Harnouphis had risen from just such contemptible conditions, risen to the rank of second servant of one of the greatest temples of Egypt. Now, all he had achieved seemed threatened, all his further ambitions a heap of ashes.

Wincing, Harnouphis forced himself to reason, to consider his plight with detachment. In the game of pharaohs and wizards, Harnouphis considered himself a serpent. Appropriately, his magical ally was Nebt-het, a cobra spirit. Yes, Harnouphis decided, he must consult Nebt-het.

The high priest stopped in his tracks and stood perfectly still. An adept of his attainment could summon an ally simply by willing it. With slow breathing he quelled his mind, then called the spirit to him.

"O Hooded One," he uttered softly, "I, Harnouphis, know your true name and call you now."

A voice whispered inside his skull: "I am here at your bidding, O priest."

Harnouphis opened his eyes and walked again, treading carefully on the slippery mud. "As you can see, Nebt-het, I am filled with vexation and despair."

"You have been attacked. When attacked there are only two choices: slither away, or strike and kill."

True, Harnouphis thought. Perhaps he had bided his time for too long. Perhaps he needed to attack his rivals. But where and how were they vulnerable?

"I have studied and worked many years to gain power. When the Greek scribe came into my possession, I sensed him to be a key. I have used him to foresee events. I have used his openness to travel the mazes of the gods, to enter their sanctuaries and absorb a portion of their power. I believed myself to be gaining potency and stature. But now this disaster has struck, and all my hopes seem threatened."

"Perhaps the time has come to choose a new ally."

"What do you mean?"

"You *have* grown in power, Harnouphis. Your sojourns to the secret houses of the gods have not gone unnoticed. There is another, far greater than I, who would be your ally, if you desire it."

Harnouphis ceased walking and spoke aloud. "Really? Who is this one?"

In the moment he awaited an answer, a commotion on the shoreline drew his attention. Young boys rushed from the water, shouting in alarm. A woman shrieked, dashed to the river's edge to snatch up a baby, then carried it running to higher ground. Peering through the dusk, Harnouphis spied the cause of the disturbance. The dark form of a crocodile slithered through the current.

Harnouphis jerked himself erect, thunderstruck. What better ally to strike down his enemies than the terrible Lord of the Abyss? Had such a lucky twist of the game truly come his way?

And would he dare to grasp it?

Chapter Nineteen

White smoke drifted up from the incense burner, misty veils surrounding the statuette. The painted figure of Isis, with wings of gold, stood on the shelf in Korax's room. He bowed his head and prayed the words Itaji had taught him.

> O Holy One of Heaven
> Rose of the Desert
> Moonlight on the Nile
> Savior from the Scorpion
> Mother and Queen:
> Accept my offering
> Hear my prayer.

As he had for many nights, he implored her to speak to him, to guide him, to relieve his suffering, to help him find his way. Eyelids resting closed, he listened for a time, hoping to hear her voice.

Only silence.

Wearily, he extinguished his lamp and lay down to sleep.

She came to him in a dream. He walked through the sacred hall, where he had last seen her, at the culmination of the initiation rite. All around him, hieroglyphs gleamed, pulsing and shifting on the walls and pillars. Isis gazed down at him—still, remote, gentle.

"What would you ask of me, child?"

His voice was a hoarse whisper. "O Goddess, I am so lost. I have tried to follow the path that you—that I believed you set before me. But there is so much to understand, and the learning takes so long."

"The path of magic requires both dedication and patience. You have studied for less than a year."

"I know. I am impatient and rash. But I long for my home, for the man I was—or believe I was."

She peered down at him for a long moment. "I am called Savior from the Scorpion because I draw out poison. When you invoked divine power for cruel and selfish ends, you poisoned yourself. Your suffering now is the drawing out of that venom. It must continue, if you are to be cured."

Korax lowered his head in remorse. He could not deny the truth of her words, however painful. *But how long must the suffering continue?* Did he dare to even ask?

"There is more," Isis said, eyes unfocused now like a seer. "The forces of chaos and law struggle eternally in all the worlds. We gods are mighty, but we can only act in your world through mortal vessels. I see a time of testing before you. You will be called to serve as vessel to powers both good and evil. Then, you must hold with all your strength to Maat. Fail, and you will be lost. But if you succeed, you may not only expiate your past errors, but gain the power to shape your life as you wish."

Her hand moved at her side, and Korax saw that she held a scroll. The dream shifted, and he was tilting forward, about to fall.

His eyes popped open. He sat up, instantly alert.

The power of her magic flowed through him—sweet, effortless, mighty, like the endless flow of the river.

A tiered game-board of painted cedarwood rested on the ebony table in Harnouphis' study. Korax examined the board curiously. He had frequently observed his fellow scribes playing the game they called *sennet*, but the board for that game was simpler. This board comprised four levels of nine-by-nine squares, supported by pillars in the form of miniature lotus columns. Tiny statuettes stood on many of the squares. Wax figures on the lowest levels appeared to represent men, while figures of wood and ivory on the three upper tiers bore the forms of animals or gods.

"We are going to play a little game this evening," Harnouphis said with his benign smile. "Please be seated."

Korax sat on a stool before the game-board. Attempting to guess the purpose of the elaborate setup, he glanced at Mehen who occupied a nearby chair. But the chief scribe's stolid expression betrayed no hint.

Harnouphis pushed a candle in front of Korax. "Gaze at the flame and relax yourself."

Though uneasy, Korax obeyed. Harnouphis sang a muted chant, and soon his rhythmic voice sounded far away. Korax drifted into a vision.

His mind fluttered like a moth among towering statues, granite images of men and of strange, misshapen beings. His vision darted upward, looping to another level, then another. Here the light shone brighter, like the sheen of sunlight on high gray clouds. Korax flew among statues of gods and goddesses, some of whom he recognized, others not. There stood Anubis with his jackal face and gleaming eyes, there Sekhet the tawny lioness, there ibis-headed Thoth.

The flight of his vision looped again. He approached a being he did not know. This one had the tall, broad-shouldered body of a god, but its black head was a bizarre amalgam of beasts—a long pointed snout, tall square-cropped ears, the slitted eyes of a serpent. In aspect, this god felt archaic, mysterious, dreadful. The moth-Korax swooped in and settled on this dark god's shoulder.

A pain burst in the palm of his hand. His brain writhed in a welter for several moments. Then Korax awoke, staring down at a tiny puncture wound in his palm. Startled, he looked at the game-board. On the top-level stood a figure like the god of his vision, a droplet of blood staining its black head.

"You've played our little game very well." Harnouphis chuckled with approval.

The high priest handed him a tumbler of wine. Korax didn't bother asking the meaning of the vision. He knew Harnouphis would not disclose any pertinent answers. Feeling slightly sick, Korax put down the wine and asked permission to retire.

When the Greek scribe had departed, Harnouphis reverently picked up the bloodied game-piece.

"There can be no doubt," he murmured.

"It might have been a trick," Mehen ventured. "The Greek is deceitful. Perhaps he was not in trance at all and knew which piece he selected."

Harnouphis shook his head with flat certainty. "No, Mehen. I realize our young scribe is crafty. He pushes his studies far beyond what he wishes me to know. But I assure you, he was truly in trance. Besides, what I did not tell you earlier is that this," he lifted the tiny god, "only confirms my own vision."

Mehen's lips quivered. "You mean, your Excellency has—"

"Yes. Set the Destroyer, the slayer of Osiris, has revealed himself to me. He has offered to become my ally."

Mehen slumped in his chair as though his spine had turned flaccid.

Harnouphis delicately laid the game piece back on the board. "An awful thing to contemplate, is it not? A god so reviled, detested as the Father of All Evil. Yet, it was not always so. Once he was worshipped just like other gods—the principle of darkness that complements the light. Sometimes destruction is necessary, so that new structures can arise."

Mehen stared mutely, his narrow face aghast.

"What an extraordinary opportunity I am offered!" Harnouphis spread his arms in an expansive gesture. "To have a god as an ally, and such a god! I am sensible to the dangers, of course. But what man of ambition could reject such an offer?"

Mehen struggled to speak. "Then you have decided?"

Harnouphis gazed at him with fevered eyes. "I do not ask you to follow me down this path, Mehen. I cannot guarantee your safety any more than my own. I will gladly request a new mentor for you, if you wish."

Mehen hesitated, like a man contemplating the edge of a precipice. With trembling arms he raised himself from the chair. He crossed the space between them, dropped to his knees and kissed the high priest's hand.

"I am your servant, my lord," he cried fervently. "Now and always."

Korax sat cross-legged on the grass, carefully drawing hieroglyphs on a papyrus. Beside him lay his pallet with its twin inkwells and stock of reed pens. In his left hand was the sheet that he copied, a spell for consecrating a certain amulet.

Before him, the bathing pool rippled gently in the twilight. Soon, regrettably, it would be too dark to read, and he would have to go back to the House of Life. Korax preferred the solitude of this garden by the pool. The trickle of the sacred spring calmed his balky nerves and helped him concentrate.

"I hope it won't disturb your study if I have a quick bath."

Korax turned his head to see Amasis approaching, a lantern in hand. At once, Korax clambered to his feet and bowed.

"Of course not, your Excellency. Would you prefer if I withdrew?"

"No, no. Not necessary."

The hierogrammat walked with an unaccustomed heaviness, shoulders slumped. He set down his lantern and discarded his kilt.

"You seem tired, Excellency," Korax remarked. "If you will forgive the observation."

Stepping gingerly down the ramp, Amasis chuckled. "That's what I like about you, grandson. No other young scribe would dare make such a comment to me, for fear of being impertinent. But you Greeks seem to lack such qualms."

"I beg your pardon if I spoke improperly."

"Not at all. I appreciate your concern. I *am* a bit tired, I admit." He sighed as he settled into the water. "May I speak with you in confidence, grandson?"

"Of course, Excellency. You honor me to ask."

"Well, there is a certain turmoil in the Inner Circle of late— concerns about Pharaoh's new taxes, arguments over how we should respond. As you are a Greek, what do your people say about King Ptolemy? Is he a hard man?"

Korax searched his memory. "I know little of his character, I fear. They do say he is an intellectual, a lover of learning. It is also said that his sister and queen, Arsinoe, is the stronger ruler, that Ptolemy defers to her on all matters of state."

Amasis rubbed a chunk of natron over his skin. "I have heard that as well but doubted whether to believe it. Well, our council must decide whether or not to oppose the king's new edicts, and if so, by what means." He shook his head. "From what I can discern, the portents seem unfavorable no matter which path we choose. I fear we are moving into a time of upheaval and danger."

A fear prickled on Korax's scalp. The Apis Bull had made a similar forecast, and Harnouphis had greeted the idea with excitement.

"But enough of my troubles, grandson. Tell me how your studies are progressing."

Since his last session with Harnouphis, his mind had been fretful and distracted. But even as he thought of this, he felt an inner prohibition against revealing his unease. Instead, he lifted the papyrus in his hand. "My studies go well enough, I suppose. Presently I am copying the *Book of Investing the Sacred Scarab with Fortitude for Crossing the Waters of Khemu*."

"Ah," Amasis said. "I have prepared that amulet several times."

"Indeed?"

"Oh, yes. As chief lector priest, it is my duty to officiate at the embalming rites whenever a member of the Inner Circle passes from this life."

Korax reflected. "May I ask a question?"

"Of course."

"The way most amulets are described, it seems they are meant to invest a living person with protection or power. And yet, I know that mostly they are used in the mummification rites, to provide for the souls of the deceased. Similarly, from what I have read of *The Books of Passage in the Otherworld*, they sound much like the initiation I received when entering the House of Life. It seems that every spell and ritual has a dual purpose."

"That is exactly correct."

"But then, how does one distinguish what magic is meant for the living and what for the dead?"

Amasis paused in his scrubbing and grinned. "One does not. Instead, you must seek to understand how each text applies to both conditions. Our sacred wisdom is meant to teach the soul how to advance through the spheres of creation. The soul seeks that advancement in the next life as well as in this one. In the end, grandson, there is no real distinction."

"No distinction between living and dead?"

"Ha-ha! I suggest that you ponder this mystery."

"I promise you, I shall," Korax affirmed. But now that he had Amasis conversing on such matters, he was not one to waste the opportunity. "As an example, take the scene in the Judgment Hall, where the god Anubis weighs the heart of the deceased against the feather of Maat. If the heart balances, the person is justified and enters the Hall of the Gods. If not, the person is devoured by the Eater of Souls."

"Yes. So what is your question?"

"How does that lesson apply to the living?"

Amasis tossed aside the natron cake and relaxed, floating on his back. "Well, you know from your studies that the feather of Maat symbolizes righteousness and truth. But laying that aside, simply consider what is pictured. If you would be one with the gods, whether in this life or the next, your heart must be light as a feather—that is, unencumbered, free of all attachment, all fear, all desire."

Korax put a hand to his chin. "Can any mortal accomplish that, to make the heart so pure?"

"In certain moments, yes. For example, in meditation and ritual. Our rites of worship are designed for that purpose, to help us shed all thought and emotion except reverence for the Divine. In those moments, the heart is pure and light."

"I see," Korax said. "But to hold that ideal consistently ... ?"

"Ah, that is the challenge, is it not?" Amasis stood waist deep in the pool. "Perhaps it can be done—over many lifetimes. If you ever meet such a person in *this life*, grandson, do them homage. For they are truly holy and not likely to pass through this world again."

Chapter Twenty

Nine days after the incident with the game-board, Korax was commanded to accompany Harnouphis on a journey outside the temple. The high priest came to the House of Records dressed in a black robe and carrying a staff topped by an ivory serpent. He directed Korax to fetch a wig and to bring a cloak to go over his tunic.

"Of course, Excellency. Where are we going?"

"You'll see."

Harnouphis' eyes were sunken, his cheeks hollow—the results of a prolonged fast, Korax surmised, such as priests sometimes observed before important rituals.

They departed from the Mansion of Ptah in the late afternoon. They walked along a broad processional avenue until arriving at the western wall of the city. There, in front of towering gates, they met Mehen and two porters. Mehen wore a skullcap and plain tunic, with no sash or badge of office. The porters Korax did not recognize. They were sinewy, bearded, sunburned men—Bedouins of the desert. Clad in ankle-length robes, they bore curved daggers and short swords in their belts. Between them, on their shoulders, they held a carrier pole from which depended a number of bundles. The oddest of these was a woven basket, which snorted as it swung from the pole. Through the open mesh, Korax glimpsed the fat, bristly shape of a piglet.

"All has been arranged as you commanded," Mehen told Harnouphis.

The high priest nodded once and gestured with his staff. The peculiar entourage followed him through the city gates and up the sandy road.

The orange sun hovered in the west, spreading an eerie glow over the monuments and obelisks of the great necropolis. Soon the party left behind the habitations of men and came to a dusty crossroads. To north and south, the road became a donkey trail winding away into distance. Ahead, the way crossed an ancient bridge over a dry streambed, then climbed a stone causeway up to the plateau. Without pausing, Harnouphis led them across the bridge.

The travelers picked their way carefully over broken stone pavement. The causeway had been repaired many times over the centuries. Before them, a huge crumbling step-pyramid loomed on the horizon. But instead of approaching it, they turned north, crossing an avenue of sphinxes and entering a labyrinthine complex of tombs and mortuary temples. In his bones, Korax sensed the presence of countless past ages, innumerable ghosts. A faint breeze whispered among the fabulous ruins. The skin on the back of his skull tingled.

At last, they arrived before a façade of thick-hewn black columns, partially buried in drifted sand. The edifice seemed neither temple nor tomb, simply a gallery built against the face of a rugged mound. Peering at the dark, half-buried portal, Korax shivered. It resembled a door to the Underworld.

The carriers set down their burden and untied the bundles. Harnouphis unwrapped ceremonial implements, including a bronze hand-axe, which he slid into his belt. Mehen lit two torches and handed one to Korax.

"Don't be afraid, Seshsetem," Harnouphis said. "We are merely going to perform a ritual, like any other."

Korax scarcely felt reassured. Still, he knew his place well enough to leave his skepticism unspoken. Besides, his fear now mingled with a powerful curiosity.

The high priest lit a chunk of incense in a long-handled censer. He waved the instrument in an intricate pattern before the doorway, praying silently. From a faience flask he sprinkled water over the threshold.

They left the two porters to guard the entrance. Mehen led the way inside, carrying a torch and the basket containing the sacrifice. Next went Harnouphis, quietly muttering incantations and swinging the censer. Korax brought up the rear, his torch blazing.

They crossed a low-roofed hall, crowded with squat black columns identical to the ones outside. In the torchlight, Korax could not tell how far the hall extended. He saw that many of the columns had once contained inscriptions, but that these had been deliberately and crudely chiseled away. At the front of the hall stood a ruined shrine. An imposing statue of a seated god had been toppled and smashed to pieces. Not enough remained for Korax to recognize the deity's shape.

Harnouphis swept incense smoke through the air and scattered droplets of the lustral water. Then he removed a silver plate and chalice from his bundle and set them before the pedestal of the fallen god. He placed honey cakes on the plate and poured red wine from a flask. Standing before the offerings, he lifted his hands and chanted a prayer in deep, hollow tones. Many of his words Korax did not recognize, but their aim seemed to be to summon a great being out of darkness. At last, the high priest finished the prayer and lowered his arms, much to Korax's relief.

But the relief proved of short duration. Instead of heading back to the daylight, Harnouphis picked up his gear and led the two scribes along the front of the hall. He stopped before a lintel and posts of rough granite. At first glance, Korax thought it a false doorway, since a stone slab completely blocked the space. But Harnouphis slid his hand behind one post and pulled a series of levers. Then, bracing his feet, he pushed on one side of the slab. With a grating noise the stone swung inward, pivoting on a center axis.

Harnouphis took the torch from Mehen and led them inside. After a few steps, the path dropped into a steep, winding stair. Down and down it curled, past several landings that gave access to unlighted passageways. As they descended, Korax smelled only dust and dry decay. But when they reached the bottom at last, the air bristled with a taint of wet sand, a hint of water.

The party traversed a low corridor carved from the rock, with crumbled plaster littering the floor. In those few places where the plaster still adhered, Korax glimpsed fragments of murals and hieroglyphs, but had no time to decipher their import. The passage cornered repeatedly, each time slanting further down. Finally, they came to what seemed a dead end. But Harnouphis worked another set of hidden levers and pushed the slab door open.

They entered a broad chamber, their torchlight flickering dimly on a high, cavernous roof. The flagstone floor ended halfway across the chamber at the curling rim of a black pool. Whether the pool was fed by an underground desert spring or some wandering subterranean arm of the Nile, Korax could not guess. At the water's edge stood a figure carved of gray basalt—a god with some nameless animal for its head.

Korax stared up at the grim, implacable visage. Was this the same fearsome god he had met in his vision of the game-board? His memory was too dim to be sure, but his fear was rising.

"What animal does he wear?" he asked aloud.

"Silence!" Harnouphis hissed. "Do not speak so heedlessly of him." He touched his heart and lowered his head in a pious gesture. "His sacred animal was driven from Egypt long ago. In these times, the god may incarnate in many forms: serpent, wild ass, boar, crocodile."

Harnouphis ordered Korax to place his torch in a bracket beside the pool. Mehen did likewise, so that the statue of the god was flanked by the two sputtering flames. Harnouphis added an incense cake to his censer and walked about, fumigating the area. Mehen set the basket containing the piglet on an altar stone in front of the statue, then backed away, bending low at the waist.

Harnouphis set a hand on Korax's shoulder and ordered him to breathe deeply. Korax wanted to turn and flee. But staring into the high priest's eyes drained his will. As Harnouphis droned an incantation, Korax slipped into a deep trance.

With Seshsetem's awareness subdued, Harnouphis turned to face the statue of the god. He thrust up his arms in supplication.

"Homage to you, O great god of the Palaces of Night, I know you and know your names: Terrible Lord of the Abyss, Set, Bebht, Smy, Apep, Typhon, Suti, Nupti. I, Harnouphis, High Priest of Ptah in his Mansion of Mem-Nephir, call to you now." His hand clapped down on Seshsetem's collar-bone. "Come into this human vessel, O god, that I may speak with you and do you honor."

The Greek's body shuddered and convulsed. After a few moments, his jaws parted and a deep voice issued from his throat: "I wake."

The basket shuddered on the altar, the piglet squealing in fear. Off in the corner, Mehen dropped to his knees and covered his face with a forearm.

Exultant, Harnouphis gazed at the god, his hands still lifted in the gesture of worship. "I, Harnouphis, bid you welcome, terrible lord. I have heard your call across the gulf of the years. In this age when your holy name is scorned and your rites neglected, I offer you due honors and worship."

The god's life burned behind the Greek's eyes. "You wish me as your ally, Harnouphis, priest of Ptah. It can be so. But have you searched your heart sufficiently? Can you say with certainty that is your desire?"

"I can." Harnouphis lowered his hands. "I have labored many years in faithful service to the Temple of Ptah, only to see myself shamed, my efforts scorned by lesser men who possess higher rank and privilege by virtue of birth. I have had my fill of these vain, petty priests. Force is needed to sweep them away. Your power is needed."

"Then we both will benefit. So be it." The Greek's head swiveled to scan the chamber. "You did well to bring me a sacrifice. But who are these others? That one cowering in the shadows?"

"He is Mehen, my loyal acolyte. He is bound to me as I now bind myself to you."

"Stand up, Mehen," the god said. "Have no fear. I am to be your master's ally."

Timidly, Mehen climbed to his feet and took a step forward.

The god regarded him piercingly for a long moment, then continued: "And this vessel that I inhabit. He is not of the Land."

"No. He is a barbarian, of the sea peoples, a slave that I use as a conduit."

The god stared down at the youth's hands, fingers and arm muscles taut. "My power has been driven far away. It will take time for my strength to grow in you, Harnouphis. Till then, this one will serve. But he is not without abilities. His brain is supple and keen. Each time you invoke me to possess him, you must ensure that he remembers nothing of it later."

"So it will be done, my lord Set," Harnouphis vowed. "Now that we have spoken, what further steps must I take?"

"Observe my worship at every sundown, and call me to your mind. Be careful to always work in secret, for my presence must be hidden. As you continue to bind yourself to me, I will be able to influence your world. Once events are set in motion, they will run quickly in your favor." The god turned his eyes hungrily on the altar. "And now, the sacrifice ..."

Harnouphis gestured Mehen to come forward and assist him. Together, the two men pulled the struggling piglet from the basket and held it flat against the altar stone. Mouthing ritual words, Harnouphis seized the axe from his belt. He lifted it high and brought it down on the animal's neck.

The creature wheezed and struggled wildly in a fountain of blood. It took four heavy blows of the axe before the piglet lay still. Dazed and covered in gore, the high priest deliberately hacked the carcass to pieces.

The cake of natron spewed fizzing bubbles that rose to the water's surface and hissed in the air. Standing chest-high in the bathing pool, Korax breathed in the salty aroma. He pressed the natron against his skin and rubbed vigorously, working it over his chest, arms, and lower body.

No matter how thoroughly he washed, he still felt unclean.

Something had happened that night outside the city, something that left him feeling defiled. He remembered nothing about it, from the time they had left the city gates until he woke the next morning in his bed. He had risen to find his tunic splashed with blood stains.

Shuddering at the recollection, Korax continued washing. By the time he climbed out of the bathing pool, the sun was already rising over the temple roofs. He had lain in bed late after yet another fitful night. But today would be a busy one in the House of Records. He shaved and dressed quickly, then hurried to the scriptorium.

Reporting to Katep's station, Korax found the scribe talking to three young men dressed in white kilts and holding wax tablets.

"There you are, Seshsetem," Katep said with a sly smile. "Here are three new scribes for us to train. Do any of them look familiar?"

Korax examined them closely, then laughed and laid his hand of the shoulder of young Baufre. He had not recognized Katep's son without his sidelock. The boy had come of age and now his head was fully-shaved.

"What do you think?" Katep cried proudly. "Baufre has been accepted as an apprentice scribe."

"Congratulations," Korax said. "To all of you."

The three young men bowed to him respectfully.

"Thank you, sir." Baufre peered at him with earnest eyes. "I look forward to learning from you. I am especially eager to gain proficiency in the Greek writing."

Katep laughed. "Baufre hopes one day to work in Alexandria."

"Indeed?" Korax said.

Baufre modestly lowered his gaze. "Yes, sir. Perhaps even to travel to other lands."

"I fear your tales have filled my son with wanderlust," Katep remarked.

Korax touched the boy affectionately on the shoulder. "I hope all of your dreams are fulfilled, young Baufre."

"These would be our three new trainees."

Everyone turned to Mehen, who had approached without notice. Korax and Katep bowed to the chief scribe, and the three apprentices instinctively did the same.

Katep pronounced a formal introduction: "I present Chief Scribe Mehen, supervisor of the House of Records."

"I welcome you, young scribes," Mehen declared. "And I remind you of the honor that has been bestowed upon you. The life of a scribe in service to our god is a great privilege. Always be aware that it is a privilege you must earn by your labor. You must be diligent in all your studies and follow the instructions of your tutors with care. Remember, in our tradition, a scribe who does not learn quickly enough suffers the lessons of the rod."

Eyeing the boys severely, Mehen allowed his admonishments to sink in. Then he turned and walked back toward his office, leaving a much-dampened atmosphere behind

Chapter Twenty-One

Near the center of Memphis, at the river's edge, stood an ancient obelisk of red sandstone. Lines chiseled in the stone over many centuries recorded the height of each year's inundation. This year, the Nile's cresting waters reached only a low place on the obelisk—in the range that historically forecast a paltry harvest and likely famine the following year. As the waters began to recede, a mood of worry settled over the city.

That worry plunged to a bleak foreboding when it became known that, unexpectedly, the Apis Bull had died. Not only the sacred animal's death, but the bizarre manner of death heightened the people's anxiety. According to rumor, Apis had left his stall in the middle of the night and wandered into the exercise yard. The god-bull was found in the morning with half his body submerged in the alabaster drinking trough: Apis had drowned.

On the day of the bull's demise, Korax received a summons from his master Harnouphis. This time, instead of going to the high priest's apartments, Korax followed a messenger through a series of passages in a building adjacent to the House of Records. He had not seen Harnouphis since that night outside the city, and a feeling of dread lingered in him, an instinctive urge to shield his soul from the high priest's intrusions.

If only that were possible.

He found Harnouphis standing alone in an airy chamber lit by a high-set clerestory. On a sprawling table-top lay a map representing the whole of Egypt. From the Delta to the cataracts, every nome, every city, every known village was marked and named. Korax had seen maps and navigational charts often in his life, but nothing so huge and detailed as this.

"You have heard the news about Apis?" Harnouphis inquired.

"Yes, your Excellency." Korax kept his eyes lowered.

"A pity we could not foresee this event," Harnouphis said. "Still, it may yet turn to our advantage."

Harnouphis was changing. Absent now was the amiable mask of friendliness and charm. The high priest appeared solemn, abrupt, as though spurred by a relentless inner force.

"Do you understand what happens at the death of the sacred bull?"

"I know that a new one must be found," Korax said. "A new calf."

"That is correct. There will be fear and consternation across the land until the reincarnated god is found. And great honor and status will attend the servants of Ptah who find the calf. Do you know by what mystic signs Apis is recognized?"

"No, your Excellency."

"Then listen well and picture them in your mind. His hide is black. On his forehead, there is a white triangle, on his back, a vulture with outstretched wings. On his right flank is a crescent moon, and on the top of his tongue, the image of a scarab. Finally, the hairs of his tail must be double. Can you remember and envision all of these signs?"

Korax had fixed them in his mind. "Yes, Excellency."

"Good. Now I shall place you under a mild enchantment. In your vision you will see the time and place where the sacred calf is to be born. You will show it to me on this map and tell me the month and day."

Harnouphis set a hand on his shoulder.

Reluctantly, Korax looked into the high priest's eyes. The familiar, dreamy haze seeped into his brain.

Three days later, Harnouphis departed from Memphis. He commissioned one of the smaller temple barges and, attended by a handful of porters and servants, set sail in the early morning.

When he returned from upriver one month later, a cheering throng met his ship at the quay. Runners had been dispatched the day before to inform the temple hierarchy that the sacred calf Apis had been found. At Harnouphis' instructions, the runners made no effort to conceal the joyous news from the folk they met along the way. The crowd sang hymns as the barge floated into its mooring. They broke into exultant cries when the calf appeared, draped in flowers and was led down the gangway by Harnouphis himself.

Of course, Harnouphis understood that the calf could not be proclaimed the true Apis until certified by a panel of expert priests. He apologized profusely to his superiors that word of the calf's arrival had somehow spread to the population at large. But he also understood how difficult it would be for the panel not to certify the calf, now that the people of Mem-Nephir had recognized the animal as their incarnate god.

Fortunately for all concerned, the examination did not take long. The calf was led into the temple yard, while hushed, anxious onlookers crowded the seats and swarmed against the fences. Wielding ceremonial implements, the priests measured the holy markings and compared them to images on the antique scrolls. Perhaps the vulture mark looked more like a lopsided insect, and the scarab on the tongue might have been a sore. Still, no calf was perfect. Most of the experts had seen worse approximations. After a brief, tense discussion, the priests flung their hands in the air and shouted out the happy news.

The god Apis had returned to Mem-Nephir.

Harnouphis enjoyed abundant acclaim for finding the incarnate god so expeditiously. His annual salary was increased and banquets held in his honor. He officiated at the ceremonies investing the new Apis with magical powers. He received accolades and gifts from city officials and village leaders all over the region.

His disgrace at the council two months past now appeared completely forgotten. Indeed, the blustery talk of mounting resistance to Pharaoh's taxes had mostly evaporated. Only two detailed strategies had been submitted, including the one by Paramses. Both were rejected by the conservative majority of the Inner Circle.

Harnouphis used his rising fortunes to strengthen his alliances on the council and to further ingratiate himself with the first servants. His daily contact with the god Set imbued him with rising confidence. He sensed that more and more events would swing in his favor and that soon, at long last, his moment would come.

Korax thrust hard, knees bent, hands gripping the wooden shaft. The blunt end struck the wall with a thud, denting the soft brick, making fragments of dust fall to the floor. He leaned back with a hiss.

Must be more quiet, more cautious. Must not wake his neighbors.

The wall on that side of his room was scarred with numerous marks from his improvised weapons. On sleepless nights, he no longer wandered the temple grounds. Instead, he practiced the arms training he had learned at school in Rhodos. A fallen acacia branch, picked up in a temple grove, served as a spear. Now he leaned it in the corner and picked up a short rod, the broken end of a discarded walking stick. Striding to the center of the floor he spread his feet, lifted an imaginary shield, and began a regimen of sword practice. Silently he wheeled, ducked, slashed, and thrust, stepping lightly, always balanced on the balls of his feet.

These drills calmed his mind much better than forlorn wandering in the night. They reminded him of his past, of Korax the son of Leontes, who he had been. His body was still paunchy, with spindly limbs. But at least he felt more invigorated and alive.

Sometimes, after practicing in this way, he would sit in bed with a wax tablet, writing as best he could remember passages from Plato, verses of Euripides and Homer. He was determined to preserve both body and mind, to not let his Greek self fade to nothing.

Of course, he also still practiced the visualizations of light, continued to pray and burn incense to Isis. He had vowed to her that he would walk the path of the sacred knowledge with all the patience and dedication required. That vow, that path, sometimes seemed opposed to his urge to return to the Greek world. Other times, he thought that it must *be* the path that would eventually lead him to freedom.

Isis had warned him that a time of testing would come. Korax knew that his master Harnouphis had used him more than once for evil—in ways he could not remember, but that certainly left him defiled.

Teeth clenched, he stabbed the air hard.

Perhaps the day would come when he would kill Harnouphis. Perhaps that was the duty the gods would set before him.

He pivoted and slashed with a growl.

Whatever his fate, he promised himself he would face it not as Seshsetem the slave, but as Korax, son of Leontes—Korax of Rhodes.

The immense procession crawled ponderously from the gates of the Temple of Ptah and down the long avenue of sphinxes. A somber crowd lined the steps and galleries to watch the funeral of the deceased Apis Bull. Eighty days had elapsed since the bull's death—the period required for mummification.

To Harnouphis, it seemed another eighty days would pass before this tedious ritual finished. He stepped along in a place of honor, leading the new incarnation of the god by a tether woven of rushes cut from all the nomes of Egypt. In front of him, the enormous painted coffin rode on a gilded cart in the shape of a boat. Around the cart walked flutists playing a dirge and priests who beat their breasts and wailed lamentations. A team of oxen pulled the cart, led by the chief lector priest Amasis, who wore the jackal-head of Anubis.

But the cause of the infuriatingly torpid pace moved at the very front of the procession. Neksapthis, the feeble Sem-priest, bedecked in yellow vestments and a ceremonial leopard-skin, crept along like a crippled dog—too old to lead such a long ritual, too vain and stubborn to step aside for a fitter man. Harnouphis cursed the ancient Master of Artisans vehemently under his breath. His muttering brought a look of solemn sympathy from Mehen, who marched along at his shoulder, sharing in his honors and the concurrent discomforts.

By the time the procession had passed through the Saqqarah gates and approached the vast city of the dead, the sun blazed high overhead. The sweltering heat forced a number of mourners to stop and rest by the roadside. Elderly and overweight priests sat gasping and sweating in their bright ceremonial gowns, like so many dying fish washed up on a riverbank.

Deep in the necropolis, the procession halted at a complex of temples and shrines dedicated to the cult of Osiris-Apis—the bull in his deceased and resurrected form. Here the columns and facades gleamed with freshly-painted reliefs. Ramps and stairs stood littered with jars of offerings. By an odd twist of theology, the Greeks had identified Osiris-Apis with Serapis, a new god they worshipped in Alexandria. Under the Ptolemies, his cult had burgeoned, and so this dilapidated burial complex had been refurbished.

Tottering about the courtyard in the harsh sun, Neksapthis uttered interminable prayers. Subordinates swarmed after him, censing the air with perfumed smoke, sprinkling holy water, carrying his scrolls and wands, or simply standing ready to catch him if he fell over. Other priests, in masks and orange gowns, beat tambourines and performed a curious, hopping dance. The new Apis calf, impatient with the blazing heat, began to struggle and bellow loudly. Everyone regarded this as a propitious omen.

Finally, the exterior ceremonies were concluded. The oxen were unhitched from the funeral cart and priests of Ptah took their place. They dragged the cart up a long ramp, across a towering portico, and into a dim hypostyle hall. Here at least the air was cooler.

The heat diminished further as the procession descended a series of zigzagging ramps into the vast subterranean catacombs. Hundreds of cressets lit the way as the mourners marched slowly through the ancient labyrinth, where countless generations of mummified bulls lay interred.

Finally, the mourners stopped before a niche newly-carved in the rock. Still, Harnouphis lamented, the funeral was far from over. Another whole liturgy of prayers and incantations must now be performed to ensure the bull's successful journey into the afterlife.

But as he stepped forward to resume the rites, Neksapthis faltered. Lifting a lotus wand high overhead, he suddenly grew stiff and emitted a loud wheeze. Before the startled subalterns could react, the Sem-priest dropped to his knees, then fell on his face.

Immediately priests surrounded him, and the tunnel filled with a rising din. Smelling distress, the Apis calf mooed plaintively. Harnouphis and Mehen exchanged wide-eyed expressions.

"If the Master of Artisans has died in the midst of performing the funeral rites," Mehen muttered under his breath. "That is an ill omen indeed."

Harnouphis gazed inward. After a moment he whispered, "On the contrary. For us, it is a prelude to glory."

Chapter Twenty-Two

The embalming rites for Neksapthis had scarcely begun when the Inner Circle elected his replacement. After meeting for only half a day, the eight surviving first servants choose Peherenptah as the new Master of Artisans.

Clever and robust, in his mid-forties, Peherenptah was a popular choice. He boasted an ancient priestly lineage and had distinguished himself as both a skilled administrator and a potent ritual celebrant. He enjoyed universal respect, though some high priests privately voiced reservations over his dissolute temperament. A man of wealth, he indulged himself with three wives and a harem of concubines. He drank expensive wines and kept a household chef who had trained in Alexandria. Most disturbing of all to narrow traditionalists, Peherenptah had been known to take part in the sensualistic rites of Hathor, the goddess of love and pleasure.

For seven days, the first servants performed intense and elaborate rituals to invest the new Sem-priest with the symbols and potencies of his office. During this time Peherenptah was required to fast, drink only water, and of course abstain from all congress with women. When the final rites of Investiture were complete, Peherenptah's first act was to celebrate with an extravagant banquet in his own honor.

A terraced courtyard was converted to a sumptuous dining pavilion. Curtains of flimsy, embroidered linen fluttered in the cool evening breezes. Lanterns sparkled cheerfully amid rows of tables and couches. An army of entertainers had been hired and dancing girls pressed into service as waitresses. In scanty mesh costumes, they carried platters of goose and lamb basted with complex sauces. They poured wine from painted jars and mixed it with spices from tiny silver ewers. According to the gossip, one hundred jars of imported wine had been purchased—an extravagance indeed considering Ptolemy's hefty duties on foreign luxuries.

Harnouphis reclined on a couch among the second servants, observing the festivities with a serene and pleasant mien. But inwardly his thoughts simmered. The death of Neksapthis had at long last opened a place on the Dais. Harnouphis' recent success in discovering the Apis calf had been well timed to buoy his cause. Chief Treasurer Shepseskaf had even privately acknowledged Harnouphis to be the leading candidate.

Still, the appointment was far from certain. Imouthes was rumored to favor his own protégé Paramses, and Harnouphis knew that other first servants might also put forth their favorites. Doubtless, these would be men of the priestly caste, the key social advantage that Harnouphis himself lacked. He shook his head with rancorous disgust. His inner sense assured him that the vote would likely go in his favor. Yet, he had no way of knowing for sure, or knowing when the decision would come.

When the feasters had eaten their fill, Shepseskaf rose from his place among the first servants. He delivered a speech praising the inauguration of the new Sem-priest and invoking the blessings of all the gods upon his leadership.

Peherenptah himself then addressed the banquet. He spoke with remarkable fluency, Harnouphis decided, considering the quantity of wine he had consumed.

"Brothers, esteemed guests, I thank you all for the honor of your presence at this modest celebration. And, as I have many times these past days, I humbly thank my fellow first servants for the trust they have placed in my hands. The mansion of our god faces formidable challenges in these times. But I assure you, I will do all in my power to protect and preserve our sacred heritage.

And I am confident that, with your help, we will not only maintain our glorious traditions, but usher in a new era of prominence and prosperity for our temple, our city, and our god."

As though at a prearranged signal, a number of priests leaped up and applauded crisply. Soon the entire banquet rose to imitate their actions. Grudgingly, Harnouphis stood up with the rest. Peherenptah patiently waited for the acclamation to subside.

"Tonight, as a sign of the new alacrity I plan to instill in the temple's governance, I am pleased to announce the appointment of our newest first servant. With his addition, the Inner Circle is once more complete ..."

This unexpected announcement incited murmurs of surprise and anticipation. Shocked, Harnouphis stood rigid as an obelisk.

"It may appear to some that we moved hastily in this appointment," Peherenptah continued. "But I assure you, he is a high priest of such incomparable qualifications that the Inner Circle saw no reason to delay. Tonight, it is my great privilege to present to you, for the first time as a member of the Inner Circle, our brother Paramses!"

To Harnouphis it seemed as though a jagged boulder had materialized inside his belly. He could barely stop himself from doubling over and howling in anguish.

Grinning amid the cheers and shouts of congratulations, Paramses jaunted to the foremost terrace and took his place among the first servants. Conscious of the furtive glances cast his way, Harnouphis regained his composure and stiffly joined in the applause.

Peherenptah smiled and lifted a gem-inlaid goblet. "And now, priests of Ptah, I command you to drink wine and be merry! For we are blessed men and should honor the gods by relishing our blessings to the fullest!"

The drinking and entertainment continued, but presently Harnouphis retired to his own apartments. After dismissing his servants and concubine for the night, he carried a burning lamp to his study and locked the door.

Along one wall stood a niche designed to house a modest shrine. Recently, Harnouphis had commissioned a carpenter to enclose the niche in a cabinet of fine cedarwood. The elegant doors closed with an iron latch, to which Harnouphis held the only key.

Now he unlocked the cabinet and swung the doors wide. Inside, on the altar shelf stood a figure of Set a cubit tall, which Harnouphis had fashioned of wax and coated with lampblack. Before the god's implacable figure lay candles, a censer, and the ceremonial axe.

Harnouphis lit four candles and placed them in lamps of red glass. He fired a lump of frankincense, and the dense smoke writhed before the visage of the god. Far away, Harnouphis could hear the lively music of the banquet, mingled with bursts of laughter. The sounds of merriment fueled his fury.

"Homage to you, O great god of the Palaces of Night, I know you and know your names: Set, Bebht, Smy, Typhon, Suti, Nupti, I, Harnouphis, call you now."

The soft, subtle voice came into his head: "I am here."

Harnouphis controlled his emotion with a supreme effort. "I greet you, Lord Set. We have suffered a ... setback, in terms of—"

"You are enraged, Harnouphis. That is good. Rage properly channeled can bring forth momentous results."

"I ... did not expect this failure!"

"There is no failure. I have not forgotten my promise to you. This is only one move in the game."

"But this was the first opening to appear in fifteen years. Now it is lost!"

"Heed my words, Harnouphis. I can only approach the game from the pre-existing arrangement of the board. The piece called Paramses has always stood in your way. Now it is positioned for removal."

"I do not understand."

"Look into your heart. Power arises from will, and will springs from desire. What do you desire now, at this moment?"

Blood, Harnouphis thought. He had sunk to such a pit of frustration and hate that his soul cried out for the death of Paramses.

"You see?" said the god. "You have the desire. Do you also have the will to make it manifest?"

Did he? To murder a fellow priest—a monstrous crime. And yet, to shrink from the act would mean denying all his aspirations, all he would become—all he had already become.

"I have the will."

"Then listen carefully. Your chance will come at the next full moon. You must employ the young scribe as my vessel, for I will need a firm grasp to tighten the snare...."

The first thing Korax noticed on entering the high priest's study was the air of tension. Harnouphis and Mehen awaited him, both dressed for ritual in glossy black gowns and heavy pectoral collars. Both wore folded scarves on their heads and amulets of black obsidian in settings of jagged gold.

The next thing Korax noticed was the game board on the ebony table. Today only two pieces stood on the board: a small, waxen figure of a man on the lowest level and an animal-headed god on the upper tier.

"Sit down, Seshsetem," Harnouphis told him curtly. "Drink this."

Korax received the tumbler and eyed it mistrustfully. When Harnouphis presented him with wine before a ritual, the drink always contained a drug.

"Just a mild potion to help you relax," Harnouphis said with a brittle smile.

With sullen resignation, Korax swallowed the draught. Harnouphis and Mehen began to chant. Korax stared at the god-figure on top of the board, with its unrecognizable animal head. The image sparked a simmering fear. He had seen that image before, but the memory had gotten lost—or been stolen from him.

Beyond the table, the terrace opened onto a quiet afternoon. The day was cool and overcast, a rarity for Egypt even in mid-winter. As the deep, rolling chant continued, Korax gazed into the gray sky.

Presently, his vision drifted off across the terrace. It floated higher, a leaf borne aloft by wind, high over the walls and courts, across the broad, shimmering expanse of the Nile. It streamed out over the desert, a scarred terrain of broken rocks, withered grass and low, sandy hills.

Abruptly, his awareness swooped down and blinked off.

Stunningly, he came awake in the body of an animal, a huge predator cat. Air bristled on sensitive whiskers and filled his brain with overpowering smells. Sand yielded under his paws as he prowled, sure-footed, on coiling, powerful legs.

Topping a ridge, he lifted his muzzle to the wind. A new smell reached him—salty, musky, the scent of prey. A ferocious hunger burned in his belly.

He ran down the hill, loping, gathering speed.

Over the next rise the prey came into view: a group of men, two horses. Korax feared they were too many. But the cat charged, heedless of any danger. The men appeared to be a hunting party, a noble and his attendants. They huddled around a chariot, examining a broken wheel.

Smelling the approaching cat, the horses neighed and reared. The nobleman tried to grab the reins, but in their terror the horses knocked him to the ground. They ran off, dragging the broken cart amid shouts of confusion. The attendants saw the charging cat, but instead of rushing for weapons, they stood gaping, paralyzed. In a moment, they broke and fled in panic.

The nobleman scrambled to his knees, looked about desperately. But his javelins had been carried off in the chariot. The man screamed as the cat sprang.

His teeth sank into flesh, tearing tendons. Warm, delicious blood gushed over his tongue.

The man gave a horrible scream and batted at the cat. Growling, the beast pressed the struggling body to the earth with a paw and bit deeper into the throat. The struggles weakened. The body spasmed and lay still. The cat raised his gory muzzle, peered about and growled, then bent his head to feed....

Writhing, yowling, Korax awoke. He knelt on all fours on a colorful carpet—his master's study. Harnouphis and Mehen stood over him with gleaming eyes and enthralled expressions. Past their shoulders, Korax glimpsed the game board. The god-figure now stood on the bottom level, over the wax man-piece, which had been torn in half.

Korax stared at Harnouphis, a sickening comprehension rising in his mind. Perhaps the fury of the predator still lingered, or perhaps only his mortal outrage impelled him.

Howling, he sprang at the high priest and sank fingers like claws into the neck. Locked together, they staggered back against the table, Harnouphis grunting.

"What have you done to me?" Korax screamed. "What have you done?"

Mehen came to his master's aid. Together, he and Harnouphis pried Korax's hands loose, allowing the high priest to slide away.

Korax collapsed over the table, wailing. "No more! You won't use me again for your crimes!" He thrust out his arms and swept the game-board from the table. It fell to the floor, shattering.

Harnouphis had snatched up a ceremonial staff. When Korax straightened and tensed to attack again, the high priest was ready. The butt of the staff sprang out and struck Korax between the eyes.

Korax sank to his knees, stunned, clutching his brow. But in a moment he lowered his hands, murderous rage burning in his heart.

"Stay down!" Harnouphis commanded, brandishing the staff before the Greek's face.

Korax struggled to rise. Harnouphis' eyes stabbed into his soul. Korax stared back, blazing with wrath and hate. Straining, he pulled his feet under him. But as he tried to straighten up, his sinews turned to water. He collapsed onto his elbows and knees.

"Foolish young man! Do you think to match wills with me?"

The staff struck the back of his head. Korax dropped on his belly, groaning.

"Do you think because the god uses you as a vessel that you have any power? You are nothing! You are a reed I use to write with, and like a reed I can snap you at will. Do you hear me?"

A serpent of fire slithered around Korax's spine and squeezed. He writhed on the floor, screaming in agony.

"Do you hear me?"

"Yes. Yes."

"Then listen well, Seshsetem. You will forget everything that happened since you swallowed the wine. You will remember *nothing* of this! In a few moments, the pain will subside. Then you will rise and leave my chambers. You will go quietly, and be ready to come again when you are called."

Chapter Twenty-Three

News of the death of Paramses spread like a contagion through the Mansion of Ptah. To lose a first servant so soon after his appointment, and a man so robust and talented—this was a great calamity indeed. For long hours, the Inner Circle met in their sanctuary to discuss the implications of the terrible event, seek to divine its meaning, and reach some conclusion about what to say to the populace.

Harnouphis kept his countenance somber and went quietly about his duties. But he could hardly contain his excitement when, three days after the tragedy, he was summoned to the private apartments of the new first servant Peherenptah.

The Sem-priest rested on a tiled balcony, watching the sunset from a broad, silk-covered couch. With his silver gown, fringed wig, and kohl-darkened eyes, he cut a figure of opulent repose. Behind him, a slave girl attended with ostrich-plume fans, ready to stir the air should it suddenly turn unpleasantly warm. Near the couch, four voluptuous concubines knelt on cushions, dressed in gold pectoral collars and little else. Seated by the balustrade, a pretty musician in a sheer gown gently plucked the strings of a lute.

"Welcome, Harnouphis. Thank you for coming. Please ..." Peherenptah waved a ringed hand at a couch only a bit smaller than his own.

Harnouphis sat down facing the Sem-priest.

"Some pomegranate wine, perhaps." Peherenptah crooked a finger and a slave girl presented Harnouphis with a painted, gold-rimmed cup.

Peherenptah sighed and sat upright. "I need to speak with you regarding this terrible accident."

Harnouphis stared soberly into his wine. "Such a shock."

"Certainly. And so unusual for an experienced huntsman like Paramses. From what we know, a whole series of mishaps conspired together. First the wheel of his chariot broke at the hub. While they were trying to fix it, the animal came. The men all agreed that the cat was huge, a black leopard—extremely rare in these parts. Still, it does not explain why experienced retainers fled, nor could they explain it themselves. And then, instead of carrying off the body, the cat devoured only a small part of it and left the rest." He shook his head in bafflement. "Very hard to understand."

Harnouphis kept his expression dutifully grave.

"But we must look to the future," Peherenptah declared. "No doubt you have noticed how my governing style differs from that of my predecessor. I insist on attacking problems, not letting them fester. That is why I moved with such dispatch to appoint Paramses. And that is why you are here now."

Harnouphis experienced a flutter of anticipation but kept his expression neutral.

"I will speak frankly. Paramses was chosen over you—and the vote was close—because some of us felt that he would function better as part of the Inner Circle. I'm sure you know that in group ritual, smooth interaction of personalities is crucial. You, Harnouphis, have always struck some of us as a mystery man, a bit of a loner."

You mean low-born, Harnouphis thought bitterly. *Not of your class.*

"Now, obviously, we must again fill an open chair on the Dais. I tell you frankly, Harnouphis, no other second servant approaches you in qualifications. The appointment can be yours. Are you interested?"

"Of course. I would welcome the opportunity to rise in service to our god."

"Excellent." Peherenptah smiled and leaned back on the couch. "I only need to assure myself that you are a man we can all work with. That is why I invited you to my residence, so we could talk privately ... socially, as it were."

Taking the cue, Harnouphis reclined on his elbow. "I thank your Excellency. What can I say or do to assure you that I would be a worthy choice?"

"Well, there is the question of your assignment for one. When I advanced to Sem-priest, it left the job of chief steward open. Brother Shepseskaf graciously agreed to step into that toilsome post. Of course, that left the opening at chief treasurer, which we expected Paramses to fill. Naturally, you are even better qualified, having served as Shepseskaf's subordinate all these years. I would hope you would accept that position."

Harnouphis smiled easily. "It seems eminently suited to my experience."

"Exactly!" Peherenptah sat up again. "Now as chief treasurer, you would administer both revenues and expenditures. In the time I've had to review our budgets, I've noticed a number of areas where I believe improvements are needed. In fact, I intend to reorganize all of the temple's finances eventually. As chief treasurer, I would rely on your support."

"Of course. I would consider that my role."

"Some accounts need immediate attention," Peherenptah stressed. "In particular, there is the budget for the Sem-priest's household—woefully inadequate. Our departed brother Neksapthis must have practiced an amazingly penurious existence. I assure you, I have no intention of doing likewise."

Harnouphis tilted his head with mild surprise. The petty libertine's first concern was that the temple support his own lavish lifestyle. Well, the answer was obvious.

"I promise you, Excellency, my gratitude to a Sem-priest who sponsored my candidacy would compel me to ensure that all his needs were met to his complete satisfaction."

"A wise and perfect answer," Peherenptah exclaimed happily. "I can see you are a man we can work with very well. But let's not talk any more business tonight. Rather, let us relax as two gentlemen and enjoy ourselves."

He clapped his hands smartly and the concubines glided from their cushions. The lute came to life as the four women paraded sinuously toward their master.

"Do you like what you see, Harnouphis?"

Sexual congress as a social pastime was an imported custom, practiced by only the most decadent of the Egyptian upper class. Harnouphis found the notion distasteful—but not so distasteful that he would dream of rejecting the Sem-priest's hospitality, especially on this occasion. Besides, Peherenptah's concubines were magnificent.

"Your women are most enchanting, Excellency. You are a very lucky man."

Peherenptah smiled effusively as he stroked a naked thigh. "And I enjoy sharing my good fortune with my friends."

Tiers of white candles blazed and danced before the statue of the goddess. Wrapped in her golden wings, Isis gazed down serenely from her pedestal at the front of the chapel.

Korax had placed his mat against the rear wall so he could rest his back. The chapel was located off a back corridor of the House of Life, a place for initiates to meditate and commune with the goddess. Lately, Korax had come here every evening, attempting to settle his mind sufficiently for study. Some nights, he remained in the chapel till dawn.

Most of the candles were burning low, and Korax was alone in the darkened shrine. It must have been some hours past midnight when Amasis entered. Wearily, the old priest trudged to the front of the chapel, raised his hands in supplication, and prayed quietly. Korax shifted into deeper shadow, gripped by an unreasonable terror that the hierogrammat would spot him. He wondered if he could slip out without being noticed.

But already Amasis had turned. He crossed toward the door, then stopped and looked at Korax. After a moment, he nodded slightly and moved on.

Then he halted a second time, shoulders tensing. He peered intently at Korax, who climbed reluctantly to his feet.

"You are here very late, grandson," Amasis whispered as he approached.

"Yes, Excellency."

"Pardon my noticing, but you seem disturbed."

Korax quivered slightly, too afraid to answer.

Amasis tilted back and covered his heart with a hand. "What is troubling you?" he demanded.

"I don't know ... I cannot tell." Korax's tone revealed desperation. "My spirit is consumed with grief and dread ... but it has no cause, no sanity."

"How long has this been so?"

"I-I cannot say. I have no rest. And when I do sleep, I wake from horrible dreams."

"Of what do you dream?"

"I cannot remember."

Frowning, Amasis grasped the young man's wrist and peered into his eyes. "Don't look away," he ordered, when Korax instinctively lowered his face.

Blinking, Korax obeyed. Amasis' eyes narrowed with concentration, then widened with empathy and worry. When he released his grip, his face evinced a troubled confusion.

"Have you asked the goddess to intercede?"

"I pray to her every day, morning and night."

"And has she answered you?"

"She came to me once, in a dream. But that was months ago. Since then, she is silent. I feel so terribly lost."

Amasis pursed his lips. He pondered for an interval, then seemed to decide something. "Continue to pray to her, grandson. If there is a cure for any sorrow of this world, she in her mercy provides it."

Amasis turned to leave, then paused with another thought. "You know, it is permissible to fall asleep in the chapel. Perhaps you could rest more peacefully here."

Korax nodded, and the high priest withdrew.

Alone again, Korax sat slumped against the wall. His distraction and fear had grown worse than ever, worse even than his days in the slave yards. At times he felt so troubled he thought he would weep. But the release of tears never came.

He watched the statue of Isis for some time, praying for mercy, for his suffering to ease. Then he prayed for her guidance, that she show him the path he must take. Eventually drowsiness overtook him, and he fell into a sleep.

He woke in the morning, startled to find himself still in the chapel. Gray daylight slanted through narrow windows beneath the roof, illuminating the goddess and her altar.

Korax noticed a scroll lying at his side. Bewildered, he unrolled it and read the hieroglyphs of the title:

The Book of Calling the Magical Ally.

Below the House of Life, a secret stair of rough-cut stone descended many levels. It led deep underground to the mortuary vaults, where Amasis worked the magical funeral rites.

Accompanied by torch-bearers ahead and behind, Peherenptah descended the steps with a perturbed and irritated air. For three days running, Amasis had dispatched messengers to beg that the Sem-priest meet him here—and come alone. Naturally, as chief lector priest, Amasis could not absent himself from the embalming rituals during certain periods. But over a three-day span he surely could have slipped away for a short time, if he chose. No, Amasis had some other motive. Peherenptah had finally relented, as much out of curiosity as deference to the old hierogrammat.

Still, Peherenptah resented being dragged into the mortuary vaults. For all his schooling in the sacred arts, this place of death appalled him. A true Egyptian, he clung to his belief in the afterlife, but hoped to postpone it as long as possible.

At the base of the steps, Peherenptah followed the attendants across a painted foyer and into a broad sanctuary. The air reeked of salty natron and putrefying body fluids. In an island of lamplight at the center, priests and embalmers stood clustered around a tilted stone table. Looking past them, Peherenptah shuddered and took an involuntary step back.

On the table lay the deceased Paramses. The body had already been eviscerated, the organs placed in sealed jars, the cavity packed with natron. At present, two embalmers leaned over the head. They manipulated long bronze tweezers up the nostrils and carefully picked out the brains.

A slender figure wearing the jackal-head of Anubis detached himself from the group. "Thank you for coming, my brother,"

Amasis said, after pulling the dark mask over his head and handing it to a subaltern. "I apologize for the inconvenience of meeting in this place."

Peherenptah had regained a measure of composure. "On the contrary, esteemed Amasis, I regret that pressing duties prevented me from responding more promptly to your summons."

Amasis inclined his head toward the table. "Curious, don't you think, how the predator left most of the body intact."

Only parts of the neck and shoulder had been eaten, the missing flesh now packed in bandages.

Peherenptah winced and averted his gaze. "May I ask why you needed to speak with me, Amasis?"

"Of course. Please."

The old man led the way to a dim corridor. Some distance along the relief-covered wall, they came to a candle-lit chapel. The shrine stood empty except for an enthroned statue of Osiris, green-skinned and robed in gold, the beloved god of the dead.

Amasis pitched his voice just above a whisper. "I wanted you to see for yourself how little had been devoured. Does that not seem strange to you? As if the leopard's purpose was purely to kill, not eat?"

The Sem-priest scowled, perplexed and unhappy. "What are you meaning to imply?"

"That perhaps Paramses was killed by magic."

A series of troubled emotions flicked over Peherenptah's face. "But ... that would take potent machinations indeed."

"It would explain the bizarre circumstances."

"Yes, but so much influence brought to bear? Who? ... You suspect Harnouphis?"

The first servants stared at each other in the shuddering candlelight.

Amasis said: "I've watched him curiously for some time. That Greek scribe of his has unusual gifts. Harnouphis uses him as a seer—Who knows what else? I thought little of it until recently. Then I encountered the Greek late at night in the Chapel of Isis. He was in a very bad way. My inner sense told me he had been possessed—by something very dark and powerful."

After pondering a few seconds, Peherenptah shook his head. "That is not much evidence to accuse Harnouphis—and of such an abominable crime."

"I do not accuse." Amasis lifted his palms. "I merely read events and suggest an interpretation."

"Indeed, that is your proper role," Peherenptah muttered. "But there certainly could be other interpretations. The leopard might have been frightened away before it could feed. The size and sudden appearance of the cat might have panicked the attendants. As for the Greek, well, who knows what mental diseases may plague a foreigner? Then there is the fact that we have already voted Harnouphis onto the Dais. His investiture is set for two days hence. Without strong evidence, we cannot rescind his appointment."

"Agreed," Amasis said. "Still, I felt it my duty to apprise you of my suspicions."

Peherenptah nodded. "What is your counsel?"

"That we be on our guard, observe Harnouphis for any sign of tainted practice or abnormal powers."

"Very well."

"One other thing: you might want to increase your own magical protections."

"Me? Why?"

"Well, if Harnouphis *is* a murderer, and his ambitions are not yet slaked, who else would be the next target?"

"Thank you." The Sem-priest sighed morosely. "On that unpleasant note, I will leave you."

The first servants exchanged bows. Peherenptah hastened away, anxious to return to the daylight.

Climbing the steps, he pondered the implications. Having Harnouphis in the Inner Circle might actually prove an advantage, making him easier to watch. On the other hand, the whole idea seemed fantastic. Harnouphis, the boorish uncultured administrator, a master of nefarious magic? Perhaps Amasis was spending too much time in the mortuary vaults. Such morbid duty might bend a man's imagination. And Amasis was old, nearly as old as the lamented Neksapthis. The time might be near to gently suggest that the hierogrammat consider retirement.

By the time he topped the stairs, Peherenptah had concluded irritably that he really needed to keep an eye on both Harnouphis and Amasis.

Chapter Twenty-Four

O n the appointed day, the entire priesthood of Ptah gathered to honor Harnouphis and witness his investiture. The procession formed at noon in the vast outer courtyard of the temple. To the solemn beating of clappers and drums, the priests marched past the towering obelisks and through the pylon gate.

Harnouphis trod along near the front, preceded only by the eight first servants. Each of those high priests wore ceremonial gowns of different colors, and each carried a lotus wand. Harnouphis himself was arrayed in a tunic of gold and a shawl of the finest white cambric. A towering gold headpiece crowned him, so heavy it forced him to bend his neck.

An assembled multitude of temple staff and civic officials watched the parade cross the inner courtyard and ascend the steps. Next, the procession passed through the grand hypostyle hall. Here the majority of the priests would stop, forming ranks to wait in mute attention while the ceremony took place within.

"Are you happy Harnouphis?"

Exultant, my lord Set. And filled with gratitude toward you, of course.

Giddy with triumph, Harnouphis proceeded into the next hall, with its rows of painted columns and larger-than-life statues. The measured drumming continued as the second and third servants of Ptah filed in behind him.

At the front of the hall stood the embossed gold doors and the inner sanctuary, where only first servants might enter. Harnouphis stopped at the foot of the dais. The eight first servants mounted the steps and then turned to face the assembly. They intoned prayers in the old language, Peherenptah chanting and the other high priests answering in chorus. Harnouphis was censed, sprinkled with water, anointed with purifying unguents.

Then, one-by-one, the first servants stepped down from the dais and laid a hand on Harnouphis' shoulder. They spoke blessings and bestowed upon him a current of magical vigor. Harnouphis thrilled as blissful sensations rushed through his being—this moment of triumph, so long aspired to, now his at last.

"This is only one step of your journey," the voice of Set whispered in his ear. "Greater things are yet in store."

Faintly, Harnouphis wished his divine ally would depart and allow him to relish these few moments of glory.

Peherenptah, the last to confer his blessing, now gestured for Harnouphis to ascend the dais. Together, the two priests approached the gold doors of the holy of holies. Together, they broke the clay seal and pulled the great doors open.

All but the first servants averted their gazes. For the first time, Harnouphis looked within. Side-by-side with Peherenptah, he entered the sanctuary, the other first servants walking behind. The chamber was round, of pink sandstone trimmed with alabaster. Beyond the offering tables and altar stood the figure of the god, stately Ptah with his Pharaonic beard and serene countenance, fashioned of solid gold.

The first servants formed themselves into a circle with Harnouphis at the center. Led by Peherenptah and Amasis, they chanted incantations from the oldest books of the cult—verses that only first servants could utter. One by one, they pointed their lotus wands at Harnouphis and invested him with the supreme powers of Ptah.

Harnouphis emerged from the inner sanctuary in a state of sparkling exaltation. As he stepped from the dais, the voice of Set came to him again.

"Yes. Much greater things are possible for you, Harnouphis—if you have the will. But they are for later. For now, enjoy your victory. Only remember one thing: do not in your self-congratulations neglect my worship or forget the duties you owe me."

The last words sounded pointed, like spears.

Never, Lord Set. I promise you!

Korax kissed Itaji on the lips, rolled over and sat up on the edge of the bed. Before he could rise, the dancer wrapped her arms around his neck and kissed his earlobe.

"Are you getting up so soon?"

He patted her wrists. "Yes. I really must get back to my studies. Don't be cross with me, Itaji."

She flopped out on the bed, stretching sinuously. "Oh, I am not cross, Seshsetem. Only a little disappointed."

He smiled down at her. "What? Don't I please you anymore?"

The dancer giggled. "Oh, to be sure! I *did* worry about you for a while. Last month you seemed so unhappy." She jumped to her feet and hugged him. "But lately you have regained your fire. You are again my passionate Greek lover!"

He kissed the top of her head. "I was lost for a while. I thought I had lost myself entirely. But now I have found my way back to Isis."

She raised her head, delighted. "Her voice has returned to you?"

Turning away, Korax reached for his tunic. "Not her voice exactly, a more tangible gift."

"What does that mean?"

"A new path has opened in my magical work, thanks to her."

"Oh, your work again." Itaji shrugged and looked around for her clothing.

"Magical work." Korax grinned. On an impulse, he embraced her tenderly. "Thanks to her and thanks to you, who taught me her worship. You have not only been a lovely mistress, but a true friend to me."

She stiffened in his arms, turned up her face, suspicious. "You talk as though you are finished with me."

"Oh, no. Not at all." He pulled the tunic over his head, avoiding her gaze. "But in fact, I won't be able to see you for a while. At this next phase of my studies, I must abstain from lovemaking."

"Abstain! I hate that word." She gave him a petulant scowl. "And just when you've regained your energy."

He laughed fondly. "I am sorry. It cannot be helped."

"How long?" she asked. "For how long must you *abstain*?"

Korax considered. "Ten days, I think. We need not mention it to anyone. So of course, you will still be paid."

She stepped close, brushed a fingertip over his earlobe. "Paid with coin, yes. But not with the pleasure of your kisses."

He laughed and gave her an extra payment.

A short time later, at the opposite end of the same apartment block, a slender figure walked lightly up to a door. A child-like hand reached out and knocked. In a few moments, a bald manservant pulled the door open. He looked down at the young woman, smiled appreciatively, then stepped back for her to enter.

Itaji stepped into the foyer, nervously tapping her fingers together. Leaving her to wait, the servant shuffled off into the dark interior of the apartment. The dancer paced back and forth, rising on her toes as she pivoted.

Presently, another man approached her from the inner chamber. "Yes. What is your report?"

"Oh, the harvest looks weak, and the river runs low, so the prices of bread and beer will doubtless run higher."

"Stupid girl! Speak plainly." Chief Scribe Mehen was not a man who appreciated clever repartee.

"Yes, sir," she answered, chastened. "Well, as I told you last time, he has not seemed so miserable of late. This continues. In fact, these past few times he's been strangely elated, full of energy, and yet … preoccupied. Tonight he asked me to leave as soon as we finished, saying he needed to study. Oh, and he will not see me for the next ten days. 'Abstaining' is the word he used."

"Did he indeed? Did you ask him to explain?"

"Of course I did. He answered that it was a phase of his studies."

Mehen stroked his pointy chin. "Visit him in three nights, as usual. Ask if he's changed his mind. Ask him to show you what magic he is working. I must know what he is up to."

He counted out three copper coins and dropped them into her palm.

Itaji scowled. "My usual fee is seven, sir."

"Seven is for sleeping with him *and* bringing me news of his intentions. You've only done the former."

Sullenly, Itaji slipped the coins into her girdle. "If you're going to cheat me of my fee, I'm not sure I'll come back here at all. I told you before, I have no taste for spying on him."

Mehen showed her the back of his hand. "Your tastes do not interest me, harlot. Only the information you bring. My master Harnouphis is now the chief treasurer of the temple. Do you really wish to invite his displeasure?"

"Of course not."

"Then do as you are told. Bring me *useful* information next time, and your fee will be restored. Now leave."

Mehen opened the door with a thin-lipped sneer of contempt. Itaji wrapped her shawl around her shoulders and marched indignantly from the apartment.

When the door had shut she paused, looking in both directions. She spat emphatically on the doorstep before hurrying away.

Chapter Twenty-Five

Korax studied the lines of text, anxious that he had neglected none of the intricate preparations. The noon hour approached on this day of the full moon.

The timing of the ceremony was crucial.

That the papyrus was written in the most archaic hieroglyphs compounded his problem. Many of the symbols could assume multiple meanings, and Korax was far from expert.

Some of the instructions read plainly enough: for three days the magician must fast, taking only water; for eight days he must abstain from sexual contact; on the morning of the ceremony, he must bathe three times in clean water, then put on a white garment never worn before.

But other directions were abstruse and perplexing. To successfully call an ally, the magician must "sacrifice the edifice of his former life" and "offer up a torn and penitent heart." Well, Korax felt ready enough to sacrifice his present existence. And if the text meant a heart broken by the trials of life, then surely he qualified as well as most.

A glance at the terrace showed that the shadows had dwindled to their minimum length. Ready or not, he had run out of time. He rolled up the papyrus and slipped it inside his new tunic. He took his reading lamp from its stand and carried it up the ladder, emerging in the brilliant sunlight.

The roof of the apartment block was furnished with screens of woven matting, affording privacy so tenants could sleep outside in hot weather. Korax had set up screens on all four sides to hide the artifacts of his spell. Within the enclosure he had placed a straw met, a walking stick, a small brazier with charcoal, a reed pen with ink and papyrus.

He knelt on the mat and stilled his mind, breathing quietly. Presently, he lifted the walking stick—his makeshift wand—and traced sigils in the air: the Eye of Horus for power and protection, the Ankh for eternal life. He used the lamp to fire the charcoal in the brazier. As it began to burn, he picked up the pen and wrote carefully on a clean sheet of papyrus:

Korax, son of Leontes
Seshsetem, scribe of Ptah

All of his past self must be sacrificed, consecrated to the gods in flame. Only then would his soul be purified, his spirit renewed. Only then would he be worthy of the power bestowed by a magical ally.

Only when your heart is light as a feather can you enter the sphere of the gods.

Deliberately, he folded the sheet in three places. He lifted it up toward the sun, then carefully placed it on the fire.

Next, he unrolled the *Book of Calling the Magical Ally* and began to recite the incantation.

I place myself on the altar of Ra
I arise triumphant in the light
I create myself in the image of the gods
I am formed of the atoms of all the gods
In the radiance of Ptah I come forth into being

I am the hawk that flies in the circle of Nut
I am the great fish that swims in the Khemu
I am the ibis that treads the edges of the Land
I am the bull whose loins are mighty

I am established in the wisdom of Thoth
Isis has taught me her secrets
I am arrayed in the robes of Maat
Osiris now sends me an ally
Ptah endows me with one to command

Over and over, Korax repeated these verses, until the fire had burned down to ashes. Then he lay down, flat on his back, arms flung wide, and turned his face to the burning sun.

Eyes closed, he waited.

Time passed. The sun seared the unprotected skin of his face and feet. According to the book, his ally should now appear at any moment.

But Korax experienced no divine illumination, no voice or inner message, no sign.

In the late afternoon, he finally admitted failure. Head throbbing, weak from hunger and fatigue, he cleaned up the remnants of the ceremony. He carried the implements down the ladder and stored them away. He spread ointment on his sunburned skin, then went and ate some supper.

Returning to his quarters at twilight, he reread the book. Had he done something wrong? Or did he simply lack sufficient ability? He judged the latter more likely but could not tell for sure.

Gloomy and forlorn, he extinguished the lamp and went to bed.

He had only just drifted off when a noise woke him—the cry of a bird close by. Startled, he bounded from his bed and gazed out at the small terrace. An ibis had landed there, a water bird strayed from its usual haunts. The bird stared directly at him and arched its wings in the glimmering moonlight.

Korax whirled, sensing something behind him.

In his room stood a being, pale and translucent as the moonglow. Korax blinked deliberately, but the spirit remained—tall and angular, ibis-headed.

Korax seized hold of his courage. "What are you?"

"Don't you know? You called me." The voice rolled deep and powerful as the river, yet carried a hint of mirth like froth on the surface.

"I summoned a magical ally. But you *appear* to be Thoth, the god of scribes and magicians."

"So you do know me. I am relieved."

"I am not," Korax replied. "I have been troubled with madness in my time, and now I do not trust what I see. Are you saying *you* are my ally?"

"So it would appear."

"But—I am an untutored neophyte. How can I merit the Lord of All Magic as ally?"

"I am surprised myself, yet here I am." Thoth spread his long, long arms as if to demonstrate the fact.

Korax stared, a dawning elation warring with awe and distrust. Thoth was the great god of magic, the founder of all the mental arts. The Greeks identified him with Hermes, but Korax knew him to be—like all Egyptian gods—more mysterious and elemental than the corresponding Greek deity.

Thoth said: "An aspirant attracts an ally according to his ability and the tasks set before him by fate. I would conjecture that you have significant talent—and also a difficult path ahead."

Korax touched fingers to his sunburned cheek. "If you are really my ally, then you must assist me to manifest my will."

The ibis-head nodded. "That is my role. What is your will?"

"To free myself," Korax asserted. "My master Harnouphis uses me for evil purposes, then steals the memories. I must escape his control."

"I expect that can be done."

"And there is more," Korax said with rising excitement. "I wish to leave this place, go home to Rhodes, regain my former life."

"Ah." Thoth seemed amused. "But in the ceremony to call a magical ally, did you not sacrifice the edifice of your former life?"

Korax was struck dumb. How could he have missed so obvious a pitfall? He had trapped himself by the very ritual he hoped would set him free.

"I see your point," he muttered. "Indeed, I have been a monstrous fool."

Thoth's exhalation sounded like a laugh. "Oh, you are very young. Do not look so crestfallen. The sacrifice must have been successful, or else I would not be here. Now the way is open to you."

"I do not understand you. What way do you mean, if I cannot restore my former life?"

"That depends on your will. The river has risen and fallen more than once since you left your island. Much may have changed there. More importantly, *you* have changed—by your study and practice of the sacred arts. The truth of it is, you cannot return to your past, but you *can* choose your future."

Hope rekindled in his heart. "So then, you *can* help me to escape from Memphis? To return to the Greek world?"

"If that is your will."

"Excellent! I will need a plan for leaving the temple, sufficient coin to pay my expenses, spells to avoid recapture."

"You have thought the problem through. That is promising."

"Yes. How long? How long, do you suppose, before I can leave?"

"Well, that depends on you—how hard you are willing to work, how quickly you can learn. I can see you are adept at learning. If you are willing to apply yourself, I think a month should be sufficient. Yes, the next full moon, when the tides of energy once more run high."

How wonderful! A month and he could be free. But even as the prize seemed in reach, another doubt dragged him back. "I have one other concern. I believe the Goddess Isis guides me, and that she has some service she will require of me. Perhaps finding you as my ally is part of her plan—No doubt it is. Yet I feel there must be more to it."

"Oh, I wouldn't worry about that," Thoth answered. "If Isis has a task for you, you can be sure she will let you know."

"I warned you this day would come. I've voiced the warning for many years."

Imouthes' pronouncement somehow conveyed both smug satisfaction and fearful dismay. Harnouphis' scorn for the man had crystallized into a perfect loathing.

All morning the first servants had listened with mounting alarm to the reports of assessors from their widespread estates. With the harvest due to begin in less than a month, the forecast was even worse than expected. Now, they had convened in the sanctuary to discuss the dire ramifications. The only one missing was Amasis, whose duties at the mummification rites of both Neksapthis and Paramses still required him constantly in the underground.

Harnouphis' glance darted from one solemn face to another. His countenance remained neutral, masking the contempt he felt for every one of these men.

"I see no cause for panic," Peherenptah the Sem-priest maintained. "Granted the harvest looks weak, but not so weak as to indicate wide-spread starvation."

"You underestimate the problem," Shepseskaf answered with unmitigated gloom. "If we pay Pharaoh his full grain quota, it will result in such shortages as will cause food riots across the region.

If we convince him to accept a lesser portion, so enough remains to feed the peasants, Pharaoh will demand increased taxes on our pressed oil and manufactured goods—which in turn will drive us deeper into debt."

Frowning, Peherenptah scratched the skin beneath his wig. "Do you agree Harnouphis?"

Harnouphis sat expressionless on his throne. "Brother Shepseskaf's assessment matches my own."

"You see?" the volatile Imouthes cried. "After years of being rescued by bountiful harvests, we've arrived at the place I've predicted all along: bankruptcy."

"You predicted it all along," Shepseskaf chided, "but never offered a practical solution, only illusory fantasies of rebellion."

Imouthes bolted to his feet. "Your implications are insufferable! At least I had the courage to warn where we were headed, where we were being led by do-nothings of your ilk!"

"Brothers!" Peherenptah shouted. "This bickering gains us nothing. Please sit down, Imouthes." He waited for the First Warrior of Ptah to comply. "It appears we are at a point of crisis. We can either pay the full grain tax and risk an uprising, or withhold a portion for the peasants and risk Pharaoh's wrath. Harnouphis, you have dealt with Ptolemy's ministers more than any of us. What is your recommendation?"

"Perhaps we should prepare for both eventualities."

"How do you mean?" the Sem-priest asked.

"I suggest we withhold a percentage of the tax quota in our granaries—enough to stave off famine. By the time the auditors' reports reach Alexandria, the Synod will have convened. There we can explain our reasons and leave the next step to Ptolemy. If he wants his full share of the grain, he can send troops to seize it. Then, if there are riots, at least his soldiers will be here to bear the brunt of putting them down."

In the silence, Peherenptah scanned the faces of the others, then nodded thoughtfully.

"Of course," Harnouphis added, "this will also allow time for our chief steward's men to transfer the temple's grain allotment to our own cellars."

"So even if the peasants starve," Shepseskaf observed, "our own bread will be assured. A rather cold-blooded plan, I must say."

"I disagree," Harnouphis answered quietly. "Merely realistic."

Chapter Twenty-Six

The temple treasury stood in a central courtyard not far from the House of Records. Unlike the surrounding offices of brick and plaster, the treasury was built of granite blocks—sure to prevent thieves from digging through the walls. In his time at the temple, Korax had passed the building often, but had never gone inside. Now, called from his work in the scriptorium at midday, he approached the entrance in the company of a treasury clerk.

Eight days had passed since his calling of Thoth. The presence of a magical ally had opened whole new channels of power in him. Inspired by the god, he had begun new exercises to summon and direct the power, and to write the spells and chants he would use in his grand undertaking, his journey out of Egypt. Now, for the first time since acquiring his ally, he would face Harnouphis. He knew he must hide his awakened capacity. At the same time, he was determined to shield his mind, protect his soul from further defilement. Inwardly, he spoke a charm:

The strength of Sekhet is in my heart
My vision is clear in the Eye of Horus
My secrets are hidden from my enemy

Two sentries guarded the broad, iron-ribbed door, burly men in kilts with short-swords hanging from their hips. They crossed their spears to bar the way, staring belligerently at Korax.

"He is Seshsetem," the clerk explained, "the scribe the chief treasurer sent for."

The guards looked him over, committing his face and name to memory, Korax realized. They uncrossed their spears without a word. One of them turned and unlocked the door with an iron key from his belt.

JACK MASSA

When the heavy door clattered shut behind them, darkness engulfed the long hallway, penetrated only by dim gray light at the opposite end. Along the corridor, they passed closed doors, which Korax imagined must lead to treasure vaults. At the far end of the hall, they stepped into a counting room. Daylight filtered in through narrow windows set near the ceiling and protected with iron bars. Clerks sat on mats at low tables, tallying piles of coins and recording the amounts.

Here was the money he needed—the thought flashed in Korax's brain. His summons here was no accident. It was his magic working, the gods revealing his way.

"Come along," the clerk prodded, as Korax had paused unwittingly to scrutinize the money tables.

Harnouphis awaited them in his office, a spacious chamber full of fine furniture and cluttered with gold and silver vessels. Broad windows admitted ample daylight, though they also were sealed by iron bars set in the masonry. Murals adorned the walls, depicting pharaohs, high priests, and gods presenting each other with boxes of treasure. Korax suspected the chamber must contain a secret entrance for convenience sake. But if so, the portal was well disguised by the wall paintings. Or perhaps a trap door was concealed under one of the opulent carpets.

"We have much work today." Harnouphis was already mixing drops of oil into an alabaster bowl. "I wish to know what you foresee regarding the harvest yields at each of the temple's estates."

Warily, Korax sat down in the place indicated. Avoiding the high priest's eyes, he continued to repeat the inner charm. *His mind was his own, his powers hidden.*

The high priest set the scrying bowl on the table. The clerk sat nearby with palette and papyrus, ready to record the prognostications. Korax took a deep breath. He dutifully stared at

Harnouphis' eyes. But he kept his mind in focus, ignored the priest's chanting, and brought *himself* into the receptive state for scrying.

Throughout the afternoon, Korax gazed into the bowl and described his visions. Harnouphis questioned him exhaustively regarding each crop at each farm and plantation. The yield of emmer from the temple's fields at Narm-atep would come in one tenth below the assessors' forecasts. The yield of barley would be one third lower.

When the harvest forecasts were finally complete, Harnouphis asked for more general predictions. What events could be seen surrounding the granaries in the months following the harvest? What about the Synod in Alexandria?

Dark and violent visions stirred themselves in response to the first question. Korax saw riots unfolding, mobs rampaging through the streets of towns and villages, troops of cavalry riding them down. But in Alexandria, the outlook was sunnier. Harnouphis, bedecked in ceremonial regalia, spoke convincingly with priests from other temples and made winning appeals to Pharaoh's officials. Always, at his shoulder, hovered a shadowy figure, a tall, lean god with the black head of a nameless beast.

At last, the surface of the scrying bowl lay still. Harnouphis stared at it contemplatively. Korax watched him, and for a moment the two locked eyes.

Then Harnouphis blinked and rose from his chair. He waved a hand, muttered a spell, and commanded Korax to forget all that he had seen.

Korax blinked and pretended to come out of trance. As he crossed the counting room and passed down the dim corridor, he reflected on what he had seen—satisfying himself that he remembered every detail.

His vision was clear in the Eye of Horus.

Deliberately, Harnouphis closed the doors of the shrine to Set and turned the key in the lock. Brow furrowed, he walked across his study to the curtained doorway. Mehen awaited him in the antechamber, seated on a stool, stiff and erect. Harnouphis gestured for him to enter.

Harnouphis poured two tumblers of wine and set them on the ebony table. By the time Mehen sat down, the high priest had already drained his cup and was pouring again. Mehen said nothing, only waited with somber countenance.

"Lord Set confirms the forecasts and predictions," Harnouphis said, tracing a finger over the rim of his cup. "We stand on the verge of tumultuous days. There will be famine and violence in Egypt. To a degree, the current structures may be broken and swept away." A ravenous light burned in his eyes. "Such times cast aside the weak and cowardly. But they can lift strong men to undreamt heights. You and I, Mehen, can rise on the crest of the flood—if we have the will and courage."

His fervor touched a spark in the dry tinder of Mehen's soul. "What must we do?"

"Lord Set has gifted me with a vision. What I am about to confide, you absolutely must not repeat."

Mehen replied with a wounded tone. "Does your Excellency doubt that I am trustworthy?"

Harnouphis' stare made the scribe shift uncomfortably. "I know you would never betray me, Mehen. You would not dare. I speak only to reiterate the need for utter secrecy, for the steps I mean us to take are both daring and dangerous." Harnouphis took another swallow. "The Inner Circle has agreed to my suggestion that we withhold a portion of Pharaoh's grain. I am to explain our reasons and plead our case at the Synod. Set has promised to bend the events in Alexandria to our advantage. But they will go to *our* advantage, not that of the Inner Circle."

"How do you mean?"

Harnouphis shook his head. "Ptolemy and his sister will never stand for less than the full allotment. They will send soldiers to claim the rest. But I have friends among the king's ministers and advisors, men I have cultivated for years. I will convince them that the Inner Circle is plotting against Pharaoh, working to stir up rebellion. I will offer to expose the traitors and show where they have hidden the stores of grain. In exchange, I will ask that Pharaoh, by his divine authority, abolish the Inner Circle and appoint me supreme cleric of the temple."

Harnouphis paused to gauge the scribe's reaction. A faint, avid smile lifted the corners of Mehen's mouth.

"Think of it, Mehen. I shall return to Mem-Nephir with an army. At last, we will sweep away this corrupt, stagnant priesthood and establish a new temple—one capable of reasserting the honor of our land and our ancient gods, *all* of our gods. I shall lead this new order and you, as always, will be my lieutenant, my loyal and able right hand."

"What must I do to assist you?" Mehen cried. "Command me, and I will do it."

"I will need you here while I am in Alexandria, to keep me apprised of events and to prepare the ground for my return. There might be rumors I want you to plant, documents to prepare to incriminate certain men. We will plan the details carefully between now and the Synod."

Mehen nodded. For the first time, he sipped from his cup.

Harnouphis drained his tumbler. "There is one other task. I would not dare any of this without the assurance of the god's aid. But, as always, his power comes with a price. He is no longer content with the sacrifices we offer each moon. In exchange for his help, Set requires that his cult be reestablished in its original, archaic form."

Mehen responded with a note of worry: "What does that imply?"

"He demands a human life."

Mehen's long face turned pale.

"Many will die in the violence ahead," Harnouphis asserted. "What is the sacrifice of one life balanced against the good we will forge? With us in control of the temple, and Set's strength behind us, Mem-Nephir will no longer have to grovel to Pharaoh. We will establish a new balance of power between Egyptian and Greek, to the benefit of our gods and our people. But to accomplish all this, we must act now with ruthless courage. Our duty requires it." Harnouphis gazed resolutely. "I will not shirk my duty."

"Who?—How will we choose?" Mehen asked.

Harnouphis refilled his cup yet again. "The god's desires are specific. The sacrifice must be worthy. He demands a bright, intelligent soul, but above all, innocent and pure."

Five nights before the next full moon, Korax rose from his bed at a late hour. He stepped quietly into his sitting room, where a black cloth covered a short table set against the wall.

Carefully, he lifted the cover, revealing his magical tools and implements: a candle and brass brazier, some lotus petals, papyrus sheets that his ally had led him to find and copy in the House of Life. In the table's center stood a small wax figure of Thoth that he had fashioned with the best skill he possessed.

Sitting on his heels, Korax lit the candle from his lamp, then fired a charcoal from the candle. He set the charcoal in the brazier and added a wafer of incense. As the smoke thickened, he stared at the figure and summoned Thoth to his mind.

"It is time to begin," Korax whispered.

"Then begin."

"I hope this works as you predicted."

"It will not work if you harbor doubts."

Korax knew that to be true. He must banish all doubt from his heart.

"Remember that you speak the Great Word of Ptah," Thoth told him, "whose sound underlies all creation. You only need to bend the perceptions of two ordinary mortals—and that only briefly. Not a difficult deed for one possessing such power."

Korax clenched his lips and nodded. He had studied the sacred arts long and hard. Time at last to put his magic to the test.

He fanned the brazier with his hand until it glowed bright orange. Speaking a blessing, he dropped three lotus petals into the fire. As they curled and blackened, he unrolled one of the papyruses: *The Book of Not Being Halted at the Gates of Khem-Aataat.*

Korax formed in his mind a vision of the two sentries he must pass. Then he read the text aloud, in the portentous voice Thoth had taught him to practice—the same voice Thoth claimed to have taught to Isis, the voice for speaking words of power so that those who heard must obey.

> The spear of Sekhet is in my hand
> The word of Ptah is on my lips
> I am strong, I am mighty, I am not to be resisted
> I come and I go wheresoever I wish

Setting down the papyrus, Korax rose. He picked up a satchel of coarse linen and a walking stick, which he had made into a wand by carving on it certain words and symbols sacred to Thoth. Leaving the brazier and the candle burning, he left his apartment.

The gibbous moon rode high, lighting his way as he moved through the gardens and galleries. He passed the House of

Records and came to the courtyard where the treasury stood. Just as he had pictured in his mind, two sentries guarded the door in the dancing light of torches. Korax dared not pause for fear his nerve would falter. With a brisk and determined gait, he strode across the courtyard and up the steps.

"Who are you?"

The guards crossed their spears in front of the locked door.

Korax pitched his voice to a note of impatient command. "Imbeciles! Don't you recognize Harnouphis, chief treasurer of the temple?"

The two men exchanged glances, baffled and uneasy.

Korax thrust out his wand to part their spears. "Open the door! There are documents I must retrieve."

After a breathless second, the guards stepped aside. One of them took a key from his belt and turned it in the lock.

Korax pushed past him with an irritated air. "Leave it unlocked. I will only be a few moments."

Heart pounding, Korax hurried down the corridor. The door to the counting room was shut, but he had ascertained on his previous visit that the door had no lock. Feeling in the dark, he found the handle and lifted the latch.

He slipped inside and surveyed the chamber. The barred windows beneath the ceiling admitted narrow shafts of moonlight—enough so he could see the stacks and piles of glimmering coins.

A twinge of avarice heightened his excitement. Enough money lay here to make him a wealthy man in Rhodos or even Alexandria. But he immediately put down the greedy thought. Keeping to his plan, he moved from table to table, taking only a few copper and silver coins from the uncounted piles. Korax had copied enough financial reports to know the inefficiency of the temple's accounting practices. The money he stashed in his satchel would be more than adequate for his needs. But, with any luck, its disappearance would go unnoticed or, at worst, result in a cursory and fruitless internal audit.

He emerged on the porch a short time later. He watched, frowning, while the sentry dutifully locked the door.

"No need to mention that I was here tonight and that you failed to recognize me," he said. "We won't add a black mark for stupidity to your records—this time."

The guards looked at each other, faces brightening with relief.

"No, your Excellency."

"Thank you, your Excellency."

Korax nodded brusquely and descended the steps. He marched across the courtyard and disappeared into the shadows.

Chapter Twenty-Seven

Next day, Korax left the scriptorium in the early afternoon, feigning illness. Returning to his apartment, he dressed in a wig and a plain tunic with his green sash, and slung the satchel over his shoulder. He left the temple through a postern gate and headed for the marketplace in the center of the city.

In a mood of high elation, he ranged among the stalls, carefully picking out what he needed, haggling over prices, joking with the shopkeepers. His longed-for day of freedom was at last nearly at hand.

First, he bought a donkey, small but young and fit, a foul-tempered creature that he named Mehen. He loaded Mehen's back with his other purchases—a blanket, a light cloak with a hood, sacks for storing food, two large water-skins. At a cobbler's stall he bought a pair of boots suitable for rough ground.

Any pursuit by the temple police would probably concentrate on the river. So, Korax had decided to go overland, along the fringe of the desert. The disadvantage of this way—aside from the length and discomfort of the journey—would be the risk of meeting bandits. Korax purchased a short sword, dagger, and a hefty staff of tamarisk wood. He trusted that these weapons, along with the magic inspired by Thoth, would provide sufficient protection.

He stabled the donkey and stowed his gear at a caravansary near the Saqqarah gate. He instructed the proprietor to have the beast loaded with provisions and ready to travel in the afternoon three days hence. He promised the man an extra drachma to guarantee these arrangements.

With the preparations complete, Korax returned to the temple. He changed into his scribe's kilt and took supper at the dining hall. Then he retired to his quarters and lit his reading lamps.

Tonight, and the three nights after, he had more spells to weave—enchantments to conceal his escape, to protect him on the journey, to guard against recapture.

He had just lit the first candles when a knock sounded on his front door. He snuffed the wicks with his fingers, jumped up, and pulled the black covering over the table. Opening the door, he sighed with relief to find Itaji. Since acquiring his magical ally, he had started sleeping with the dancer again. But he had completely forgotten her visit tonight.

"What's wrong?" she asked. "Aren't you going to let me in?"

"Actually, no. Tonight it is not convenient."

"What? Don't tell me you're *abstaining* again."

"Not exactly. But I am deeply engrossed in my studies."

"Oh, you study too much." She slipped under his arm and into the narrow foyer. She twirled to face him, then playfully dropped her veil. "Don't you like me anymore?"

"Of course." He gripped her shoulders to prevent her undressing further. "But I really cannot see you tonight. In fact, I'm going to be very busy till after the full moon."

She frowned petulantly. "Do you have another girl?"

"No! I promise. Darling, Itaji, you are the only one. But my studies are in a critical phase."

Her eyebrows lifted. "You are doing magic? Show me!"

"No."

She crossed her arms defiantly. "I won't leave unless you at least show me what you are doing."

Her stubbornness made him suspicious. Quietly, he asked, "Why are you so insistent?"

She averted her gaze. "Oh ... I am just curious."

Suddenly Korax knew the truth, and his belly twisted. "No. It is more than that." He grabbed her arm, dragged her over to the shelf before the figure of Isis.

"Ow, you are hurting me!"

He loosened his grip. "I want you to swear before the goddess that you are not spying on me."

She gaped at him, shocked. She began to protest, then swallowed the words. Casting down her eyes, she said: "I-I cannot."

The betrayal enraged him, but he kept his composure. "For Harnouphis," he stated coldly.

"Yes, I suppose. I only speak with his pet vulture, Mehen." She looked at him, wincing, eyes watering. "I never wanted to! At first he just paid me to visit you. But then he insisted I come to his apartment and tell him how you were. It seemed harmless at first. Oh, Seshsetem, I am sorry. I am so ashamed."

She covered her face and sobbed. Her abject tears touched him, and the rage vanished, replaced by pity. She too was a victim of the evil machinations of Harnouphis and Mehen. He took her in his arms, his tone soothing. "I understand, Itaji. You are not to blame. They are cruel and cunning men. But now you see why I cannot show you what I am doing. That way, you can honestly tell Mehen that you do not know."

She sniffled, nodded. "Yes. I will go now."

Korax walked her to the foyer. "Wait a moment." He went to the satchel and took a silver drachma from his purse. He showed her the coin, and pressed it into her hand.

"To thank you for your honesty. And to show I am not angry with you."

"What?" Itaji scrutinized the drachma, then tested it with her small white teeth. "But it is real."

"Of course." Korax laughed as he opened the door. He let the tone of subtle command enter his voice. "Remember, you will say honestly that you were unable to learn *anything* about my studies."

Itaji nodded, started to leave, then stiffened and faced him. "I know I must not ask. But I have a feeling I will not see you again."

Korax stared at her, refusing to answer, refusing to look away.

She searched his eyes, her expression thoughtful. Then she smiled sadly, stood on her toes and kissed him.

"Goodbye, Seshsetem."

In a corner of the scriptorium, Korax scrutinized an inventory report. A stack of similar documents lay beside his mat. As the authority on Greek, he commonly reviewed the writing of his fellow scribes. With the harvest about to begin, the number of reports and correspondences was already mounting.

He glanced out at the garden to check the angle of the sun. This day could not pass quickly enough. If all went according to plan, it was the next-to-last day he would ever spend in the House of Records.

The past two nights he had woven magic spells to aid his escape. The first rite was entitled *On Making the Walker Invisible to His Enemies*. The second night, he had cast a charm called *Protecting One on His Passage Through the Twelve Halls of Annu*. Tonight, he had one more ritual to perform: *On Changing into a Falcon and Flying Forth by Day*.

Tomorrow, the day of the full moon, he would leave the scriptorium in the afternoon. He would pick up his donkey and gear and be out the Saqqarah gate before sunset. Most likely, his disappearance would go unnoticed until at least the following morning. By then, he planned to be many miles north of Memphis.

For now, he studiously fixed his will on his work, cautious to avoid any unusual behavior, any hint of his inner excitement. He had nearly finished reviewing the stack of documents when an urgent whisper interrupted him.

"Seshsetem, I must speak with you."

"Katep." Korax's quick smile immediately drooped. Katep appeared pale, his normally jolly face tortured. "What is wrong?"

"We'll speak outside. Please."

Korax followed him across the colonnade and down into the garden. They sat at the edge of the lotus pool, Katep glancing about to verify their privacy.

"What is troubling you so?" Korax demanded.

"It concerns Baufre." Katep's voice trembled. "You know he has been working with some of the other apprentices, under Chief Scribe Mehen."

"I heard something of it," Korax acknowledged. Lately he hadn't paid much attention to events in the scriptorium outside of his own assignments.

"I thought it a bit unusual," Katep said, "but saw nothing wrong until ... Two days ago, Baufre told me he had to work late, that Mehen had assigned him special duties. He seemed thrilled and delighted. But that night, he never came home. Nor did he appear in the scriptorium the next morning. I asked Mehen where my son was, and he told me Baufre was working for his Excellency Harnouphis, and would be for several more days. That was yesterday. Baufre did not come home again last night. My wife is almost mad with worry. Today, Mehen was not in his office, so I went to look for Harnouphis. I finally found my way to his residence. Mehen and Harnouphis both were there. They informed me that Baufre was within, but that he was doing important work for the first servants, that I must not interfere. I insisted on seeing my son, and finally they allowed him to come to the door. But he seemed changed, distant. He hardly knew me, his own father. He claimed he had been promoted to an important post, that I must not stand in his way. He reminded me that he is of age now and can do as he wishes. Then Mehen ordered me back to work and shut the door."

Katep's eyes shone moist, his jaw quivering. "I know this sounds mad, Seshsetem, but I think they have bewitched my son."

"Not mad," Korax muttered. "I fear it could be true."

Katep gripped his bald scalp with both hands. "But a first servant of Ptah ... It sounds fantastic, like a tale from Hetepher's imagination. But if you could have seen him, the coldness in his eyes ..."

"I believe you," Korax said. He knew Harnouphis capable of pernicious magic. Lately, more and more evil fragments had surfaced in his memory. But what could Harnouphis want with young Baufre?

"What am I to do?" Katep cried. "I have no lawful complaint. Baufre is of age. Besides, Harnouphis is a high priest, and I am only a scribe. You're the only friend I have who has even initiated in the House of Life. I have no one else to turn to, Seshsetem. What am I do?"

Korax gripped the scribe's forearm. "Give me tonight to investigate. Go home to your wife, and try not to worry. Come to the scriptorium tomorrow as usual. I will hope to have news for you then."

"Thank you, my friend!" Katep seized Korax's hand and kissed it, fighting to hold back his tears.

Korax's first impulse was to take the problem to Amasis. If a high priest of Ptah was performing evil sorcery, it seemed proper that the master of the House of Life should handle the matter. But these days Amasis seldom emerged from the mortuary vaults. The months-long embalming rites for the two deceased first servants approached their culmination. As Korax understood it, the rituals now required the chief lector priest's presence almost constantly. Even if Korax dared disturb the rituals, the stairways to the underground lay behind secret doors whose locations he did not know. Instead, he hastened to his own apartment and summoned his ally.

"A new problem has appeared," he told Thoth. "An emergency, I think."

"I can ascertain the matter from your thoughts."

"Can you tell what Harnouphis wants with the boy?"

"I can. But better to allow you to see for yourself. This only requires that certain submerged memories be restored to you. This is happening gradually already, but I can accelerate the process. Be warned, however, breaking the barriers all at once will engender distress."

"Proceed," Korax said. "Whatever Harnouphis stole from me, I want returned."

A jolt dropped him to his knees. He sank in blackness for a moment, then visions rushed into his mind: his hand bloodied on the game piece of a black-headed god; a piglet hacked to pieces on the altar of that same god, in a cave beside a stygian pool; a black leopard tasting the blood of a dying priest at dusk on the desert plain ...

Slowly, Korax regained his senses. As he rose to his feet, another dire image came to him: *That same underground altar would soon run with Baufre's blood.*

"The god is Set," Thoth informed him. "To the people of the Land, he is the Father of All Evil."

Pain throbbed in Korax's skull. "Does Harnouphis' villainy run so deep?"

Thoth allowed the images to speak for themselves.

"What can be done?" Korax asked.

Again, his ally remained silent.

"You mean, *I* must stop him?"

"That is for you to decide. I am your ally, not your master."

Korax recalled how Harnouphis' power had made him convulse in agony on the floor. True, his own abilities had blossomed since then. But at best he was a talented neophyte, hardly capable of challenging both his master and his master's god.

He grimaced, rubbing the back of his head. He planned to depart tomorrow—his longed-for escape. But how could he go now, abandoning Baufre to death, Katep and Hetepher to inconsolable grief?

"You are not without allies of your own," Thoth reminded him.

At that, Korax thought of Isis and felt her benefic presence. Long ago, she had set a path before him, and a question: Was he willing to serve the gods?

Now, at last, the test had come.

He gazed steadfastly at the figure of Thoth on his altar. "I will rescue Baufre. Kindly advise me how best to proceed."

Chapter Twenty-Eight

L ate that night, Korax crept across the temple grounds. He carried the wand of Thoth in his hand and words of power on his lips.

Approaching the precinct of the high priests' apartments, he crouched behind a corner of the garden path. Ahead, two sentries stood before an arched gate. Moonlight gleamed on the points of their spears.

Eyes shut, Korax envisioned himself walking past the sentries without their notice. Simultaneously, he whispered his charm:

The word of Ptah is on my lips
I pass as a whisper passes on the wind
I walk unseen among my foes
I come and I go wheresoever I wish

Quiet as a cat, he stood and walked toward the gate. As he approached, one of the guards shifted, frowning, as if disturbed by a nagging thought. But neither man looked at him as Korax brushed quickly past their spears.

He crossed the inner garden and raced up the flights of steps. He stalked along the high gallery toward Harnouphis' door. No sentries patrolled here, but as he expected Korax found the door locked. Casting a quick look around, he sat down in the shadow of the balustrade and folded his legs.

He took long breaths to quiet his mind, then cast his thoughts through the door and into the apartment. He had walked that way many times, when summoned to scry for Harnouphis, so he could picture the foyer and paneled corridor with ease.

In the anteroom to the high priest's study he discovered Baufre, lying asleep on a couch. In his vision, Korax leaned over and whispered in the boy's ear.

Baufre. Wake up. It is time to leave now.

The young scribe moaned quietly, but did not move. Korax pressed harder, calling again and mentally closing his fingers to tug on Baufre's ear.

"What?" Baufre sat up, awake and confused.

Korax poured his voice into the boy's mind. *Get up, Baufre. You are in danger. Come to the front door.*

"Seshsetem? I cannot see you."

Hear my words and trust them. I speak as your friend. Rise and walk to the door.

Sluggishly, Baufre got up and tied on his kilt.

Nevermind your sandals, Korax told him. *Hurry.*

The boy shuffled sleepily down the corridor and across the foyer.

On the terrace, Korax opened his eyes and leaped up. He reached the door just as it started to open. Baufre blinked at him in puzzlement. Korax pushed the door wider and grabbed the boy's arm.

"Hurry."

But Baufre resisted, pulling back. "No! I cannot leave."

"Yes, you can. You must." Korax tugged harder. He dragged Baufre half-way across the threshold.

The door flew open. Strong hands seized Korax by the arm and neck. A lamp appeared inside the apartment. Baufre was shoved aside and another set of hands grabbed Korax. Struggling, he was yanked across the foyer and flung to the floor. Scrambling to his feet, he faced his attackers: dark and sinewy men, the two Bedouin tribesmen. He remembered them from that afternoon in the necropolis.

The chamber was flooded with light now, as Mehen and two servants had appeared, all carrying lamps. Behind them stood Harnouphis, holding a serpent-headed staff.

Surrounded, Korax gave up any hope of fighting. He stood with shoulders slack.

"Bind him," Harnouphis commanded his henchmen. "Don't harm him, unless he resists."

The desert men tugged Korax's arms behind his back and tied his wrists with leather cord. They shoved him down on his belly and bound his legs at the ankles and knees. Finally, they bent up his knees and used more cord to connect the bonds of his wrists and ankles.

Standing against the foyer wall, Baufre watched with a dull, confused expression.

"Return to sleep, my son." Harnouphis ushered him across the room. "To you, this is only a strange dream. You'll forget it all by morning."

The high priest dispatched one of his servants to see Baufre to bed. He turned his attention back to Korax.

"You made a remarkable attempt, Seshsetem. Your abilities are far advanced over what I expected. But it was preposterous arrogance to believe you could overmatch my power."

"Arrogance indeed, your Excellency." Mehen handed him Korax's stick, which had been dropped in the struggle. "He deems himself worthy to bear the Wand of Thoth."

Harnouphis examined the stick with a scornful smile, then broke it over his knee.

"My ally foresaw your coming here," he told Korax. "And my loyal Mehen has warned me often that you are treacherous. He did well to have an informer keep close watch on your activities. Yes, your little dancer. She tried to conceal what she had guessed of your intentions. But her shallow mind was easy for Mehen to read. Based on what he discerned, Mehen searched your residence yesterday. He found scrolls far too advanced for a neophyte. Those, and a cache of coins, which I suspect you stole from the treasury. Mehen wanted to arrest you at once, but Set assured me we could avoid the disturbance if we only waited. And so, you have come to us."

"You think you know all my secrets," Korax said venomously. "But I also know some of yours. I remember how you made me to murder the priest in the desert. And I know how you intend to murder Baufre. What has turned you into such a monster, Harnouphis?"

The high priest paused, seriously pondering the question. "Desire," he replied. "And will." He turned abruptly to the Bedouins. "One of you keep watch over him tonight. And make sure you stay awake."

The taller of the tribesmen frowned. "Wouldn't it be simpler just to cut his throat?"

"Simple, but unwise," Harnouphis said. "Awkward to have to remove a corpse from my residence." He leaned over and brushed Korax's brow. "Besides, Seshsetem is a useful tool—only one whose care I have neglected. With a little grinding and polishing, I will make him useful again."

Korax glared his defiance. "Perhaps the tool will cut off your fingers."

"Put a gag in his mouth." Harnouphis straightened. "And make sure it's tight. Make sure he cannot speak."

Knotted firmly around his skull, the gag filled his mouth and pulled the flesh painfully against his teeth. Korax lay with his chin on the tile floor, staring up at the Bedouin. The man sat on a stool, long legs and arms crossed, watching him impassively.

Korax could move his arms and feet a little, roll over from his side to his belly, nothing more. Soon he gave up struggling.

Toward dawn, despite the cramped position enforced by the bonds, he fell asleep from exhaustion.

He woke later as the two Bedouins carried him down the corridor. They dumped him on the floor of the antechamber, just as Harnouphis was emerging from his study. The high priest was dressed for traveling, in a plain tunic and head-scarf. He gave Korax a perfunctory glance as he crossed the chamber.

Korax rolled over so he could see the corridor. He watched as the Bedouins moved back and forth, carrying gear toward the foyer. He saw Mehen walk past, with Baufre following dutifully behind. A while later Harnouphis returned, leading a spearman who wore the collar and headdress of the treasury guard.

"Here is the prisoner. Watch him well. Do not remove his gag under any circumstances. Another man will relieve you at sundown."

"Of course, Excellency." The guard peered dubiously at Korax. "But, wouldn't it be better to confine him in the jail?"

"No," Harnouphis snapped. "I want him here, so I can interrogate him when I return. Do not question my orders, sergeant, obey them."

"Yes, Excellency. Your pardon."

The guard bowed low as Harnouphis swept brusquely past him. He frowned at Korax, then set his spear on the floor and assumed the erect posture of attention.

Korax heard Harnouphis issuing final instructions to a servant, then the footsteps of the party leaving the apartment: Harnouphis, Mehen, the two tribesmen, and Baufre, bound for the necropolis and the ruined Temple of Set.

Korax closed his eyes, sickened by hopelessness and grief. Not only had he failed to save Baufre, he had gambled his chance at freedom and lost. Grunting, he tugged at the bonds, but it was pointless. His spine and shoulders only burned with new pain, before fading back into numbness.

Where was his ally? He called Thoth to his mind. His tongue moved against the gag, silently uttering the words of summons.

No answer.

Too tense. He calmed himself, breathed deliberately. Gradually, he drifted into a half-sleep. There, amid the gently shimmering colors of dream, the ibis head appeared.

"Awake! You have work to do."

How? I am helpless.

"Not completely. You can still use your will."

How?

The god instructed him, formed the ideas in his mind. He must reach out with his will to the guard, bend all his mental powers on the man, touch his mind, surround it, envision the five components of his soul, and one by one overpower them. Then he could take control of the body.

The idea sounded impossible.

But Korax had nothing else to occupy his time.

He poured his will into the task, saw his mental force flowing like a stream of light across the space between him and the guard. He envisioned the guard's nerve centers, pulsing, radiant spheres at his brain, throat, and heart. Korax thrust his mind into those centers, piercing them, slowly filling them.

An hour passed.

Korax directed his will against the guard's will, like water dripping on a wall of sand, gradually making it crumble.

The guard's name was Kahmose. He was thirty years old. He loved beer and flute music.

Korax kept his eyes closed, his brow beaded with sweat.

Another hour.

Kahmose lived with his aged mother, a toothless, embittered woman. Kahmose's wife found the old woman intolerable and complained vehemently. Kahmose longed for a tranquil home; he felt very tired. Korax pulled the threads of that weariness, binding them to his purpose.

Near noon, the guard snuck out to relieve himself and drink a little water. He returned refreshed and stood more erect.

Korax had to start again.

But the power flowed more readily now. Korax had gained practice, and Kahmose's resistance had weakened.

Two more hours came and went.

Kahmose decided he could risk sitting down. He pulled a low stool against the wall.

Another hour, and he leaned his head back, feeling more and more drowsy.

The sweat had dried on Korax's face, his throat now unbearably dry. He strove to ignore the varied agonies of his body, to focus instead on squeezing away the last of Kahmose's will.

Suddenly it was gone, like a candle flicking out.

Looking up, Korax saw the sentry slumped against the wall, deep asleep. Swiftly, he shut his eyes and concentrated on the next task. Again, he envisioned the stream of light flowing from him to Kahmose. But now he thrust himself into that stream, like a man rushing across a falling bridge.

He opened his eyes. He was in Kahmose's body.

This was magic indeed!

"Don't hesitate," Thoth warned him. "Act while the power holds."

Korax struggled out of the seat, reaching for the sword at the guard's hip. He fell to the floor, crawled to where his own body lay.

The short sword was designed for thrusting, not cutting. Its iron edge was woefully dull. Korax sawed desperately at the leather cords binding his wrists, then picked at the knots with the sword point. Finally, he tore them lose, then started sawing the cords at his knees.

"No," Thoth told him. "You can free yourself now. Return to your own body. Lie down on the floor. Make sure you leave the man asleep."

Korax laid the sentry on his back beside his own motionless body. He draped Kahmose's arm over Korax's back. Then he relaxed, loosening his hold on the guard's muscles and will. He used Kahmose's arm as a bridge to pour himself back into his own resting body.

He awoke to glittering pain, his nerves screaming. He sat up and furiously rubbed the life back into his shoulders and wrists.

Beside him, Kahmose began to snore.

Korax freed himself from the gag. With the sword he cut and tore the cords from his legs. Quickly, he used the same cords to bind Kahmose's wrists and ankles. The guard groaned a little as Korax gagged him, then returned to his restful slumber. Korax slid the man's sword into the sash of his tunic and picked up the heavy spear.

He staggered across the antechamber and into Harnouphis' study. He found a jug of water and quenched his desperate thirst.

Some instinct drew his attention to the wall shrine with its dark, cedarwood cabinet.

"Open it," Thoth urged.

Korax tested the lock with his hands, then used the spear point to pry the latch. The iron lock wouldn't give. Korax hung his whole weight on the spear haft, and the door tore off its hinges, clattering as it struck the floor.

Inside stood a statue of Set, tall as a man's forearm. The image made Korax shudder.

"Destroy it," Thoth told him. "That will weaken Set's hold on the priest."

Korax swept the statue from the shelf with the spear, then stamped it into the floor, grinding it to pieces under his heels.

Chapter Twenty-Nine

Outside, the afternoon shone bright and quiet. Harnouphis would not begin his ritual before moonrise. Korax still had time to save Baufre.

He slipped through the antechamber and glanced down the corridor. Kahmose lay deep asleep, and Harnouphis' servants were nowhere in sight. Korax left the apartment through the front door and hastened along the gallery.

Swiftly, he made his way back to his rooms. He packed his magic scrolls in the satchel, along with his cache of money and the small wax figure of Thoth. One way or the other, he had no intention of returning to the Mansion of Ptah.

He ran to the House of Records and marched into the scriptorium. Row on row, the scribes stopped their work and stared at him in bewilderment and wonder. What was Seshsetem doing with sword and spear? Ignoring them, Korax found Katep and signaled him to come outside. The corpulent scribe climbed to his feet and hurried after Korax. The two men stopped to talk on the portico.

"What news? What has happened?" Katep demanded.

"I am going to rescue Baufre."

"He is in danger? Where?"

"Listen and do as I say. After work, leave the city by the Saqqarah gate. Go to the crossroads just before the bridge that leads to the necropolis. Wait for me there. I will bring him to you during the night."

Katep's face contorted with anguish. "Do you go alone? No! I am no warrior, but if my son is in peril, I will go with you."

Korax shook his head emphatically. "You would hold me back. Trust me, and do as I say. I will bring your son, I promise it on my life."

He squeezed Katep's arm, then whirled and hurried away.

Crossing the outer precincts of the temple, Korax departed through a postern gate. He ran along the avenue, drawing curious glances from passers-by. The sun blazed in the western quarter of the sky: still at least two hours till sunset. Breathless, Korax slowed his pace. He had eaten nothing since yesterday, and his strength was failing.

He made his way to the caravansary. As arranged, his donkey was packed and ready for travel. Korax paid the proprietor and led the beast out into the courtyard. He put on his new boots and the light, hooded cloak. He discarded the guard's sword and replaced it with the iron short sword he had purchased. He unpacked some dry bread and munched it as he led the donkey along the streets.

He passed through the Saqqarah gate and headed up the road. The sun hovered cool and orange, slipping toward the horizon. Korax yanked the reins to force the donkey to a trot. Mehen brayed in complaint but obeyed.

He left the donkey tethered behind a mortuary temple a short distance inside the necropolis. The beast was slowing him down. Besides, he would need to approach his foes in silence.

Hefting the spear, Korax trotted along the sandy streets of the city of the dead. He had journeyed this way only once, and that memory had been sponged away by Harnouphis. But he knew the route with certainty. All his memories had returned and besides, Thoth guided him.

Thoth, and another.

Words from one of the scrolls ran through his mind: *I am Horus of the Horizon, Horus the avenger.*

The hawk-headed son of Isis and Osiris—the mighty warrior god. In the myth, Horus battled Set for nine days and nights before vanquishing him, thus avenging the murder of his father. Korax sensed the strength of Horus coursing in his blood. The god had come to him, sent by Isis, for the purpose of battling Set once again, in this time, this world. Korax felt no fear, no anger, only a grim, irresistible purpose.

The sun settled on the red horizon. In the fading light, Korax approached the ruined Temple of Set. Torches stuck in the sand blazed before the black colonnade. The two Bedouins stood guard at the entrance, a pair of donkeys tethered nearby. Korax whispered a quick prayer to the gods of Greece and Egypt. He lowered his spear and advanced across the courtyard.

He came within a few yards before the henchmen noticed him. One of the Bedouins pointed his spear; the other drew his sword. Korax stepped closer and the men shifted, ready to attack.

"Stop!" Korax ordered, in the voice Thoth had taught him. "You see who I am. You thought I was vanquished, but you were wrong. I have stronger magic than your master. Thoth and Isis and Horus himself fight on my side. I am going to kill Harnouphis and Mehen. I can kill you as well, or you can take the donkeys and whatever is on them, and leave this place. The choice is yours."

Brows high, the two men glanced at each other.

"Choose quickly!" Korax commanded.

"No reprisals," the taller henchman said. "No curses. We go in peace?"

Korax nodded. "Leave one of the torches."

The Bedouins put away their weapons. They bowed their heads and touched fists to their lips. They moved from Korax's path and scurried over to unhitch the donkeys.

Korax watched until the men had started across the courtyard. Then he plucked the torch from the ground. He trudged over the drifted sand and through the portal.

Holding the torch and spear before him, he traversed the ancient hall with its squat black columns. He passed the broken statue of the god and approached the secret door.

The pivoting slab stood ajar. Korax leaned his head inside and listened. He heard nothing, only smelled the cool air rising. He stalked inside and descended the spiraling steps.

Reaching the bottom, he set the torch in a bracket and proceeded in the dark. His best hope lay in taking his foes by surprise, striking before they could react. He didn't remember all the turns in the passageway, but his inner sense and the scent of moisture guided him.

Soon he rounded a corner and saw flickering light in the distance. He crept noiselessly to the next intersection and peered around the wall. Ahead stood the chamber of the black pool, lit by fluttering torchlight.

Korax edged along the wall. Staring past the stone door, he spied Harnouphis. Bedecked in black and gold, the high priest waved a long censer in front of the statue of Set. Baufre knelt beside him, naked and still. The bronze axe rested on the altar slab.

Korax leaned back, catching site of Mehen. The scribe moved along the edge of the pool, scattering lustral water. Korax slipped back into the shadows, waiting, hoping to catch both men with their backs turned.

The preparations continued. Mehen walked to the front of the altar, sprinkled the stone, then dashed a few drops over Baufre's head. Harnouphis lit two red lanterns. He nodded solemnly at Mehen, then faced the god and raised his hands in adoration.

Mehen took a final look around. He hastened across the floor and took a position midway between the altar and portal.

In the passageway, Korax leveled his spear.

Harnouphis lifted the serpent staff and called out to his ally. "Homage to you, O great god of the Palaces of Night ..."

Mehen raised his hands in worship and sank to his knees.

"... Terrible Lord of the Abyss ..."

Korax charged out of the tunnel. He aimed to drive the spear through Mehen's back. But midway, he changed his mind.

"... Set, Bebht, Smy ..."

If the point went deep, the spear might be impossible to free in time to wield it against Harnouphis.

"... Apep, Typhon ..."

Running, Korax twirled the spear around. He thrust the butt hard into the back of Mehen's neck. Mehen collapsed with a muffled cry. Harnouphis heard and whirled around. Korax pointed the spear and rushed him.

"No! You cannot!" Harnouphis roared, brandishing his staff.

The power of his voice stunned Korax, and he stumbled. As he scrambled to his knees he glimpsed Baufre, snapped from his trance, peering about in confusion. Then Harnouphis stood over Korax, the serpent-headed staff leveled at his face.

"You cannot challenge me. You cannot challenge the god!"

Korax's arms went numb, the spear slipping from his fingers.

But then his own power surged through his nerves. He lifted his voice in defiance. "I am Horus of the Horizon."

Doubt flickered over the high priest's face.

"Horus the avenger!"

Korax snatched up the spear and stabbed with all his strength. The point pierced Harnouphis in the belly. He staggered back, lost his feet, fell hard on his backside. His hands clutched the wound, blood seeping between his fingers.

Korax jumped up and lifted the spear, ready to finish his enemy.

A loud splashing made him spin in the other direction.

A crocodile had clambered out of the pool. The enormous creature stalked toward the place where Baufre stood, while the boy watched in amazed horror.

Set had taken a new form, determined not to lose his offering.

Shocked for just a second, Korax leveled the spear and charged at the crocodile. Weapons-training from the school fields of Rhodos guided him—the proper alignment of legs and shoulders, the savage yell unleashing all strength to the thrust.

The monster turned its head to face him, jaws opening. Korax plunged the point deep down the throat. The jaws snapped and the head twisted, tearing the spear from Korax's hands and flinging him to the ground. The beast rolled over in frenzy, struggling to shake the weapon loose.

Korax gained his feet, ran to Baufre, shook him by the shoulders. "Run for the door, Baufre. There!"

The boy blinked, nodded, started to run.

Korax wheeled and drew his sword. Harnouphis was on his knees by the altar, face ashen, struggling to rise.

The crocodile smashed its head on the edge of the pool, knocking the spear free. The creature rolled onto its feet. It eyed both Korax and Harnouphis.

Korax glanced down at his sword. *It would not be enough.* He turned and fled.

Mehen had regained his senses. On hands and knees, he had caught Baufre by the foot and tripped him. Now he grasped an ankle as the boy tried to pull free.

Korax skidded to a halt. He swung the sword over his head and chopped down, cleaving Mehen's forearm to the bone. Mehen screamed and let go of Baufre.

Korax picked the boy up and they ran. He thrust Baufre ahead of him into the passageway, then turned and shoved hard against the pivoting door.

As the slab moved, Korax glanced back into the chamber. The crocodile stalked menacingly across the floor, in between the two men. Mehen had seen it now and was backing stiffly away. Harnouphis leaned on the altar, clutching his stomach, eyes wild.

Abruptly, Mehen gave a shriek of terror and bolted for the tunnel. Korax closed the door just before Mehen could reach it.

Leaning his weight against the stone, Korax searched for the hidden levers. As he pulled them one by one, he could hear Mehen wailing within.

Soon there came other, louder sounds—screaming, roaring, snapping and chomping. Korax kept his shoulder braced against the stone until all was still, until he knew for certain that no one— no being—was coming out.

Then he found Baufre's hand in the darkness and led the boy out of the underworld.

Chapter Thirty

The disk of the moon rode high above the desert, spreading a pale glimmer over the temples and crumbling ruins of the necropolis. Korax walked along the ancient causeway, leading his donkey Mehen. Beside him walked Baufre, dressed in sandals and spare tunic from Korax's pack. The boy's terror and relief had flooded together into a wild elation. He chattered incessantly.

"I knew what was happening all along, but I couldn't help myself. I said and did whatever Harnouphis wanted, even though I tried not to. I was like a puppet, like a piece on a game board."

"I've been under his control myself," Korax answered. "That you were even aware of it and struggled testifies to the strength of your mind."

"I could see him, the god Set, hovering behind Harnouphis' like a ghost. And then, when you arrived in the vault, I saw Horus swooping in behind you. Horus and Set fought each other, just like in the stories."

"Indeed, they did."

"You are a great warrior and a mighty magician, Seshsetem."

"Oh, well ..." He laughed quietly. "Call me Korax. That is my true name."

"Korax! What does it mean?"

"It means blackbird, actually. My mother gave me this name because I was black-haired and swarthy, compared to her Thracian kin, who tend to a pale and ruddy complexion."

"Korax, blackbird—an excellent name!"

Ahead in the distance, a lantern burned at the crossroads. As they passed over the bridge, Korax discerned two men waiting—a round shape and a narrow one. Drawing closer, his curiosity turned to a wary surprise as he recognized Amasis standing beside Katep.

"Baufre!" Katep rumbled forward and hugged his son. "Are you all right?"

"I am now, father. Harnouphis was going to kill me, to give my blood to Set. But Korax saved my life."

"Korax?" Katep frowned in bewilderment.

"Seshsetem," Baufre laughed. "Korax is his true name."

Katep wrapped both his arms around Korax. "Thank you!" he cried, bursting into sobs. "Thank you for saving my son."

Amasis watched with a placid smile. "Ah, Korax. May I have a word with you please?"

Korax bowed to the first servant. "Your Excellency, how surprising to find you here."

"I am sure."

Amasis inclined his head for Korax to follow. They walked off a little distance. Amasis spoke in a muted voice.

"Can you perhaps tell me the whereabouts of Chief Treasurer Harnouphis?"

Korax sighed. "He is in a chamber under the ruined Temple of Set. Or, he is in the belly of a crocodile, which might *be* Set. Either way, I expect he is dead, along with Mehen, his servant in villainy."

Amasis nodded, somber but serene. "You have done well, grandson. Somehow, I knew I could count on you. I only regret I could not help you more."

"What do you mean?" Korax demanded.

"Well, at my age, a man is no longer of much use in battle—be it a struggle of arms or of magic. But he can still oppose evil in more subtle ways. Fortunately, I am still capable enough to attract the aid of powerful beings."

"You left me the papyrus in the Chapel of Isis," Korax realized. "You gave me Thoth."

"Thoth, is it?" The old priest's eye popped open in surprise.

"Yes, my magical ally."

"Well, grandson. You never fail to amaze me. But, no. I only gave you the scroll. Thoth came as your ally because you are gifted—even more than I had guessed."

Korax bowed his head. "I owe you a great debt, esteemed Amasis."

"On the contrary. It is I, and the Mansion of Ptah, who owe you thanks. You have destroyed a great evil that might have strangled us all. But what happens now, Korax? I could not help but notice that you appear decked out for travel."

Korax straightened his shoulders. "I am leaving Mem-Nephir. I am going back to the Greek world."

"Hmm." The old priest squinted. "I don't suppose I could convince you to reconsider? There is much you could learn in the House of Life. For a young man of your talent, the possibilities are boundless."

Korax had already weighed the idea of changing his plans. With Harnouphis and Mehen gone, his life here would be much easier. Perhaps Amasis himself would act as his mentor. The learning he might acquire was immensely tempting.

But no. If he stayed, he reckoned that Korax the Greek would disappear forever. His memories were still incomplete. He needed to discover who he was really was. Perhaps it was the divine energy of Horus that lingered in him. But above all he yearned for freedom, to spread his wings and fly.

"I appreciate the offer—more than I can say. And I do thank you for all you have taught me. But my heart was never in this place."

"Oh, well. I expected as much," Amasis replied. "Fear not, I will do all I can to assure that no one searches for a runaway slave named Seshsetem. Also, I packed a few papyruses for you, magical texts you might find useful." He removed a satchel from his shoulder and handed it to Korax. "There's also some silver, to help cover your expenses. I really ought not to give you that, with the temple finances in such poor condition. But it's a paltry amount in the scale of things, and I'm sure our Sem-priest can cut back a little on his personal expenses."

Korax dropped to his knees and kissed the high priest's hand. "Honored lord, I will always remember your kindness to me, and your wisdom."

"Remember to seek the guidance of Maat, grandson. *That* will do me honor."

They strolled back toward the lantern, where Katep and Baufre waited.

"It's a pity you won't change your mind about leaving," Amasis said. "With the harvest on us and Harnouphis and Mehen both gone, think of the workload you're leaving in the House of Records for poor Katep and your fellows."

"Not for me," Katep answered. "Your pardon, Amasis, but I am leaving Mem-Nephir also. My wife, Hetepher, has long wished that we should move to one of the new cities of the Fayum. From now on, I am going to be ruled by her judgment."

"You are wise, my friend," Korax clasped his hand. "Give my respects to your lady and to your little girls."

"You will be cherished in our hearts forever, Seshsetem."

"Korax, father!" Baufre cried. "His name is Korax."

With a nod to Amasis, Korax picked up the donkey's tether and pulled. "Come on, Mehen."

"Mehen?" Katep exclaimed. "You named your ass Mehen?"

"He has the same sweet temperament," Korax answered with a shrug.

Katep and Baufre started laughing, and soon Amasis joined in. Korax walked his donkey over the ridge and down into the dry streambed. The laughter of his friends followed as he walked off under the moon.

Korax followed the streambed north for many miles, walking between the fertile land and the desert, the villages of the living and the city of the dead. The peace of Isis filled his heart. He feared neither man nor ghost nor god, for Thoth's wisdom reigned in his mind and the courage of Horus in his body.

At sunup, he reached the plateau of Giza, the place of the great pyramids. He scrambled up a hill of loose sand and stood facing an enormous sphinx. Peeling paint marred the face of an ancient king. Only the head and shoulders stood above the drifted sand.

Korax had been told that Bedouins and Egyptians both shunned the environs of the Great Sphinx, believing it haunted. This made it the perfect place for him to stop and rest for the day. He unpacked the donkey and tossed the bundles in the bowl of sand under the statue's head. He gave Mehen water, tied on his feed bag, secured his tether. After feeding himself on bread, figs, and dried cheese, he curled up under his cloak and slept.

He awoke in the late afternoon, exhilarated by the unfamiliar taste of freedom. For a long time he gazed down at the dark, fertile valley and the silver sweep of the river.

Twilight gathered. Time to go on soon ... but where? He had not exactly decided.

The moon appeared on the horizon. The presence of Thoth slipped into his mind.

"Great god of magic, you are still with me?"

The translucent, ibis-headed figure hovered before him in the moonlight. "I am your ally."

"Where should I go, now that I am free?"

"What is your will?"

Korax pondered. "I wish to go home to Rhodes and find my family, to learn why my ransom was never paid, if that is in fact what happened. Indeed, I need to discover if my memories of family and home are even true. And yet, if what I recall *is* true, I have enemies in Rhodes ... And I do not feel ready."

"What will you need to be ready?"

"To master my magic." He gazed down at his hands and arms. "And, I need to find a gymnasium and transform this pudgy Egyptian back into a Greek gentleman. And, I need—I wish—to enjoy myself, to watch plays, to kiss pretty girls, to play music."

"Hmm. Magic, exercise, culture, pleasure." The ibis-headed god folded in the air, transforming himself into human shape. A curly-haired, keen-eyed youth, he smiled sardonically—Hermes of the Greeks.

"There is one city above all others in the world that I would recommend to you. Luckily, it is not far."

"Yes," Korax whispered. "Alexandria."

JACK MASSA

Excerpt from

The Lights of Alexandria

A Conjurer of Rhodes, Book 2

Following his escape from the Temple of Ptah, Korax has come to the new Greek capital of Egypt, Alexandria. As a runaway slave, he has deemed it wise to concoct a new identity. His hair grown, his body honed by the gymnasium, fashionably dressed, he now displays the appearance of a young Greek gentleman. He has dispatched letters to the family he remembers in Rhodes and, while awaiting a reply, has determined to pursue his study of magic.

The Paneum was a curious, tall, circular structure, resembling nothing so much as a gigantic pinecone. Neither Greek nor Egyptian in design, its architecture echoed certain hive-like mounds known in Ionia and the islands of the North Aegean—shrines dedicated to the worship of archaic gods. But the structure raised by the Ptolemies was far grander than those. A colossal mound of gray and white stones, it towered nearly eighty feet against the limpid Alexandrian sky.

Korax arrived there in mid-afternoon, having retraced his steps along the Canopic Way and trekked past the Tomb of Alexander. The grounds of the Paneum bordered on the winding streets of Rhakotis, the old Egyptian quarter. A rugged stone fence enclosed a park of sloping lawns dotted with stands of cypress and sycamore, tiny shrines, and grottos. At the center, a spiral ramp led up the outside of the giant mound, rising to the top where priests conducted the rites of Pan.

The summit afforded a spectacular view of the city and the sea, and had become an attraction for tourists and idlers. Wandering across the grounds, Korax passed many who fit that description, but spotted no one who seemed to have official connection with the temple. He entered a small columned pavilion near the base of the mound but found it empty save for a granite statue of Pan, laughing deviously over his pipes.

Pan, the shepherd's god, was a special patron of Ptolemy's Macedonian ancestors. The Paneum, with its artificial mountain wilderness, reflected that overt aspect of the god. But Korax understood that in philosophic circles Pan carried another, esoteric meaning. He embodied the concept of all the gods or, alternately, the God of All. It stood to reason that a society of scholars pursuing the Mysteries would choose his temple as their meeting place.

But how to find them? The grinning face of the god offered no clue.

Korax set a coin at the feet of the statue. He uttered a brief prayer, asking Pan for his blessing and guidance. Then he returned to the daylight.

Lacking another plan, he started to climb the spiraling path of the mound. From the base he could see that it circled seven times before reaching the summit. In places among the boulders, grass and shrubs clung to the steep slope, adding to the naturalistic effect. Korax half-expected a mountain goat to come romping down the trail.

He had completed the fourth circuit when he passed a narrow recess. Under a rock lintel, a small door of blackened bronze led inside the mound. Korax surmised the door must lead to a storage vault, perhaps used for groundskeepers' tools. But an inner prompting tugged him from the path. He stepped down into the recess and tried the door. After a firm shake of the handle, the latch gave and the door creaked open. Cool air flowed from the blackness within. Korax decided to investigate.

A short distance down the passage he faced a wall formed of the same rough boulders as the exterior. But a slender stairway opened to the right. More cool air drifted up the stairs, carrying a veiled scent of perfume or incense.

Korax felt his way along the wall, since the light from the open doorway was lost to him now. The steps curled down, then ended in a corridor with smooth masonry walls. The floor slanted gently upward as the passage turned, mirroring the outer curve of the mound. All was silent.

Korax groped along the tunnel for some time. Then a light appeared ahead, a blurred flickering of candle or lamp. As his vision improved, he strode forward confidently. The light came from a portal of smooth-cut stone. Korax rounded the corner and stopped.

He stood on a gallery that circled the inner core of the mound— an enormous hollow chamber. Spots of daylight shone at the distant pinnacle, enough for him to tell the vast dimensions.

A clay lamp burned on the floor in front of him, set before a balustrade that lined the gallery. On the rail of the balustrade was a cushion, and on the cushion sat a young woman, cross-legged, balanced precariously. Behind her was empty air, with the floor of the vast chamber far below.

Astonished, Korax examined the woman. Her eyes were closed and her back erect: she sat in trance or deep meditation. She wore pale blue robes and yellow slippers. Her complexion was dark; she seemed Phoenician or Babylonian perhaps. She had narrow shoulders and face, with a high forehead, pointed chin, and tiny mouth. She would not be called beautiful by Greek or Egyptian standards, yet Korax found her appearance compelling. Perhaps it was her pose of meditation, but he sensed intelligence, wisdom, power. Perhaps he sensed a kindred spirit.

Abruptly, her eyes opened. Her shoulders jerked, and for an instant Korax feared she would tumble backward and fall to her death. But her hands shot down and caught the rail. Next moment, she thrust herself off the cushion and landed softly on her feet.

"Who are you? How did you get in here?"

"I apologize. I did not mean to frighten you."

"I am not frightened."

But she took a step back as Korax approached. He peered over the balustrade, glimpsing ramps and galleries at many levels. The drop ended four stories below on a black, circular floor.

"Isn't it dangerous to practice your meditations on such a perch?"

"I know what I am doing." She seemed younger than Korax had thought at first. But now she took the offensive: "Tourists are not allowed in this place."

Korax leaned back, momentarily daunted by her intensity. He leveled his voice: "I am not a tourist, only a humble seeker of wisdom."

The young woman paused. Her eyes seemed to dilate, and she scrutinized him for a long moment. "Humble? I do not think so."

Korax grinned and gave a courteous bow. "Please forgive my abrupt appearance. I am Astrametheus, a son of good family from the town of Hermopolis."

"How did you get in here?"

"Through a door on the outer path. It was unlocked."

"So, is it the custom in Hermopolis for men of good family to invade sacred grounds uninvited?"

"No." Korax smiled again. "Not so far as I know. But I came in answer to an inner call. I've heard that a company of philosophers meets in this place, practitioners of the divine arts. I greatly wish to make their acquaintance."

"To what purpose?"

Korax spread his arms. "To join them perhaps. I have some learning and experience, which I wish to augment."

"Have you indeed? From Hermopolis?"

"Well ... several places. But what of you, young-woman-whose-name-I-do-not-know? Is it the mystic arts of Babylon that teach you to sit in trance over a yawning abyss?"

The corners of her mouth twitched, the start of a smile that she quickly suppressed. "I will take you to Krateros. He will decide if your request merits consideration."

She gathered up her lamp and cushion and indicated for him to follow. They walked along the gallery of the vast, quiet chamber.

"This is truly remarkable," Korax said. "I'll wager not one person in a hundred knows that this structure has a hollow core. It was built by the first Ptolemy, so I understand. Though I do not recall the architect's name."

"Are you planning to write a travel book?" the young woman asked. "Or are you just full of prattle by nature?"

Korax winced at the gibe. "I would much rather hear your story, if you would disclose it. But so far you've not even told me your name."

"I am Miriam, daughter of Zakur."

The names sounded Phoenician or Nabataean perhaps, which would fit with her looks. "And your nationality?" he prompted.

She gave a sidewise glance, disapproving his inquisitiveness. Still, she answered, "I was born in Alexandria. My father's people came from the region of Hebron. We are Jews."

"I see." An Aramaic-speaking people—Korax knew little about them. He seemed to recall they were monotheists, worshippers of some grim, shapeless god. Their priests supposedly possessed ancient texts of powerful magic.

Miriam preceded him down a series of ramps, which connected one gallery to the next. Soon they reached the lowest level, the floor of the great hollow space. Again Korax sniffed traces of incense, more definite now. Their shuffling footsteps on the paving stones made the only noise.

Passing through a portal, they traversed a corridor illuminated by filtered daylight. Before Korax could discern the source of the light, they stepped into an even brighter chamber. It was spacious and furnished with stools, tables, and shelves full of papyrus rolls. A statue of Pan grinned down from a niche in the far wall.

Two men of middle-age sat conferring at a table spread with documents. One was dark, solemn, gray-bearded, with forehead and features resembling Miriam's. The other was Greek, likely a Macedonian—large and broad-headed, with curly brown hair and prominent eyes. Both men frowned when they saw him.

"Miriam, why are you disturbing us?" the graybeard asked. "Who is this person?"

"I am sorry, father," Miriam replied. "This one appeared out of nowhere on the gallery above. He entered through an outer door on the spiral, which he says was unlocked."

"Oh. I was responsible for sealing the doors after the last ritual," Miriam's father commented thoughtfully. "Perhaps I forgot to do that."

The chamber was lit by several large windows in the shape of multi-pointed stars. Yet these windows did not open to the outside. Stepping over to examine one, Korax saw that it contained a large mirror, which reflected daylight from an angled shaft above.

"Most ingenious."

The large Macedonian had stood and was glowering. "Who are you? For what reason do you invade our sanctuary?"

"He says he is called Astrametheus, from Hermopolis," Miriam answered before Korax could speak, "though I'm not sure I believe it. He claims to be a student seeking instruction."

"I am Krateros, high priest of Pan," the large man said. "Is Astrametheus your true name?"

"Well, I have gone by other names." Korax strolled toward the table. "For the moment, Astrametheus is the most prudent to use. I will willingly divulge my other names to you in time, should I find this company trustworthy."

Zakur slapped the tabletop. "You presume too much, young man!"

Korax halted, taken aback by the elder's anger. His pose of bluff self-confidence was being perceived as arrogance and discourtesy. He cleared his throat and gave a formal bow. "Forgive me gentlemen. I presume nothing. I apologize for my unorthodox arrival in this holy place, as I have already apologized to the young lady. I am not in the habit of breaking into temples. But I am in the habit of heeding inner guidance, which has led me to this meeting."

"I see." Krateros appraised him. "Are you an initiate?"

"Yes, of the Egyptian rites."

"Indeed?" Zakur fixed Korax with a dubious, penetrating stare. "A Greek, scarcely past twenty, yet initiated by the Egyptians. You seem to possess an unusual history."

Korax returned the gaze, unabashed.

Krateros noticed the beaded satchel, and his eyes widened as though with an insight. "Perhaps you carry something of value."

Korax pulled the bag from his shoulder. "Perhaps if I share it with you, you will welcome me into your society."

Krateros lifted a palm. "That would be for the whole group to decide. All true-hearted candidates are welcome to apply for admission." His glance fell again on the satchel. "Of course, one who is already an initiate, and who brought with him gifts of knowledge—such a candidate might find a readier welcome."

Smiling, Korax opened the bag and removed a roll, a copy of one of the magical texts given to him by Amasis, the high priest who had befriended him in Memphis. He untied the ribbon and spread the papyrus on the table. Zakur and Krateros leaned to examine it. Miriam craned her neck to peer over Korax's shoulder.

"Most interesting," Krateros said.

"It looks authentic," Zakur grunted. "Can you read it, young man?"

"Of course. I studied for more than a year in the House of Life. I will not say in which temple."

"A man of mystery," Krateros commented, half-smiling. "You do intrigue me, sir. We have several in our circle who can read the hieroglyphs, and others of us are learning. Perhaps you know enough to act as tutor."

Korax glanced at Miriam. Her expression revealed a new respect, though none of her reserve had melted.

"I am not averse to sharing what I know," Korax said. "Of course, I would hope the arrangement would be mutual."

"That is the function and purpose of our society," Krateros declared. "We are a group of scholars from many nations. Our mission is to advance knowledge of the divine arts and unravel the secrets of Nature—for the good of all peoples. That is our charter from the king, whose blessing and patronage we enjoy."

"Then you are exactly the society I hoped to find," Korax said. "I will do all in my power to prove myself worthy of your company."

He extended his hand. Krateros grasped him firmly by the wrist. Korax then turned and offered his hand to Zakur, but the graybeard merely folded his arms in his sleeves and nodded.

"As I mentioned," Krateros was saying, "all honest candidates are welcome to seek admission. The application process involves a test, administered by our entire group. If you wish, I will arrange an examination to take place at one of our general meetings."

"I could ask no more," Korax replied. "And I will leave you this text, as a gift and sign of friendship."

"We accept it," Zakur answered, his stern expression softening a little. "Miriam, please show our visitor the way to the main portal. Then, if you would, please ascertain that all the outer doors are properly locked."

"I will, father."

"Thank you, esteemed gentlemen." Korax bowed his head. "May I ask when and where the next general meeting will occur?"

"We will summon you," Krateros said. He and Zakur had resumed their seats and were scrutinizing the papyrus.

"Very well. I am staying at a small inn, on the Street of Pomegranates, west of the causeway. It might be a little hard to find."

"No matter." Krateros gestured dismissively. "You will receive our summons. If you don't ... well, no further test will be necessary."

Retrieving her lamp, Miriam conducted Korax through the corridor and across the circular chamber. In the faint light, Korax discerned life-size statues set in hollows along the walls. Otherwise, the space was empty.

He ventured to make conversation. "I gather you are an initiate in this society, Miriam. How would you recommend I prepare myself for the test Krateros mentioned?"

"You don't really expect me to answer that, do you?"

Korax smiled, shaking his head. "I confess, I don't know what to expect of a girl who practices trance in a high and dangerous place. Is that one of the arts I will learn in your group?"

She paused, near a low rounded portal of white brick. "That practice is my own invention. And please don't mention it to anyone. My father would not approve."

"Aren't you afraid of falling?"

"Of course. Don't you see that is the point?"

They passed through the portal and descended a long, slanting tunnel. Korax, walking a step behind, pondered what she had said.

"You are a curious young man," Miriam remarked. "You claim to be an initiate of the Egyptian Mysteries—which I sense to be the truth. And yet you act so frivolous, lacking all solemnity."

"Do I strike you as such? Perhaps it is merely the difference in our cultures." When Miriam made no reply, Korax reflected: "To be honest, there are parts of myself I am still seeking to discover— or rediscover, for the truth is, some of my memories are lost to me."

She might have twitched a little at this disclosure, but did not ask him to explain.

Korax sighed. "Perhaps, as you say, I am a creature of contradictions. But the same might be said of you, a Jewish maiden studying mystical arts in the Temple of Pan."

"My people worship one God," she said. "But those of us who are privileged to study the deeper wisdom understand that God shows many aspects to Creation, and there are many ladders by which man, and woman too, may ascend to comprehension of divinity."

"Yes," Korax agreed. "You remind me of the Egyptian teachings: They describe various spheres that the soul must rise through to reach the source of the divine light, or again, many halls that must be passed for one to arrive at the Hall of Truth."

They had reached the end of the passage. Miriam threw a latch and pushed open a pivoting door. Bending low, they stepped through the opening. Korax saw they were in the pillared pavilion, behind the statue of Pan where he had left the coin.

Hesitantly, Miriam extended her hand. "I bid you good day, Astrametheus of Hermopolis. I hope we will meet again."

He touched her fingertips. "Korax is my true name, Korax of Rhodes."

Afterword

The Mazes of Magic is the first book of the *Conjurer of Rhodes* series. As of this writing, the scheduled titles are:

Book 1- *The Mazes of Magic*

Book 2 - *The Lights of Alexandria*

Book 3 - *The Treasure of the Sun God*

I am very grateful to my beta readers, my marvelous editor Jaime Henriquez, and my patient and talented cover designer, Mirna Gilman of BooksGoSocial.com.

If you enjoyed this story, please consider leaving a rating and review on Amazon, as well as other sites. The algorithms of the publishing business make this extremely important to a book's success.

I love hearing from readers. You can also connect with me at:

Web: triskelionbooks.com or jackmassa.com

Facebook: https://www.facebook.com/AuthorJackMassa/

X/Twitter: @JackMassa2